THE
COYOTE
TRACKER

A Josiah Wolfe, Texas Ranger Novel

LARRY D. SWEAZY

BERKLEY BOOKS, NEW YORK

THE BERKLEY PUBLISHING GROUP
Published by the Penguin Group
Penguin Group (USA) Inc.
375 Hudson Street, New York, New York 10014, USA
Penguin Group (Canada), 90 Eglinton Avenue East, Suite 700, Toronto, Ontario M4P 2Y3, Canada
(a division of Pearson Penguin Canada Inc.) • Penguin Books Ltd., 80 Strand, London WC2R 0RL,
England • Penguin Group Ireland, 25 St. Stephen's Green, Dublin 2, Ireland (a division of Penguin
Books Ltd.) • Penguin Group (Australia), 250 Camberwell Road, Camberwell, Victoria 3124, Australia
(a division of Pearson Australia Group Pty. Ltd.) • Penguin Books India Pvt. Ltd., 11 Community
Centre, Panchsheel Park, New Delhi—110 017, India • Penguin Group (NZ), 67 Apollo Drive,
Rosedale, Auckland 0632, New Zealand (a division of Pearson New Zealand Ltd.) • Penguin Books
(South Africa) (Pty.) Ltd., 24 Sturdee Avenue, Rosebank, Johannesburg 2196, South Africa

Penguin Books Ltd., Registered Offices: 80 Strand, London WC2R 0RL, England

This is a work of fiction. Names, characters, places, and incidents either are the product of the author's
imagination or are used fictitiously, and any resemblance to actual persons, living or dead, business
establishments, events, or locales is entirely coincidental. The publisher does not have any control over
and does not assume any responsibility for author or third-party websites or their content.

THE COYOTE TRACKER

A Berkley Book / published by arrangement with the author

PUBLISHING HISTORY
Berkley edition / August 2012

ISBN: 978-0-425-25041-9

BERKLEY®
Berkley Books are published by The Berkley Publishing Group,
a division of Penguin Group (USA) Inc.,
375 Hudson Street, New York, New York 10014.
BERKLEY® is a registered trademark of Penguin Group (USA) Inc.
The "B" design is a trademark of Penguin Group (USA) Inc.

PRINTED IN THE UNITED STATES OF AMERICA

10 9 8 7 6 5 4 3 2 1

Praise for
THE COUGAR'S PREY

"[A] gem among gems. Sweazy is a superb storyteller, and this quick-moving yarn is cut from tightly woven cloth. He breathes life into the frontier, and readers are immersed in the sights, sounds, and ever-present threat of death lurking at every corner."
—Phil Dunlap, author of *Cotton's War*

"Larry D. Sweazy once again spins a fine historical adventure full of compelling characters and gritty action."
—James Reasoner, Spur Award nominee and author of *Redemption: Hunters*

THE BADGER'S REVENGE

"A richly layered story that offers twists and turns that dare the reader to speculate who is guilty and why."
—Matthew P. Mayo, author of *Haunted Old West*

"[A] fine entry to a great Western series . . . Wherever he goes, I'm on board, through thick and thin." —Bookgasm

THE SCORPION TRAIL

"Possesses the grit and swirl of dust kicked up from the heels of a galloping steed, carried swiftly on a hard West Texas wind."
—Mike Blakely, Spur Award–winning author of *A Tale Out of Luck* (with Willie Nelson)

"Larry D. Sweazy's Josiah Wolfe books promise to stand among the great Western series. Think *The Rifleman* in the deft hands of a Larry McMurtry or a Cormac McCarthy."
—Loren D. Estleman, Spur Award–winning author of *Infernal Angels*

"Larry D. Sweazy writes a lively blend of mystery, action, and historical realism."
—John D. Nesbitt, Spur Award–winning author of *Gather My Horses*

To Dr. William E. Wunder

ACKNOWLEDGMENTS

The physical production of a book from idea to bookshelf is a long process and involves a lot of talented people. The reality is that the production team often goes unnoticed, and all of the behind-the-scenes jobs—from the paper buyer's, to the cover designer's, to the editors'—rarely receive the public kudos they deserve. I hope to correct that here.

I can't tell you how many times a reader has picked up one of my books and said, "You have really great covers." What a fantastic compliment, time and time again, as the series continues. The cover artist, Bruce Emmett, has done a truly outstanding job capturing the look and feel of Josiah Wolfe's world. Each cover depicts a scene out of the book, and the final product always amazes me.

I would also like to thank Lesley Worrell, the cover designer, and Laura K. Corless, the interior text designer. My books have been consistent and inspiring because of your work. Thanks also goes to Rick Willett, my copy editor, who has made each of the Wolfe novels much better because of his sharp eye and dedication to his craft.

There are even more people who see my books through the pipeline whom I am unaware of, and too many to list here. Please know that you have my utmost gratitude.

Finally, I'm happy to have worked with Faith Black on four of the five Josiah Wolfe novels. Your enthusiasm for the series and efforts to make each book consistent and better has not only encouraged me, but greatly enhanced my maturity and skill as a writer. Thank you, Faith. It doesn't get said often enough.

As always, thanks go to my personal team as well: Liz, Chris, Cherry, and Rose, who continue to inspire me, dream with me, and walk alongside me on this journey.

AUTHOR'S NOTE

The following books and resources may be of further interest to readers seeking more information about the Texas Rangers and Texas history in general: *Texas Rangers: A Century of Frontier Defense* by Walter Prescott Webb (University of Texas Press, 2008); *Lone Star Justice: The First Century of the Texas Rangers* by Robert M. Utley (Berkley, 2002); *The Texas Rangers: Wearing the Cinco Peso, 1821–1900* by Mike Cox (Forge, 2008); *Six Years with the Texas Rangers, 1875–1881* by James B. Gillet (Bison Books, 1976); *Lone Star: A History of Texas and The Texans* by T. R. Fehrenbach (Da Capo Press, 2000); and *Frontier Texas: A History of Borderland to 1880* by Robert F. Pace and Dr. Donald S. Frazier (State House Press, 2004).

Other resources include: *The Look of the Old West* by William Foster Harris (Skyhorse Publishing, Inc., 2007); *www.texas.gov*; *The Handbook of Texas* (www.tshaonline.org/handbook/online); *The Portal to Texas History* (http://texashistory.unt.edu/); and *Texas Ranger Dispatch* magazine.

PROLOGUE

※

June 1, 1865

The footsteps behind Josiah Wolfe were close, trudging along at a steady pace, just like his. Every voice was silent, and every man in the small troop had a dry mouth, thirsty for the smallest drop of fresh water.

Nothing but the thought of home propelled them all forward, one step heavily in front of the other. Josiah was so tired, hungry, and worn down that walking another ten feet was more effort than he thought he could muster. But it was Texas air that he was breathing, and Texas dirt that he was walking on, pushing him on, encouraging him to use every bit of perseverance that remained in his mind and heart. There was no stopping him now that he was so near his home.

The hot sun beat down from a cloudless and merciless sky. Two vultures soared above, circling high overhead, their voices silent, as usual. The broad-winged birds' shadows were large and dark on the brightly lit ground, passing over the men like storm clouds spiraling rapidly out of nowhere. It seemed like death and misery were following every man home from the War Between the States, waiting to catch him at every turn, even in a carrion eater's beak if it could.

As they made their way south, deeper into Texas, the first hint of the piney woods that Josiah had hunted in as boy touched his nose and perked him up. He recognized the lay of the land, too, and the realization that he was almost home, had actually returned from the war with his life and all of his limbs, was nothing short of a dream come true. It was a mix of miracle and luck, though Josiah was not prone to believe in either, even after serving almost the entire duration of the war.

Surely the days of blood, explosions, and killing were behind him now, he thought, drawing a deep breath of air into his dry mouth.

"You got much farther to go there, Wolfe?" Calbert Jenkins, a scrawny boy of nineteen, asked as he hurried up next to Josiah.

None of the men, the seven of them, had an ounce of fat to spare. Each was gaunt, his eyes sunk in, defeat weighing heavily on his shoulders, neck, and spirit. Jenkins was the skinniest of the bunch and still smelled of blood and death.

"I hope to see my folks' cabin soon, Jenkins," Josiah said. "Up that hill and down a bit lies the town I call home. How about you?"

Jenkins smiled, showing teeth that were beginning to decay and gums that had been bleeding recently—it was a common sign of bad nutrition that they all shared. The troop had scavenged for whatever game and food they could find since Lee had surrendered in the latter part of April. Not that food had been a bounty before the war ended. Hardly. But it was worse on the trek home, left to fend for themselves as they were.

"I still got a long ways to go. Alto, you know. The rest of us, too. You're the lucky one," Jenkins said.

Josiah nodded. "I remember you talking about home. It'll be your turn soon, you'll see."

"Some of the boys are talking about meetin' up in a week or so, plottin' revenge on some of those Yankees still lingerin' around Texas. We need someone like you, Wolfe. Good in the lead and always walks out when they's supposed to."

Josiah didn't flinch, didn't take the words as a compliment. He'd just been doing his duty, just like the rest of the men of the Texas Brigade. They were first into a battle and the last men out, at least, those that were still standing. The losses suffered by the Brigade were immense. Even now, Josiah could taste and smell the odor of the battlefield—gunpowder and blood—just at the thought of it.

"The war's over for me, Jenkins. I fought more battles than I should've, and I'm lucky enough to stand here and be talking to you. I hope to never raise a gun at another man for as long as I live."

Jenkins looked like a little boy who'd just asked for a dog and been told no. His eyes drooped, and he looked away for a brief second. "You're serious, Wolfe? A man like you, layin' down the gun?"

"I sure hope to."

"That'll be the day."

It wasn't Jenkins who spoke. The scrawny boy had slowed his walk at the first utterance of Josiah's objection and was about a step and a half behind Josiah, his head lowered deeper to the ground than it had been before he spoke with the offer to keep them all together.

The voice belonged to Charlie Langdon, another Seerville boy who'd fought alongside Josiah.

They'd both joined up with the Texas Brigade on the same day, back in '61. Charlie took to the war and killing like a coyote takes to sneaking about. He was good at it. Had no conscience, or regrets, about the pain and blood he left behind. Josiah, on the other hand, had to season himself, become accustomed to taking another man's life. If that was possible. He only did what he had to to stay alive.

Josiah ignored Charlie's comment.

For a while, he'd considered Charlie Langdon his friend, even though his own mother had warned him against it. Both men had saved each other's hide more than once, but now there was a distant something growing between them, and Josiah wasn't sure what that something was, except the idea that Charlie was intent on bringing the war home with him and Josiah wasn't.

"You'll see, Wolfe. Guttin' a squirrel won't be near enough for you. You're a killer through and through. All of us are. What are you gonna do? Sit on the porch, chew grass for the rest of your life, and pretend you don't know how to do what you do best?"

Josiah felt his chest heave and caught his words in his throat. There was no use arguing with Charlie, so he just ignored him and picked up his pace, pushing to the crest of the hill that stood between him and home.

"You'll see, Wolfe. You wait and see. I'll be right. I guarantee it," Charlie Langdon said, pulling up next to Jenkins and engaging him in a conversation of whispers and encouragement.

Seerville came into view at the peak of the hill.

The small town didn't look like it had changed much. It was a stop-off point on the way to, or from, Tyler, the nearest big town. The church looked like it needed a new coat of whitewash, and one of the two liveries was shuttered, but other than that, from what Josiah could see, the town was just like he'd imagined it since he left.

Someone must have spotted them, spread the word that men from the war were coming through, because a small crowd had gathered at the entrance to the town, just off the boardwalk, in front of the bank.

Main Street was dry, the ruts hard, like rain had been sparse in the last few weeks of spring. Josiah licked his lips in anticipation of quenching his thirst and wondered how the farming was going, considering the obvious early drought. He knew he would find out soon enough.

As Josiah walked down the hill, he searched for the faces of his mother and father, but he didn't see them in the crowd. Maybe they were deeper back, standing behind someone, or maybe word had not gotten to them yet about the arrival of the soldiers.

There were some soldiers, long-returned, standing in wait, their gray coats on, some doing their best to balance themselves on one leg and a crutch, or hide the sleeve pinned to their coat from a missing arm. It was not a victorious welcome. There was a sadness on nearly every face Josiah saw.

Josiah looked the waiting soldiers in the eye, nodded, and walked on, his attention drawn away from the gloominess by the face of a girl that at once looked familiar but changed, older, sixteen or seventeen, instead of eleven or twelve, a young woman instead of a girl.

Her face was like that of an angel, alabaster white skin framed by shiny, long, brown hair, with sensitive green eyes that looked happy to see the men, especially him. She wore a wide smile and showed a row of perfect pearly white teeth that glimmered in the sun.

The girl was Lily Halverson, one of the eight Halverson children, all boys except her. It was only a hop, skip, and a jump to the Halverson farm from the Wolfe farm, so Josiah knew the girl, and her brothers, too. He had known them most all of his life, been friends with the boys, but never too close. One of the brothers stood behind Lily, his leg cut off at the knee. Josiah didn't know what had become of the rest of the boys—if they'd all lived or if there were more at home. Some of the brothers were too young to have raised a rifle in the war, so Josiah supposed they were working the farm.

Josiah smiled back at Lily, and she gazed at him in a welcoming way. His face flushed red, and he hurried his step, looking over his shoulder at her every few feet. Calbert Jenkins, Charlie Langdon, and the rest of the boys were quickly forgotten.

Lily Halverson never took her eyes off Josiah, and he couldn't wait to see her again once she disappeared from his view. She was the most beautiful thing Josiah had seen in years, since he'd left Seerville.

He knew for sure then that coming home had been worth fighting for, no matter what lay ahead of him.

CHAPTER 1

---◆◆◆◆◆---

May, 1875

Josiah Wolfe stood outside of Robertson's Mercantile on Congress Avenue, doing his best not to show his impatience. There was no way to pass the time—since he didn't smoke cigarettes, or quirlies, as his fellow Texas Ranger Scrap Elliot called them—other than to just stand there watching people, and the horse traffic, come and go in the busy city of Austin.

A streetcar lumbered up the street, garnering his attention, and nearly everyone else's who was walking along the boardwalk.

The use of streetcars was a recent development in the city. Josiah thought they were nothing more than fancy wagons with low wheels and eight benches, covered to protect the riders from the weather. The streetcar was pulled by a pair of fine-looking Springfield mules, barely lathering from the effort; the day was comfortable, cloudless, the sun not too hot—those days were coming, summer was near.

The streetcar was packed full, smiles on all of the riders' faces, like none of them had ever stepped foot on an open wagon before. You'd think they were en route to a carnival somewhere south of town, but none existed that Josiah knew of.

Along with the recent installation of gas lamps and another railroad coming to the city, there was no denying progress had found its way to the capital once again.

The Panic of '73 was finally loosening its hold on the city's financial resources. None of the recent improvements were much of a concern to Josiah, though there did seem to be something in the air that suggested more change was on the way—more than most people wanted, himself included, if truth be told.

No one paid much attention to Josiah standing in wait, literally twiddling his thumbs.

If any of the passersby did catch a direct look in the eye from him, they quickly looked away, casting their gaze down to the ground, as far away from him as possible, and didn't even mumble a simple salutation or hello.

It wasn't as if Josiah were notorious. Not like the outlaws John Wesley Hardin or Sam Bass. But he *was* known in Austin now, recognizable to strangers and every lawman in town.

Up until a few months prior, no one in Austin had known his name or what Josiah's face looked like. He'd been just another emigrant to the city, hailing from no farther away than East Texas, from Seerville, a speck of a town a little south of Tyler. He hadn't crossed an ocean or traveled across the country from the East, weary and in search of some unseen promised land. He had just left an old life in search of a new one, knowing full well that when he lit out from his childhood home, Austin was his destination. The lack of distance he'd traveled didn't seem to matter; the desire, in the end, was the same as any man seeking to change his life.

A quick series of incidents had decreased his anonymity recently, and honestly, an identity, or a degree of privacy, was not something Josiah had ever known he could lose.

In a matter of a few short months, Josiah had killed Pete

Feders, the captain of the Texas Ranger company he belonged to, then more recently, he'd killed a spy for Juan Cortina, a cattle rustler and Mexican criminal named Leathers, who had followed him up from Corpus Christi with no other intention than killing *him*. Both incidents were self-defense. Shoot or be shot.

The way Josiah saw it, he was a lucky man to be standing anywhere, no less outside of a mercantile in Austin. He should have been toes up, six feet under in the local cemetery, and nobody knew that better than he did.

From a distance, and through the narrow view of the local newspaper, the *Austin Statesman*, it looked to the general public like Josiah was nothing more than an outlaw himself, no better than Bass or Hardin. He also, according to the newspaper, was a renegade with an itchy trigger finger, hungry to make a name for himself, eager to cash in on any bit of fame that might come his way.

Nothing could have been further from the truth—at least as far as Josiah was concerned.

Still, he knew he was looked upon with great suspicion, which was why he had found himself with some extra time on his hands. Time enough to wait for a woman who was on a lazy afternoon trip to the mercantile to make a purchase of material and buttons for a variety of daily-wear dresses. Josiah shook his head at the thought.

Josiah had not been furloughed from the Rangers; he was still on the payroll. But he had received orders to stay in town and wait for the return of Captain Leander McNelly, who would, one more time, decide on Josiah's fate within the organization and the company of Rangers that McNelly headed up.

Josiah had been cleared of killing Leathers, but the notoriety of the previous event involving Captain Feders had not entirely escaped the public's mind or the *Stateman*'s printing presses. The entire Ranger organization was being brought into question because of Josiah's actions.

The noise from the street subsided as the streetcar angled south, away from the capitol building.

It was mid-afternoon, the sun high overhead, bright enough to force Josiah to cock his wool Stetson down a bit deeper to shade his eyes.

Josiah was a tall, lanky man with a head full of hair the color of summer wheat and eyes the color of blueberries. Most days he wore a day or two of whiskers on his face, but recently, since he'd been off the trail and away from duty and in the company of Pearl Fikes, the woman he was waiting on and was courting as properly as possible, his face was clean-shaven. There was no way to keep the mud from his boots, but he tried to keep them as clean as possible, too.

At the moment, his impatience was intent on getting the better of him. Courting was a recent development in Josiah's life, a matter of weeks actually. He felt a little out of sorts, wet behind the ears. He'd been married before. His wife, Lily, had borne him four children: three girls and a boy. Lily and the girls had died, taken by the flu, a little over four years prior. His son, Lyle, survived, and was most likely the only reason, along with the Rangers, that Josiah had pulled himself out of the depths of his grief and found himself in the company of another woman.

Josiah sensed the presence of someone staring at him; a passerby had stopped a few feet from him, just off to his right.

"Is that you, Wolfe?"

Josiah immediately recognized the voice. It was that of Rory Farnsworth, the sheriff of Travis County, which included the whole town of Austin and beyond.

Farnsworth was about half a head shorter than Josiah and dressed more like a dandy Yankee than a Texas sheriff. He sported a fine tailored suit that was more fitting for a politician to wear than a lawman. His finely waxed mustache seemed to glow in the sunlight, even though it was shielded slightly by a black bowler hat that matched the color of his fancy suit. Only the silver star on his chest gave any hint to his true position—that and the air of authority he carried with him. The man strutted about like he was the only rooster in Austin.

"It is, Sheriff," Josiah said, pushing away from the wall of the mercantile, tipping up his hat so he could look Farnsworth in the eye.

"Not a place I'd expect to see you," the sheriff said.

"The saloon owner kicked me out. Said I brought in the riffraff looking to make a name for themselves with a gunfight."

Farnsworth cocked his right eye quizzically. "You're kidding, of course?"

"I am," Josiah said, his voice remaining deadpan, his facial expression unmoved. "I'm actually waiting on Pearl Fikes."

Rory Farnsworth's chest heaved, and his upper lip trembled slightly before he said anything, like a thought got caught crossways between his brain and his throat. "I see."

The sheriff had been in attendance at the Fikes estate when Pete Feders, prior to his death at Josiah's hand, had publicly proposed to Pearl—a proposal which she refused by running out of the dining hall in a ball of sobs.

All of the movers and shakers of Austin had been in attendance at the dinner, too, including Richard Coke, the governor himself. The social pages had made a great drama out of the incident, and it only got worse when Josiah was left with no choice but to shoot Pete Feders.

It was not clear to Josiah if Farnsworth had ever had any designs on Pearl; as far as he knew, the sheriff was a confirmed bachelor. He had never seen the man in the company of a woman and had not lived in Austin long enough to know the scuttlebutt concerning the sheriff's social life. Even if Josiah had heard anything, he wouldn't have taken it to heart. If he'd learned anything from his own set of troubles, it was that gossip was just gossip and usually not to be believed.

"What brings you out on this fine day?" Josiah asked, hoping to veer the conversation away from Pearl. He regretted mentioning her name the moment it had slipped from his lips.

"Do you really think courting Pearl Fikes is the proper thing to do, Wolfe? I mean, really? After everything that's happened?"

Farnsworth traveled constantly in the social circles of Austin. His father, Myron, was the president of the First Bank of Austin and, by luck, chance, or hard work, was one of the wealthiest men in town.

It came as no surprise to Josiah that his relationship with Pearl appeared as bad form, but he had no immediate response to Farnsworth's query. He shrugged his shoulders. "Matters of the heart seem best left to those involved if you ask me, Sheriff. I mean, I surely wouldn't pretend to think I could have any influence on your daily life with my opinions. Or should I?"

"I would suspect not, Wolfe."

Josiah nodded. "You never answered my question."

"Oh, yes. I am out and about. Nothing of note. Are your boys in town?" He was referring to the company of McNelly's Rangers that Josiah belonged to.

"No, still south as far as I know. My son took ill, which is how I found myself back in Austin without the ranks of the Ranger company to join."

"He is better, I assume?"

"He is. Thank you for asking."

"And that business of Cortina's spy has detained you?"

"It has. I was not in the wrong."

"Rangers have a growing reputation of shooting first and asking questions later. Your actions are not making a positive contribution to the organization. You realize that, don't you, Wolfe?"

"You're the last person I would think I would have to defend the organization, or my actions, to."

The sheriff's granite facial expression didn't change. "Are you sure Austin is the right place for you, Wolfe?"

The question felt like a punch to the gut. Austin had never felt like home, but Josiah figured it would just take time. Obviously, it was going to take a lot more time than he'd given it if a man like Farnsworth could detect his discomfort with city life.

"Are you suggesting I leave town?"

Farnsworth hunched his shoulders, then looked away without answering Josiah directly.

Three wagons loaded with fresh-cut lumber passed by, heading up Congress Avenue toward the capitol building. There was no way to know for sure where the wagons were going, but the smell of fresh-cut wood reached Josiah's nose and mixed with the other hopeful reminders that spring had fully arrived. But any sign of optimism was lost on him at the moment.

"Maybe it is something you should consider, Wolfe."

"I've just recently returned from Corpus after spending more months there than I care to count, Sheriff. Am I in danger?"

"Only what you bring unto yourself."

"What do you mean by that?"

"Some rowdy cowboy would see no difference between taking your hide and John Wesley Hardin's. It won't be long before I'm collecting another dead body from the street, will it, Wolfe? You joked about it, but there is truth at the foundation of all good humor, isn't there?"

"I'm no gunslinger."

"So you say, Wolfe. So you say."

Before Josiah could respond, Pearl Fikes exited the mercantile, a small bag in her hand and a curious look on her face. "Gentlemen," she said, slipping her arm around Josiah's.

"Ma'am," Farnsworth answered with a doff of his bowler. He flashed a quick, angled leer at Josiah, then departed quickly down the boardwalk, never looking back.

"What was that all about?" Pearl asked.

"Nothing. He just stopped to say hello," Josiah said. He took a step forward, then turned, guiding Pearl in the opposite direction of Farnsworth, not sure where he was going next.

CHAPTER 2

Pearl Fikes was dressed properly for a public stroll down Congress Avenue. She wore a white outdoor dress with the overskirts caught up with black buckled ribbons. A jacket bodice made of the same expensive-looking material, with a high neckline and cuffs, was layered over the dress. The dress shimmered in the bright sunshine of the day. Pearl wore a flat-crowned straw hat tipped forward, adorned with ribbons that matched those on her dress. To the uninformed, Pearl Fikes still looked like a woman of wealth, of high social standing, an important person to step aside for. Nothing could have been further from the truth.

What Pearl wore was a remnant of her past, of a time when she was the only daughter of a Texas Ranger captain, a debutante, whose mother's main goal in life was to see her marry well and maintain the large estate they lived on and the large house they lived in.

Now the estate and the house were gone, a consequence of the Panic of '73, the death of Hiram Fikes, and a series of bad decisions and bad investments on her mother's part.

Now Pearl's mother was in a sanatorium, and Pearl was staying in a nearby boardinghouse, intent on taking up studies at the local normal school to be a schoolteacher as a way to generate some income for herself. She barely had two bits to rub together, and if it weren't for her uncle, Juan Carlos, Hiram Fikes's half brother, she would be in even worse shape financially than she currently was.

Pearl stared at Josiah with disbelief on her face. "Rory Farnsworth did not even look me in the eye before departing so quickly. Did you have words with the man, Josiah?" She seemed agitated and tense, something Josiah did not expect after a moment of shopping in the mercantile. Pearl was happy when she went in, happy to be out with him. Or so he'd thought.

"No, no, everything is fine," Josiah said, guiding Pearl down the boardwalk, away from the mercantile and Rory Farnsworth as quickly as possible.

Pearl looked over her shoulder quickly, then sighed loudly when she faced forward. "I would like to go home."

"Now? We have the whole day ahead of us. I had planned for a picnic on the banks of the river. I know it's one of your favorite places."

"Please, Josiah, just stop."

"Did something happen that I need to know about?" Josiah asked, as he ceased walking, promptly ending their departure from Farnsworth, doing as Pearl asked. He stood in the middle of the boardwalk, still as a statue, like he had just fulfilled a marching order.

"I have been shopping in Robertson's for years. My mother carried an account there and was a very, very good customer. I asked for my own account and was refused. Refused? Can you believe that?"

Josiah looked away, then back to Pearl quickly. He wasn't surprised by the news. "You can't take the rejection personally, Pearl. The man has a business to run."

Pearl's normally soft face grew hard. "Are you saying I'm a bad investment, Josiah Wolfe?"

Without knowing it, Pearl had raised her voice and was drawing attention to herself—which was very much out of her character. Or, at least, it had been before her mother was carted off kicking and screaming to the sanatorium, from a house that now belonged to the bank and stood empty.

Now that he thought about it, there had been a bit of obvious nervousness about Pearl when Josiah called on her at the boardinghouse on Second Street, Miss Amelia Angle's Home for Girls. But any discomfort seemed to have faded once they were beyond the confines of the house. Women, and their moods, had always been harder to read for Josiah than the weather, and just as unpredictable, so he wasn't surprised that he might have been wrong.

It was not the first time Josiah had met Amelia Angle or been to the house on a proper, chaperoned call, but this day was the first time he and Pearl had walked the boardwalks of Austin arm in arm, as a couple. It was less a coming out than what Pearl was accustomed to, but from all matters of form, Pearl had indicated that she was finished with the trappings of high society, with the demands her mother and the important women of Austin had placed on her previously. She relished her newfound freedom, or at least said she did.

Maybe, Josiah thought to himself before answering Pearl's question, *she was rethinking her position on being a common woman, courted by a common man.*

After all, he was not a proper gentleman. He never had been, and had never indicated that he had the desire to behave in any manner that was less than comfortable to him. Perhaps she was embarrassed by him, dressed in his finest clothes, though far from the likes of Rory Farnsworth in his neat black bowler, with his fancy Dickens chain and gold watch and tailored black suit.

"I think you are a fine investment, Pearl. How could you think otherwise?"

Pearl's cornflower blue eyes grew glassy, and she looked away from Josiah. "This is going to be harder than I thought." It was almost a whisper.

Josiah ushered Pearl to a bench in front of the shoe-maker's shop. The smell of wet leather wafted out of the door.

They sat down, and Josiah took Pearl's hand into his. If she was uncomfortable, Josiah was ten times more so. He drew his own looks from those who passed by and knew that anyone with regular reading skills who kept up with social pages knew that Pearl Fikes had fallen out of grace right along with him. And then there was the suspicion, seemingly fortified by the public show of affection between the two of them, that Josiah had actually killed Pete Feders because of his love and desire for her.

Josiah being concerned about his image, or what the pub-lic thought, was like a coyote giving up hunting and becom-ing a domesticated dog. It was an impossible act, and any wild creature could never be considered trustworthy anyway. What other people thought had never mattered to Josiah, and there had been few consequences of that attitude out on the trail alone or with the company of a few men. But that had all changed somehow once he moved to Austin.

"You're not in this alone, Pearl." Josiah had lowered his voice, too.

"I know. But my burdens are not something you should have to consider. My family's financial troubles are not yours to carry—or assume. You have your own problems."

"My troubles are not what I'm concerned about at the moment," Josiah said, cupping her face in his hands, the consciousness of the city falling away from his worry. "I don't want to be anywhere but here with you, and I will shoulder what comes from that with a deep sense of good fortune. I'm happy you're in my life, Pearl. It's been a long time since I've felt the way I do."

"I know." Pearl nodded. "I don't want to disappoint you."

Josiah had made sure that Pearl was mostly aware of his past, of his life before he moved to Austin from East Texas, of being married to Lily. Pearl also knew the sadness of the time with Lily, the loss Josiah had endured when his three daughters died from the flu, and Lily, too, leaving him to raise a newborn son with the help of a Mexican wet nurse who had come to Austin with him.

Josiah knew, too, of Pearl's past.

Neither of them was without scars. Pearl had been married before, to a man much like her father and Josiah, a veteran of the War Between the States who came home a different man, then went on to be a lawman, of sorts, whether with the State Police or locally. Her husband had been killed by a stray bullet outside a saloon about the same time Josiah's wife had died. They both had been alone for the same length of time, their grief and longing similar, but different. Josiah had loved his wife, while Pearl had told Josiah that her marriage was more of a way to appease her mother; she liked the man but was unsure if it was love she felt, and it was in Pearl's demeanor at the time to make her mother happy, regardless of her own feelings.

"The last thing you need to worry about is disappointing me," Josiah said. He was tempted to kiss her, but that would have crossed too many boundaries in the public eye—and his own.

One of the problems they faced was finding time alone. Since they were not teenagers, and had been married previously, they both understood the needs of a man and a woman and had previously found the right time and place to be intimate, to make love, before this day, though only once.

Now there were social requirements. Requirements of the boardinghouse Pearl had no choice but to live in and the restrictions in the small house that Josiah shared with his son, Lyle.

Neither Lyle nor Ofelia, the wet nurse and caretaker who had come with Josiah from Seerville, would understand the presence of a woman staying overnight and sharing his bed. And Josiah would not expect such a thing of Pearl. Not now, if ever, until their life had taken a more formal path. Courting Pearl openly was the first step on that path, and it seemed like they were getting off to a rocky start.

They had chosen a difficult time to make their relationship public, but neither of them was foolish enough to ignore the reality of the situation they had put themselves in.

"You know I want to kiss you right now, don't you?" Josiah asked.

Pearl looked Josiah directly in the eye, her face wanting and vulnerable at the same time.

He shivered at her beauty, even though she was distraught. There was no way a man like him should be courting a woman like Pearl, as far as he was concerned. His good fortune was not lost on him for one minute.

"Please don't," Pearl finally said.

Josiah smiled knowingly and was not the least bit offended. "I should take you home." He stood up, her hand in his hand.

Pearl hesitated. "I'm sorry. I have ruined the day you planned."

"As far as I'm concerned, there'll be plenty more days to come. You didn't ruin anything."

"You're sure?"

"I am," Josiah answered, helping Pearl to her feet, "absolutely sure. Now, let's get you back to Miss Angle's."

CHAPTER 3

———◆❈◆———

It was like Josiah and Pearl walked through a curtain of silence as soon as they turned the corner off Congress Avenue.

The boardwalk was full of people who had all come to a full stop, and it was eerily quiet for such a large gathering. Most of the crowd had dropped their heads at the first sign of the funeral procession, even though it was a small one, bearing very little importance or status, from the looks of it.

Stuffed near the back of the onlookers, pressed against a building, Pearl eased her hand into Josiah's. He flinched at first, then welcomed her touch, the warmth of an offer of comfort, and her need of it, too.

The coffin was made of simple, fresh-cut pine, carried on the shoulders of four hulking men, their unemotional eyes boring straight ahead, dressed like they had just stopped the day's work in a livery or roofing a new building, to make the journey to the cemetery. Their boots were muddy, their sleeves rolled up, and their shirts were sweat-stained. Hats shielded their eyes from the sun, and their guns were in open sight, holstered on their hips.

Josiah didn't recognize any of the men and found it odd that the procession had stopped everyone in his or her tracks—until he looked beyond the coffin and saw that Blanche Dumont was leading a small pack of mourners.

A sighting of Blanche Dumont was rare, though not entirely unheard of. She was, in less gentle terms, a keeper of whores, a madam. She ran a house of soiled doves in the First Ward, not far off the trail that led tired and excited cowboys alike into town in search of a good time. The cowboys were looking for a chance to blow off steam and to part with any hard-earned money in their pockets.

Blanche strived for a higher paying clientele instead of the ragtag cowpunchers who had limited finances. Instead, she catered to the likes of property owners and the well-to-do, and possibly, if scuttlebutt were to be believed, politicians, bankers, and ranch owners. Her girls were clean, well dressed, and forced to educate themselves at least an hour a day. Josiah had no idea if any of the rumors about Blanche and her house were true—he'd only seen her once himself and had never had reason to do business with her or venture inside her place of business.

Dressed in solid black from head to toe, Blanche was properly attired with a bustle and all of the accoutrements of fine and expensive women's wear; the only skin exposed for all to see, and the sun to touch, was that of her face. And it was shaded by an overly large brimmed hat and a parasol held at just the right angle to confront the bright light of the day at its most direct touch. Still, there was no way the bright afternoon sun could hide her striking eyes that looked red from grief but were redder in an odd, permanent way, focused fully ahead on the simple coffin, showing little emotion or recognition of the crowd and their stares at all. There was no sign on Blanche Dumont's statue-like face of shedding one single tear.

It was, after all, the woman's skin, more so than her occupation, that drew the stares from the crowd and had stopped them all cold in their tracks. It wasn't as if she were the only woman in Austin whose trade was whoring . . . but she *was* the only albino woman in Austin, at least that Josiah knew of.

Blanche Dumont's skin was white as snow and just as fragile as an errant flake falling from the sky in South Texas, sure to melt before it hit the ground. She was a freak of nature, an oddity of certain beauty if one got close enough to see it. And she was a bearer of strong will, good business sense, and the ability, as it was told, to keep a secret when it was required. In her business, that was most likely a daily occurrence, and a requirement of lasting concern.

She usually wore gold-rimmed glasses with soft green lenses to protect her sensitive eyes, but not today. The glasses were nowhere to be seen. It looked like she wanted to see the world clearly, and she didn't care if the world saw her or not. Each step Blanche Dumont took forward was measured and direct. She almost looked like she was floating, a wraith with a ghostly face appearing in the midst of daylight, unconcerned about the realm of the living or any danger she might encounter.

Josiah had no way to judge the woman's state of emotion, having nothing to compare it to, but if he had to guess, he would say that Blanche Dumont was angry, maybe even enraged. Her hands were balled up into tight fists, and she never let her sight leave the coffin.

Someone coughed, and the press of men, women, and children on the boardwalk brought a variety of smells to Josiah's nose; most were unpleasant but no worse than riding behind a thousand longhorns. He wasn't concerned about himself, but with Pearl and her comfort. He looked for a quick exit, but it was too late to flee, too late to backtrack and ease out the way they had come. Even more of a crowd had piled up behind them, effectively pinning them to the spot they presently stood in.

It was only a matter of luck that Josiah could see into the street at all. He was a head taller than those in front of him, and he could crane his neck just right to catch a passing look at Blanche Dumont's profile.

At that moment, she flinched and turned her head, as if something she did not like, or feared, had caught her attention.

It looked like she was staring directly at Josiah. They made eye contact, and at that moment, the keeper of soiled doves slowed her pace.

Blanche Dumont's chest heaved forward, and she arched her back straighter than it already it was, then suddenly broke away from the other mourners, three young women all dressed similarly to her, only without parasols and extra big black hats.

Those women looked hot and sweaty, uncomfortable in the sun, and with the stares of what must have felt like the whole city gazing at them.

Josiah took a deep breath, then relaxed when Blanche Dumont broke eye contact with him and veered back about ten feet. It was not him she was interested in, after all.

He stood up on his tiptoes, just able to see a man he recognized standing at the edge of the street—and the object of Blanche's destination.

The man was Rory Farnsworth.

Everyone standing next to the sheriff pushed away in a wave, leaving him to face the pale, enraged madam on his own.

To his credit, the sheriff didn't flinch. He stood firmly planted, waiting for whatever was coming.

Surely, he and Blanche Dumont were not strangers, at least not as unconnected as she and Josiah were. The sheriff had to know of her activities and source of income as much as any other man in Austin.

Blanche Dumont walked up to Rory Farnsworth without saying a word and stopped firmly within two feet of him.

With no warning, or change of expression, she spit in his face.

The sheriff had obviously not expected such a vile act, as the spit struck him with the speed of a bullet just below his right nostril.

A look of horror crossed his face as he twisted back, angling away from Blanche, reaching for a handkerchief from his back pocket. He was not fast enough. The woman spit at him again, her face arched like a pure white snake's, spewing venom just before it clamped down on its intended victim. Her tongue was every bit as red as her eyes.

The second volley of anger and hate smacked Rory Farnsworth upside the head, just at his temple. He protested with a loud retort that was not quite a scream but a throaty, non-vocal protest of disgust and surprise.

The crowd gasped and drew backward, farther away from the pair, leaving them exposed and visible to almost everyone.

Mumbling and whispers washed up and down the boardwalk, like a wave, pushing the news of the woman's action in every direction. "She spit him in the face, she spit him in the face . . ."

A slight smile rippled across Blanche Dumont's stark white face, and with that, she spun around and walked calmly back to the band of mourners, who had kept pace with the coffin.

"You'll regret that, Blanche Dumont! Mark my word, I'll not soon forget this," Rory Farnsworth shouted, wiping his face dry as quickly as he could.

Blanche Dumont did not flinch, did not act as if she heard Rory Farnsworth's threat—but everybody else did, loud and clear.

Farnsworth's face suddenly lost all of its color, almost matching the hue of Blanche Dumont's skin. A look of embarrassment washed over the sheriff as he stuffed the handkerchief back into his pocket.

He cowered slightly, acted like he was going to say something else then decided better of it, and eased backward into the crowd, quickly disappearing from Josiah's sight.

"What was that about?" Pearl asked. "I couldn't see a thing."

"I'm not sure," Josiah answered, able to move forward now as the crowd broke apart, going back to the shops, saloons, and offices that they had been drawn out of. "It has nothing to do with us, just something with the sheriff."

"I never trusted that man," Pearl said softly, under her breath.

Josiah said nothing. He didn't acknowledge Pearl's pronouncement, but he was surprised by it.

With her arm hooked in his, he headed toward the boardinghouse, looking quickly over his shoulder, catching a fleeting glimpse of Blanche Dumont and the funeral procession turning a corner and stepping solemnly toward the cemetery.

Josiah found the whole encounter between Rory Farnsworth and Blanche Dumont a little confusing. Something had obviously happened between the two of them. Something extremely powerful for Blanche to show herself in poor light in front of the crowd, but the message was loud and clear: The sheriff was beneath her, and she was displeased with him in a bad way.

He repeated to himself silently what he had said to Pearl: *It has nothing to do with us.*

But something told him, considering his earlier confrontation with the sheriff, that that just might not be entirely true.

CHAPTER 4

—◆◆◆◆—

The rules at Miss Amelia Angle's Home for Girls were extremely strict. The fact that Josiah and Pearl were allowed to walk the streets, her arm in his arm, touching in any way, unchaperoned, was only due to Pearl's advanced age and status as a widow. Given her family's rapid fall from grace, her prospects of attracting a suitor of any worth had been judged by Miss Amelia Angle as poor to impossible.

The reality that a man, any man, had showed an interest in courting Pearl was seen by most of the women and girls in the house as a near miracle, regardless of her beauty or how she carried herself.

Josiah was aware of all of this only because Pearl had told him . . . in a soft kind of way, educating him in the ways and rules of courting and the power of a group of women's whispers.

The house was three storeys tall, built in the style of a lot of recently constructed homes: high peaks, gingerbread lattice tacked to the eaves, a red brick turret on the ground rising up past the second-floor parlor with its grand piano, and a long wraparound porch, the woodwork just as fancy as the lattice.

A black wrought iron fence bordered the yard, which measured about a quarter of the block that it sat on. Other houses of like build up and down the street matched Miss Amelia's, though two blocks away was a host of saloons and houses, much like Blanche Dumont's, that catered to the cowboys wandering into town off the trail or getting ready to leave. The debauchery and rowdiness might as well have been a world away, though. There was no sign of it on the genteel street.

The trees in the yard were well pruned, and urns filled with blooming spring flowers dotted the house's long porch. Smaller urns lined the steps that led up to the double front doors.

The air surrounding the house always smelled like it had been touched with a hint of toilet water, a fancy fragrance that was not quite identifiable to the uneducated, such as Josiah. The fragrance was not quite natural to him, forced by human intervention, unlike the fresh smell of country air.

Josiah and Pearl stopped at the gate. A sign on it said: "NO SUITORS AFTER 5 P.M."

"I could entertain you in the parlor with some tea. We still have time," Pearl said. Her voice was wistful, tinted with regret. She had slipped her arm out of Josiah's about a half a block from Miss Amelia's. There was no explanation needed. Josiah knew Pearl wanted to avoid judgment and disdain as often as possible. Her reaction to the treatment she'd received in the mercantile was proof enough of that for him.

Josiah shook his head no. "I think it's best if I go home."

"I understand."

"Do you?"

"Not really."

Josiah exhaled and looked away from Pearl's disappointed face as quickly as possible. "I'm not sure I can be as proper as I need to be, as I should be."

A sly look flashed in Pearl's summer sky blue eyes. "Are you suggesting we need to be improper?"

Josiah's face flushed then. "No, I'm just not . . ."

". . . comfortable?"

He nodded.

Pearl stepped forward, lowered her head, and whispered, "I'd rather be improper."

Josiah smiled and drew in a deep breath of relief. Her fragrance was more familiar now, distinguishable from the surrounding air, and it left him wanting her even more than he had the second before. "We've rushed into that need, maybe quicker than we should have."

Disappointment crossed Pearl's face and settled there, not promising to leave any time soon. "I can't wait much longer."

"I want to do this right," Josiah said.

"I know."

"Be patient. We'll find our time, our place."

"I will be . . . as patient as I can."

"I have to go," Josiah said, knowing full well that if he didn't leave at that very moment, he would scoop up Pearl and run off with her, not stopping until they found a private place where they could shred each other's clothes off and never look back.

"When will I see you again?" Pearl asked.

"Soon. I promise. Soon."

The house was empty. Ofelia, the wet nurse, had taken Lyle to her home in Little Mexico, the area of Austin that was populated mostly by Mexicans and was not all that welcoming to Anglos. Josiah didn't worry about Lyle's safety. Not there, not with Ofelia—he was certain she would shield the boy from any harm, putting her own life at risk before anything happened to Lyle.

It was a small house, just a box really, with one small bedroom that Josiah shared with Lyle and a kitchen and living area all in one room, a little bigger than a horse stall, with a privy out back, along with a chicken coop and a small garden that Ofelia tended to. Cool weather plants, like lettuce and carrots, were already reacting to the May sun, cowering back, wilting, but still edible.

The house was a couple of blocks from the train tracks, and sometimes in the middle of the night, the whole place rattled and threatened to collapse as the trains came and went.

A new track was being laid for the Great Northern Railroad, coming in through town, in the opposite direction, cutting through the residential area right down the middle of Cypress Avenue. Some houses had already been demolished, with more to come, and the tenants displaced.

The new railroad would be far enough away not to threaten the existence of Josiah's house, but he wondered how much more noise the train would add to his life. City life was difficult—and loud—enough for him the way it was.

He was glad to be home, and even happier to have a moment or two alone—which was a rare occurrence when he was off the trail, not riding with the company of Rangers that were his friends as well as his comrades.

Josiah unbuckled his gun belt and placed it gently on the bureau that took up nearly one whole wall of the bedroom.

He had worn a swivel rig since he'd joined the Frontier Battalion. It was a more casual, and more dangerous, way to wear a gun than a standard belt holster, but the rig had its advantages.

A lot of the boys in the Texas Rangers wore swivel rigs, which were nothing more than a metal plate attached to their belts with the stud head of an extra-long hammer screw slipped into a slot. The stud stuck out, and the gun rested just back of the trigger guard, allowing it to be quickly swung upward without having to draw it out of a holster. He could shoot through the open toe of the leather holster. Saving seconds meant saving lives—usually his own.

Perhaps it was the way he carried the Peacemaker, a Colt .45 single-action Army, that had prompted Rory Farnsworth to suggest, essentially, that Josiah was no better than a lowly gunslinger.

It was a hard accusation to swallow, and Josiah had not been able to rid himself of the depiction the entire time he'd been escorting Pearl back to Miss Amelia Angle's boardinghouse, and then on the solemn walk home.

Somehow, he'd lost the sheriff's respect, and that seemed to matter to Josiah much more than he'd thought it ever would—or should. He had to wonder if Farnsworth's opinion was the common perception people had of him in all of Austin.

Was he really just a lawless killer without any respect for the living and weak? Josiah sighed outwardly at the thought, and at the recognition that he really did care what people thought about him . . . and the Rangers. Maybe it was more that than anything.

Josiah was ashamed of dampening the reputation of the Rangers in any way. The organization had been his salvation, a place to run when he needed to start a new life. Now he had damaged the one thing that had been there for him. He wasn't sure he'd ever be able to restore his reputation, or the Rangers', in anyone's eyes.

And then, the encounter Josiah and Pearl had witnessed between Blanche Dumont and Rory Farnsworth had been even more confusing.

Josiah didn't know who had died, whose coffin was being carried to the cemetery, but something told him that Blanche Dumont thought Rory Farnsworth was responsible. Why else would she have spit on him?

He drew a deep breath then. He didn't know the answer to that question, and he hoped he didn't have a reason to care. It was just another event in the day of the city that didn't affect him, though it left him wondering, much like most events that he was witness to.

The only comfort Josiah had in the city was Ofelia, watching over Lyle. He knew when he was out on the trail that they had each other and they weren't alone.

The move to Austin had been much more difficult than he'd thought it would be, even though he'd actually spent more time away from the city, out riding with the company of Rangers, than in the small, one-bedroom clapboard house at the corner of Sixth and Pecan.

Even with his current circumstance in flux, his good standing with the Rangers in question, Josiah had little desire to move back to the small farm in Seerville from where he came.

There was no question that he missed the piney woods of East Texas and the familiarity of everything that surrounded him there, but he was never good at being a farmer, not even when Lily was alive. That's why he rode with the Rangers after coming back from the war, when they were less organized and the money was even more infrequent than it was now.

Farming was laborious, a gamble that constantly held him in a state of worry and fear. Would there be enough food, enough milk, enough of everything for his growing family to survive? And then when the State Police, promoted by the former governor of Texas, took over in the early seventies, Josiah rode with them, but only briefly, and only because of his respect for the now deceased Captain Hiram Fikes.

His most revered job was that of marshal of Seerville, the closest town to the farm. But when the railroad curved through Tyler, miles away from Seerville, the town up and died, leaving little to marshal over. Not long after, Lily and the girls died, leaving him with Lyle, under Ofelia's care.

Captain Fikes once again came to his aid, demanding he get back up in the saddle and ride with the new Frontier

Battalion, formed officially in the spring of 1874, after Governor Coke had won the election, leaving Reconstruction to the past once and for all.

Neither of them, the captain nor Josiah, knew then what fate had in store for them. It was not long after that that Captain Fikes met his death, murdered outright, the killer brought to justice—and Josiah found himself in a constant storm of trials and tribulations that made life in Seerville seem childlike and pastoral.

He had never been so unsure of his footing, and where his life was going to lead him, as he was now. The only great shining hope he could see before him was his affection for Pearl and watching Lyle grow into a well-mannered and much different boy than Josiah could have ever imagined.

He stared at the Peacemaker on the bureau and thought about its place in his life.

For as long as Josiah could remember, he had always worn a gun on his belt and always, as far as he was concerned, stood on the right side of the law.

If he was a professional at anything, then Josiah considered himself a professional lawman and nothing else. It was how he saw himself even more so the older he got, now in his mid-thirties.

It didn't matter that the Rangers didn't wear badges or have uniform requirements, keeping the peace was in his blood, and there was nothing else he would ever consider doing with his life, unless he was forced away from the Rangers. And even then, without much consideration, Josiah knew he would end up as a deputy somewhere, for a man like Rory Farnsworth, who knew too little about the human side of the law and too much about the power and prestige that he thought came along with wearing a badge.

There was no question that Josiah knew deep within himself that he was angry at Farnsworth, that he was passing judgment on the sheriff. But at one time, Josiah had thought that Rory was his friend. He wasn't so sure now.

The Peacemaker was his only trusted friend within constant reach, a permanent fixture in his life and in his house. He could not imagine his life without it.

A quick, soft touch to the barrel left his fingertips cold.

There was no life to the metal; it only breathed when it meant to destroy—or save. Then it came alive, hot for a second, and retreated to sleep, always ready, always waiting at his command.

For a brief moment then, Josiah let the regret of the past, and the silence of his own house, surround him.

He did not know how many men he had killed in his lifetime. There was no tally card, no trophy of every soul that had been lost to his bullets. War had brought the taste of killing when he was nothing more than a boy, set out on a duty-bound journey that crippled him invisibly in many ways, but left him physically whole and with all of his limbs.

Many men hobbled home on one leg and a crutch, never to be the same, never to be the man they were before the War Between the States erupted and changed everything.

Maybe, Josiah thought, stepping back, not bringing Pearl back to the house so they could share an intimate moment alone was a bigger mistake than he'd thought it was at the time.

CHAPTER 5

It was past midnight when the knock came at the door. Lyle barely stirred, and Josiah, a light sleeper himself, was glad that the boy had not been woken up. The knock was more of a tap than anything else, and when it came again, he was certain someone wanted to see him and would refuse to give up until he went to the door.

He hitched up his long johns, grabbed the Peacemaker off of the bureau, and padded to the door as quietly as he could.

After finding Josiah home, Ofelia had returned home to Little Mexico hours earlier. Everything was in its place and cleaned for the day, as it was every evening before Ofelia departed.

"Who is it?" Josiah said, loud enough for the person on the other side of the door to hear.

"It is me, señor, Juan Carlos. Juan Carlos Montegné."

Josiah didn't immediately open the door, even though Juan Carlos was a trusted friend. "How do I know it is you?"

"It is your friend, señor, Scrap Elliot. He is in trouble, and I have come for you to help him."

Josiah reached for the doorknob but still did not entirely trust the voice beyond the door, even though it sounded like Juan Carlos.

The last he had known, Juan Carlos was still in South Texas, living in a small fishing village outside of Corpus Christi. But it had been a month since he'd seen Juan Carlos there himself, and there was no doubt that with the old Mexican, change came quickly. For as long as Josiah had known Juan Carlos, he had always been a vagabond, edging the shadows, much like a possum wandering from one place to the next.

The last Josiah had heard, Scrap Elliot, a fellow Ranger and a partner in the company, was still in South Texas, too, riding with Captain Leander McNelly, taking on Juan Cortina. Or, at the very least, pushing the incursion back into Mexico.

"When did Scrap come back to Austin?" Josiah said.

"Only yesterday, señor, back with the rest of the company, and trouble found him very quickly. He is in jail for the killing of a whore."

Josiah opened the door then. He smiled slightly at the sight of his friend, then jerked his head, motioning for Juan Carlos to come inside. Happiness was not exactly what Josiah felt, considering the news he'd just been told.

It was not known to anyone how old Juan Carlos really was, but his hair was white as the snow on top of a mountain, contrasting even more brilliantly against his dark brown skin. Juan Carlos was half-Mexican and was the half brother of Hiram Fikes, Pearl's dead father and Josiah's former captain. Still able but less spry after taking a bullet near the gut in Brackett, Texas, several months prior, Juan Carlos operated in a variety of different capacities but most often as a spy for the Rangers. At least he had when his brother was alive, and more recently for Captain McNelly.

Josiah looked up and down the street to make sure Juan Carlos was alone, then closed the door softly and locked it.

Juan Carlos stood in the center of the room, a little hunched over, a natural stance not indicating pain or trouble, dressed in near rags, with no knife or gun showing. There was no question that the man was armed, just not visibly. Juan Carlos liked to fade into the crowd and not be noticed. He had saved Josiah's life on more than one occasion and had more fighting skills, and gun talents, than any one man ought to have a right to. The fool who mistook Juan Carlos for a weak old man would end up a dead fool if he pushed him around or bullied him, or anyone he cared about.

"What are you afraid of, Señor Josiah?" Juan Carlos asked, his voice low in tone, aware of Josiah's situation with Lyle.

"Nothing." Josiah laid the Peacemaker on the table in the kitchen. "Tell me about Elliot."

"Afraid of nothing? Certainly you do not expect me to believe that? Treating a friend like a stranger at the door? Life in the city has made you a nervous man, Josiah Wolfe. I am surprised by the change in you."

"It's not the city that has made me nervous." Josiah glanced unconsciously to the back room where Lyle slept.

"You fear for the safety of your son." It was not a question but a statement.

Josiah stared at the old Mexican, not acknowledging whether he was right or wrong. "I have made enemies everywhere I have gone, Juan Carlos, you know that. I can't be too careful."

"Sí, Señor Josiah, Cortina would like nothing more than to see you dead. But he has been driven deeper into Mexico by McNelly and the other company of Rangers that joined him there."

"They will go after Cortina regardless of the border."

Juan Carlos hunched his shoulders. "It is no longer my concern. I followed McNelly's company home to see my niece. Is she well?"

"I asked about Elliot." Josiah sat down at the table after lighting a hurricane lamp. The room immediately smelled of coal oil. "You said he killed a whore? That doesn't sound like something he would be involved in. Elliot's always ready for a fight, but with a man not a woman. He's scared of his own shadow around them. Even whores."

"That is why I am here, señor."

"And this is not a ruse? After everything that has happened, I'm a little suspicious of what Juan Cortina is capable of."

"You are in no danger that I know of," Juan Carlos said.

"That's good to know. But my troubles are far from cured even if Juan Cortina is hundreds of miles away. I faced down his last bounty hunter, and I'm sure there will be more. Following you, or using Elliot as a way to lure me out in the open, would not be beneath them."

"Ah," Juan Carlos said, "but very unwise since you are not alone."

"I'm sure it would be." Josiah acknowledged Juan Carlos's prowess with weapons and his fighting skill, bringing a smile to the old man's face.

"You still have troubles to face of your own. Elliot is like a bull running loose, looking for whatever he can find to break. It has caught up with him now. But I thought you should know. No matter what I think of the *niño*, I believe if you were in need of his help, he would come to your side."

Josiah nodded. "He's done so in the past. I owe him my life, but I can't let it show or his head swells even bigger than it already is."

Scrap Elliot was not much over the age of twenty years old, and Josiah had not known him prior to joining up with the Frontier Battalion in May of 1874. It had been at the start of the new Rangers, the official Rangers, organized by Governor Coke to quell the Comanche raids and restore faith and order in what was the corrupt State Police system. By all accounts, the organization had been successful, and the Comanche were nearly defeated, or at least on the run into Indian Territory.

It seemed that whenever there'd been a mission, Josiah had been paired with Elliot. The boy was one of the best shots Josiah had ever seen, and a fine horseman, too. But he was brash, quick-mouthed, and a hothead, always looking, as Juan Carlos had pointed out, for nothing but trouble.

"The Rangers came into town early this evening," Juan Carlos said.

Josiah didn't say anything, but he was relieved at the news, glad that he would be able to face Captain McNelly after the latest incident and find out what his status with the Rangers was once and for all.

"I followed at a distance," Juan Carlos continued. "It was time for me to leave the seashore. There was too much sadness there for me to bear. And it was no longer safe for me. Mexicans are being killed for no other reason than the color of their skin, and the words that escape their tongues. I could not hide behind my Anglo blood. It shows itself poorly. Besides, the village was convinced I had brought them trouble, a curse on their way of life. The fish had abandoned them, and my presence was to blame, or so they said."

After Cortina had raided Corpus Christi earlier in the month, several vigilantes got together, calling themselves minute groups, to protect the city. They were nothing but thugs looking for reasons to kill Mexicans. The uprising, as well as the raid, was the main reason Governor Coke and the adjunct general, William Steele had sent McNelly's company of Rangers to South Texas in the first place and then followed up with the Frontier Battalion, doubling the punch against Cortina.

Prior to that, after Josiah had left the Frontier Battalion and joined McNelly's company, he had been assigned to the city to serve as a spy, to arrange contacts, so they could get a better understanding of the cattle rustling operations taking place and Cortina's full intentions. Lyle had taken sick, and Josiah had come home, followed by a killer enticed by Cortina's bounty. Josiah killed the man, but as far as he knew, the bounty was still valid. The only woman, as far as Josiah knew, that Juan Carlos had loved had been killed during the raids—and Josiah had been there, had made a bad decision that had led to the woman's death. He didn't think Juan Carlos would ever forgive him, but he had, or seemed to at least.

"I'm glad to see you," Josiah said. There was no use offering up another apology. He had said he was sorry to the man more times than he could count.

"I am glad to be back in Austin. After dismounting, a few of the boys went off looking for a saloon. They stopped at the Easy Nickel," Juan Carlos said.

"I know that place." The saloon was a couple of blocks from Miss Amelia's house. "It can be a little rough for a boy like Scrap."

"I do not know the details, but I heard screams. Then I saw Scrap Elliot running down the street with blood on his hands; he was wide-eyed and pale, like a man gone loco. Suddenly, there were deputies around. They ran after him, cornered him, then took him to jail. I went asking around, but all I could find out was that the Ranger had killed a whore in the back of the Easy Nickel. It seemed very strange to me, señor."

Josiah felt numb. He could not imagine Scrap Elliot laying a violent hand on a woman. "There is nothing I can do now. I'll go down to the jail first thing in the morning."

Juan Carlos nodded and headed to the door.

"You can stay here if you want," Josiah said.

Juan Carlos smiled, nodded, then slipped out the door into the darkness, disappearing, like he always did . . . as if he had never existed in the first place.

After a moment, after the silence had completely returned to the small house, Josiah wasn't sure if he was awake or asleep, if he had dreamed the whole conversation with Juan Carlos or not.

CHAPTER 6

———◆◈◆———

The rising sun burned the back of Josiah's eyelids, forcing him awake. Sleep had been fitful, and he didn't feel rested at all. It was like he'd been fighting something, or someone, all night long, even though he couldn't remember a thing. No ghosts, no voices from the past whispering in his ear—just sore muscles and the feeling like he'd been awake for days instead of asleep for hours.

There was no question that Josiah was troubled by Juan Carlos's visit, and more than worried about Scrap—even though, given the tenuous nature of their friendship, he felt odd about that concern. Sometimes it felt to Josiah like he was more a surrogate father to Scrap than a friend or sergeant.

He sat up on the edge of his bed, wiped his eyes, took a deep breath, and then froze with panic at a sudden realization. Lyle's bed was empty, the covers twisted and rolled about. There was no sign of the little boy. Worse yet, the Peacemaker on the bureau was gone.

Fear careened through Josiah's veins like a blast of dynamite blowing open a new mine shaft.

"Lyle!" he hollered out, dashing into the front room of the house without one more thought, reacting to what he saw, instead of thinking. "Lyle!" he screamed again.

Lyle was sitting in the middle of the room. His eyes wide open, obviously startled by his father's screams. The little boy froze, like a rabbit trying to camouflage itself in the woods, unmoving at the hint of the first cry of a hawk.

"What is the matter, Señor Josiah?" Ofelia asked, annoyed by Josiah's sudden outburst, wiping her hands on her apron and rushing over to Lyle, who was now on the verge of tears.

Ofelia was at least thirty years older than Josiah. Old enough to be his mother. She was about five feet tall, and round as an October pumpkin. Her black hair was shiny, with streaks of silver zigzagging through it, and her face was almost always happy. Her wide brown eyes were more forgiving than judgmental, and she usually laughed a lot, and rarely spoke ill of anyone—even those who held a prejudice against her because she was a Mexican.

Josiah had known Ofelia since he was a little boy. She had been a *partera*, a midwife, in and around Tyler and Seerville. She had delivered all three of his daughters, and Lyle, too, into the world. Now she was much more than a *partera*; she was treated as a member of Josiah's small family. She was all that remained of his past, and he trusted her with the care and welfare of his most prized possession: Lyle Wolfe himself.

"Where is my gun?" Josiah demanded. "Lyle, what have you done with my gun? It was on the bureau when I went to bed, and now it's gone." It was Josiah's turn to act like a bull, cut loose from the herd, bucking wildly in search of a target to pierce with its horns.

The first two things that Josiah realized, after taking a deep breath, and taking in the circumstance he'd found himself in, was that Lyle was just fine and that he had slept much later than he'd thought. His heart was racing so fast he thought it was about to jump out of his chest.

The welcome smell of frying bacon hit his nose, but he was still panicked; his gun was nowhere in sight.

Ofelia had reached for Lyle with a surprising amount of grace and speed, pulling him into her arms before one tear could fall from the boy's eyes to the floor. "You have scared him. What are you thinking, yelling at the top of your lungs?"

"Where is my gun?" Josiah demanded, as he stopped in the middle of the room, about three feet from Ofelia and Lyle.

The depth of his voice echoed off the tight walls of the house, making it seem much louder than it really was. Still, he was perturbed, and scared. Though he was relieved to see his son and Ofelia in the house, acting as if nothing was amiss, the gun not a worry, or even a thought.

"I have put it away, Señor Josiah. You are not in a camp of rowdy vaqueros, where you can just *dejar las cosas laicos*." There was no mistaking the tone in Ofelia's voice. She was reprimanding Josiah. Her voice was harsh, but there was still a softness to it, a line of anger she would not allow herself to cross, though he could see she was really having to restrain herself.

Josiah glared at Ofelia. She knew full well that he did not understand her language . . . and had no interest in learning. Lyle, on the other hand, could speak Mexican just as well as he could speak English. An advantage, to Josiah's thinking, when it came to growing up in the city.

Ofelia patted Lyle's back and drew a deep breath. "You cannot leave things laying about, Señor Josiah. Lyle knows no *normas*, no rules, about such things as guns. You are not here enough for him to understand that. The *pistola* does not mean life and death to him. It means he is just like you if he carries it around. There are other ways for him to *que imitan*, to, um, how you say it? Mimic you?"

Josiah recoiled unconsciously. Ofelia was right.

"*Lo siento*. I am sorry, Señor Josiah," Ofelia continued. "I do not mean to step out of place. I came into the house this morning, and you both were sleeping. I put the *pistola* away. I should have asked you before now to be aware because Lyle is getting into everything—and I can hardly keep up with him. He *es ràpido*. Very fast for this old woman."

Lyle peered sheepishly over Ofelia's shoulder. "I din't do it, Papa."

Josiah felt himself deflate. He had acted comfortably in his own home, unaware that Lyle, who was almost four, had the strength now to carry off the gun . . . and possibly, pull the trigger. Just the thought made him shiver with fear and dread.

There were never guns lying around his own home as a child, not that he could remember anyway.

He was not allowed to touch his father's long gun that stood by the door, guarding and protecting the family, albeit coldly and silently; it would provoke a hard slap to the hand if it *was* touched. Only once, when his father was too sick to hunt, was Josiah allowed to take the long gun out of the house. And then, it was stolen by a Comanche, never to be seen again. Josiah was lucky he wasn't stolen, too, another Cynthia Ann Parker story. It seemed that the memory of guns was prolific and, at times, painful to him. And now he was giving his son a set of memories, different but the same. But hopefully not as dangerous. It was a lesson learned . . . not as hard as it could have been.

"You're right, Ofelia, I don't know what I was thinking. It won't happen again."

Ofelia nodded and let Lyle slide down out of her grip.

Josiah stood back, smiled, and opened his arms. Lyle only hesitated for a second, then ran as fast as he could to his father, jumping into the air so Josiah would catch him in a big hug.

* * *

The jail was several blocks away from Josiah's
house, and he had chosen to walk, instead of pulling Clipper
out of the livery. Spring air washed around him comfortably.
The fresh fragrance of opportunity was seemingly everywhere, like someone had kicked over an aromatic keg of
sweet-smelling liquid that had soaked thoroughly and completely into the rutted dirt streets of Austin.

The sky was clear of clouds, a perfect blue that looked
like the ocean had been cast upward and turned upside
down, the waves and tides shaken out of it in the process.

It was nearly noon, and the sun hung steady overhead,
under no threats and beaming proudly of the season it had
brought forth. The day was as perfect as one could ask for;
the only matter altering Josiah's mood was the one at hand:
finding out exactly what kind of trouble Scrap Elliot had
gotten himself into. The trouble with the gun was past; he'd
not put Lyle in harm's way again. Not if he could help it.

Josiah pulled his Stetson down to shield his eyes from
the sun and to avoid the gaze of any of the passersby, hoping
to avoid any undue recognition, or nasty snickers. His tolerance for such things was still low after his outing with Pearl
the day before.

It didn't take long to walk to the jail. It stood between
Guadalupe and San Antonio streets and between West Third
and West Fourth streets—four blocks off Congress Avenue.

Ask for directions from anyone, and you'd likely be told
it was on the Old Courthouse block, since this was the second jail Austin had seen built since the city had come into
existence. The first one had burned down in 1855.

The jail was two storeys tall, constructed of local brick,
and could hold up to thirty-four prisoners, and also held a
residence for the Travis County sheriff, Rory Farnsworth
himself.

Two square turrets bounded the building, one on each

side, and the jail was often called the "Black Hole of Calcutta," like the dungeon in India where a hundred British prisoners died in one night several years before. That grisly tale had somehow made its way to Texas and settled as a moniker for the jail. Josiah didn't know why.

It looked like a fortress, a brooding gray building with water stains seeping downward from the roof that seemed like long, dried, black tears. There were no trees, no plants growing up and around the place. It looked like nothing could, or wanted to, live on the grounds.

As it sat in the shadow of the courthouse, a white stone building that gleamed in the spring sunlight, there was no questioning that the jail had been treated with neglect and disregard by those inside and out.

It was a dangerous place. More dangerous than any saloon on a Friday night. The reputation of prisoners walking into the Black Hole on their own two feet but leaving in a pine box was well earned and caused a great deal of worry for Josiah.

He was very aware of the hard life in the jail.

It had been his charge, well over a year ago, to bring in Juan Carlos, for a crime he committed in the name of saving a man's life—Josiah's—and as a matter of fairness, when the time came to turn his head, Josiah had done so.

Juan Carlos escaped before entering the jail. The Mexican's only real crime had been the color of his skin and the accent on the end of his tongue. The sheriff in San Antonio had finally dropped those charges, at the strong urging of Captain McNelly, allowing Juan Carlos to come and go freely, though he still chose to lead a secretive life. The Mexican didn't trust the destruction of the writ, or the Anglos who put the pen to paper.

To further validate Josiah's dread of entering the jail, he found it odd that a kettle of turkey vultures were circling overhead. The birds surely smelled a chance to tear at the meat of something dead, or at least were encouraged by the opportunity of doing so relatively soon.

The sight of the death eaters, with long, black, shadowy wings, slowed Josiah in his tracks, and he sure hoped he wasn't too late. He hoped Scrap Elliot hadn't already met his maker in the violent confines of the Black Hole, the Travis County jail.

CHAPTER 7

———◆◦◆◦◆———

A desk sergeant sat just inside the tall double doors leading into the jail. He was an older man, with broomstick arms, a mustache that was neatly tended to, and eyes that looked like they could have belonged to one of the vultures overhead—black and glassy, focusing, unimpressed, on Josiah as he walked in the door.

"Remove your weapons," the sergeant demanded, then extended his hand. He was dressed in a dark brown long-sleeve shirt, wore a silver star above his heart, and was hatless.

Josiah stared at the man, sure that they hadn't met before. "I'm a Ranger."

"I don't care if you're Ulysses Simpson Grant hisself. Rules is rules. No man gets past me without checking his gun."

"Is Sheriff Farnsworth in his office?"

"Won't hep you none."

"What's your name?

"What's it matter, Ranger? If'n you really are one. I hear everything sitting here at this desk, trust me on that. You could be John Wesley Hardin for all I know, 'ceptin' I'd know that scoundrel anywheres."

Josiah shrugged. "I guess it doesn't matter. I'm not the enemy here, Sergeant, that's all."

"The name's Emery Jones, for what it's worth to you. Every man who steps in that door there might have cause for trouble. You here on official bizness?"

"No, sir. I'm here to see a friend."

"Check your weapon then. That's all there is to the matter." Jones stood up and squinted at Josiah. He wore a gun on each hip—Sheriff's Model Colts with three-inch barrels, hanging on a nicely tooled belt. "You look familiar. You ever been in here before?"

"Not recently." Josiah glanced away. There was a newspaper scattered off to the left side of the desk. His name and description had been in the *Austin Statesman* more than once in the last few months, most recently for the killing of Cortina's spy, Edgar Leatherby, aka Leathers.

The light was dim inside the foyer, only a few sconces burned along with a lamp on the desk. The ceiling was high, fourteen or fifteen feet, and the hanging lamps hung unlit. There was a musty smell mixed with an underlying odor that was not too difficult to identify. The jail smelled of human excrement, piss and shit, and the natural odor that came from warehousing men without the demand, need, or decency of washing facilities that would probably just serve as a manner of escape or violence.

"I swear you look like somebody I should know."

"I don't think we've ever met," Josiah said.

Sergeant Jones twitched quickly, casting a quick glance to the exterior wall, where all of the wanted posters hung. Satisfied that Josiah's picture wasn't there, he turned his attention back to him. "I guess you ain't John Wesley Hardin."

"It'd be a fool thing to do, walking straight into the jail, if I was an outlaw, wouldn't it?"

"It's been done. Outlaws start thinking they're smarter than the rest of us, kind of a ruse, you know. Rules is rules. No guns, no matter who you is. No knives, either." Jones nodded at the Bowie knife strapped on Josiah's belt. "You got a stingy gun hidden about, I'll need that, too."

"I only have what you see, nothing else."

"So you say."

"I suppose you're just doing your job. Can't be too careful, I expect."

"There's no supposin' to it. Who you here to see?"

"Scrap Elliot. He's a Ranger, too."

Jones shook his head no. "Ain't got no Scrap Elliot here."

"You sure?"

"Yup. Sure as it's a fine spring day and I'm stuck here inside this stinkin' hole, talkin' to the likes of you, I am."

"There's no Scrap Elliot here?" Josiah repeated.

"There's a Robert Earl Elliot. But no Scrap."

"That's him." Josiah looked to the locked door behind Jones, which obviously led to the cells. There was noise coming from behind it—hoots and hollers, laughter, and snoring. It was most likely where the smells were emanating from, too.

Just inside the foyer was a small room with another hallway leading off in the opposite direction. It held the offices, kitchen, and residence for the sheriff. Josiah had been in the sheriff's office once, but no farther than that. He had no desire to see the inside of the residence, or Rory Farnsworth for that matter. Though he doubted that there was any way around that. If he was going to help Scrap, he was certain he had to speak directly to the sheriff.

"I know who you are now. You're that Ranger who kilt his captain . . . among other things. Josiah Wolfe. That's who you are, ain't it?"

"I am."

"You're a lucky man to be walkin' around free, and still a Ranger to boot. They sure did scurry you out of the city for a while. Looks like that ploy worked, eh?"

"Don't believe everything you read."

"Why not?"

"Because what's in the papers isn't always true. It's been my experience that newspaper writers hold grudges and make things up to suit their aims."

"Really?" Jones asked sarcastically.

"Yes, really. If I killed a man unjustly, I'd be behind bars myself, or hung out in the gallows, wouldn't I? Put away in a prison instead of a jail if I was allowed to live out my days. I'm an innocent man who was just doing his duty. My guess is, my friend Elliot doesn't belong here himself."

"Rangers ain't no better'n the State Police if'n you ask me. He's here 'cause he murdered a whore, plain and simple. He'll have a noose around his neck before the week's out, Ranger or not. You wait and see."

"Nobody asked you about the Rangers, did they?" Josiah hesitated, then unbuckled his gun belt, put it on the desk with ease and respect, and followed it up with his knife. "Now, let me in to see my friend."

Jones took the weapons and walked over to the wall-sized wood armory, then unlocked it, put them in, and locked it back up. He walked back to Josiah with a frozen look on his face, void of any emotion. "Put your arms out."

"What for?"

"I need to see for myself that you're not carryin' anything else."

"I gave you my word."

"I don't trust anyone. Do as I ask or leave. It don't matter to me."

Josiah dropped his head a bit in defeat and extended his arms. "I've said those words before myself. I surely understand what you mean . . ."

Jones led Josiah down a long, dank, smelly hall with an exterior wall on one side, facing out to San Antonio

Street, and the jail cells on the other. A series of barred windows let in the light, but there were no lamps within sight or available to the prisoners, for mischief or warmth. Even in the throes of a fine spring day, there was a chill in the air that caused Josiah to shiver.

The walk garnered some attention from the prisoners, though a quiet wave followed after them as they passed by a line of twelve fully tenanted cells. There was another wing of cells behind these and one above them. There was rumor of a dungeon, a hole for solitary confinement, but Josiah had never been in the bowels of the jail, and he hoped to never have reason to be.

One man stood nervously at the front of his cell, about halfway down to the end of the hall. He was a short man, with a bald patch on the top of his head, the rest of his stringy black hair wispy and unattended. His clothes seemed to suggest nothing in particular, whether he was a saddle bum or an outlaw, but what stuck out about the man, other than a long, cold stare, was the fact that his forehead was soaked with sweat. The odd little man was either nervous or ill with a contagion, and Josiah wanted no knowledge of either cause. He hurried his step a bit to get past him.

Scrap was in the last cell, at the very end of the hall. Instead of being in line with the rest, it crooked around a corner, stuffed in an alcove, and was about half the size of the other cells.

"You got company, Robert Earl Elliot," Jones said.

Josiah stood behind the skinny sergeant, not trying to hide, but trying to get an extra second to gauge Scrap's state of mind and possibly his innocence or guilt.

Scrap was just a bit over twenty years old, maybe twenty-one, Josiah wasn't sure. He'd never asked directly. It was obvious the boy was young. He could hardly grow a full row of stubble under his nose, much less on his face, and his words and actions were mostly impulsive, lacking any wisdom or experience at all. Still, Scrap was a fine horseman and a better shot. Because of both skills, regardless of his untamed attitudes, Josiah owed the boy his life. Friendship was not an act of obligation, but respect was.

The boy was curled up on a cot at the back of the cell. Shadows fell hard in the alcove, and he looked more like a lump of grain sacks stuffed under a blanket than a body. But Jones's voice had roused him, and Scrap rolled over then sat up slowly on the edge of the cot.

He had a hard, thin face himself and a head full of unruly hair the color of coal. His eyes were blue, but distant, and he was rangy, not carrying an ounce of extra fat on his lean, muscular body. His shirt was soiled, blood-stained on the right side, and his lip was puffed, like he had taken a punch square in the mouth.

"I figured I'd see you here sooner or later, Wolfe."

"You got anyone else who knows you're here?"

"Ain't a soul in this old world that gives a hoot about what happens to me, Wolfe. You know that."

Scrap's parents had been killed in a Comanche raid when he was a few years into his teens. He was left to care for his younger sister, Myra Lynn, who was now at a convent in Dallas, serving the church and her God as an Ursuline nun. Josiah had never met Myra Lynn, but he had met Scrap's aunt Callie, who owned a boardinghouse in Fort Worth, and he knew that Scrap was, in fact, alone in the world, other than her and his relation to the Ranger company he belonged to. And there was no question that no one from the company would come to his aid, especially not if the charge of murdering a whore was true.

"I'm here," Josiah said.

Jones stepped back. "I'll leave you two to yourselves."

Josiah nodded, and Jones started to walk away, but he stopped once he was about to turn the corner. "You can see yourself back to my desk, but don't be talkin' to none of these heathens on the way out, you hear?"

"No worry there," Josiah said.

"Good." Jones walked on, eventually disappearing.

Scrap walked up to the front of the cell. "It's good to see you, Wolfe. I didn't mean nothin' by what I said."

"I know. Now, tell me what happened."

Before Scrap even got a word out of his mouth, a wave of screaming and shouting broke out, echoing back to Josiah and Scrap . . . followed by a loud, ear-shattering *boom!* An immediate rush of air pushed through the jail, followed by the quick crumbling of the exterior wall. Dust and chunks of the brick wall flew everywhere—it was like a stick of dynamite had gone off just outside the jail. A hole big enough to ride a horse through suddenly appeared on the street side of the jail.

Josiah ducked and covered, shielding himself from a thick gray cloud that had filled the hallway and from chunks of wall that were flying through the air. It was like standing in the middle of a windstorm on the driest day in the summer; he couldn't see two inches in front of his face. His ears rang from the explosion, but he was far enough away not to have been seriously injured, at least he didn't think he'd been. He could taste the dust, smell the black powder residue of the dynamite, but still feel all of his limbs.

Only one thought crossed his mind as he shoved himself into the corner of the alcove: He was in the midst of a jail-break, and there was nothing he could do. He couldn't hardly see, couldn't hardly breathe, and worst of all, he had no weapon to defend himself . . . or the jail.

CHAPTER 8

———◆※◆———

Distorted images—silhouettes of a group of men rushing into the dust cloud, and then a team of horses following, whinnying and protesting—appeared through the hole in the wall, materializing like a willful dream collaborated on by all of the hostile prisoners in the jail.

Light anxiously pushed in sharply defined rays through the eight-foot-tall hole. It was as if such bright light had never touched the inside walls of the gloomy place, even though this level of the jail wasn't the dungeon.

As the dust cleared and the images grew less distorted, and more real, Josiah knew he was right in his thinking: This *was* a jailbreak.

There was yelling and screaming everywhere. Someone fired a gun just outside of the wall. All of the sounds echoed and reverberated harshly inside the walls. Josiah's ears still rang from the initial explosion.

A rope had been tied to not one, but three horses, and two men appeared alongside the horses and simultaneously tied the rope to the metal door of one of the cells.

There was no sign of Sergeant Jones, any of the other of deputies, or the sheriff, Rory Farnsworth. They certainly had to be aware of the explosion and, more certainly, what its purpose was. Anyone within five miles had heard the rumble of the dynamite and felt the ground tremble for a second or two. Surely the jail was fortified and staffed by more men than just the grouchy old desk sergeant.

Or maybe not. The fact that it was broad daylight, coming straight up on noon, the timing of the jailbreak was brazen, and a surprise to Josiah—he would never have suspected a thing like this could happen in the middle of the day. Whoever was behind the plan must have had good reason to take such a blatant risk. Maybe the planners of the act were aware of something that Josiah was not, concerning the whereabouts of the sheriff and his men. It was the only thing that made sense.

For the moment, there was nothing Josiah could do but stay where he was and not give any indication that he had anything to do with the law.

If these men were as serious as they appeared to be, shooting a Texas Ranger would be of no consequence to them. Most likely, killing him would be just one more bloody deed to brag about after it was all said and done.

Outlaws had a mean streak that Josiah could never understand, and he hoped he didn't share any of their spiteful and heartless tendencies, like he'd been recently accused of in the newspapers.

The men on the horses were becoming clearer as the explosion and its residue quickly settled to the ground.

They were dressed in black dusters, with kerchiefs pulled up over their noses, both for protection against the dust and so they couldn't be identified. Typical. Nothing stood out. Nothing to identify them later. Even their hands were covered with black gloves. It was almost like they had uniforms on, another odd twist of forethought that stood out to Josiah, as he regained his senses and tried to pay attention to what was happening.

All of the prisoners in the cell block had recognized what was happening as Josiah had. They started shouting, banging against their metal cell doors with whatever they could find to draw attention to themselves: tin cups, pillows, shoes, their own bodies. It was an orchestra of salvation, pleas to be set free, beggars held tightly in the shackle of steel with no promise of escape, ever—until now. The voices and cries were almost as loud as the explosion.

Where was Farnsworth? Josiah wondered silently. *There was no way anyone within several blocks could not have heard the ruckus.*

None of the prisoners had any privacy in the construction of the fortress of the Black Hole of Calcutta, not that it mattered—they had all given up their rights when they committed whatever crime had landed them in the jail in the first place. There were no brick walls in between the cells, just bars, row after row, like cages set next to one another, and now that the dust had completely fallen to the floor, Josiah could see all of the way to the entrance.

Every confined prisoner was one step from madness, screaming and dancing like a fire had been lit, trapping each man even further, his life at risk—though there was no immediate threat of death, not even the slightest hint of smoke now. And the smell of freedom was an unforeseen stroke of luck that none of the prisoners could ignore. They were all in a frenzy, like someone had kicked a nest of red ants, sending them scurrying for escape.

"Let me out!" came a scream.

"Take me!" said another man.

"I'm next!" another voice shouted, rising over the rest.

The only man, it seemed, who was not excited about the break was the sweaty, mousy-looking man that Josiah had noticed as he and Jones passed by.

That man stood in the center of his cell, his head slightly down, his hands clasped in front of his waist, almost like he was looking down on a grave, praying. He was completely unaffected by the chaos around him, other than that he was sweating more profusely now. He did not share in the enthusiasm that was so palpable in the jail that it could be tasted.

"What the hell is going on, Wolfe?" Scrap whispered.

Josiah was stuffed as far back in the corner of the alcove as he could get. He held his index finger to his dry lips, hoping to avoid notice by the men conducting the jailbreak.

Scrap kicked at the ground, groaned, eyed Josiah angrily, then turned his attention back to the horses and the men standing in the blast hole.

"Pull!" came a command, and the horses danced backward with all their might, the rope on the cell wall tightening immediately.

After a quick tussle, the door popped off with a hard-fought and unifying tug from all three horses. Only after the metal fell to the ground, creating an immediate cloud of dust, did one of the horses begin to protest more strenuously than any of them had previously. Something had spooked the solid gray gelding. Fear and frustration boiled in the horse's eyes. If there was any identifiable creature among the outlaws, it was this horse.

The rider, who sat tall in the saddle, tried to calm the horse, but didn't seem to be able to get it to settle down.

"Explosion set it off," Scrap mumbled. "Damn fool's gonna let that horse hurt itself if he don't get it out of there fast."

Josiah said nothing. Just watched and kept an eye on Scrap. The boy knew horses and their behavior better than any man he knew, and the thought of one in trouble made the boy visibly nervous, agitated.

Scrap started pacing, pushing at the bars that separated him from his freedom, and from helping the horse. "You gotta get me out of here, Wolfe."

Josiah shook his head no.

"Untie the damn thing," the rider yelled. "Now. Untie it now!"

Only a few minutes had passed since the explosion, but it seemed longer. Everything was happening at lightning speed. The gang of men looked well rehearsed, with distinct roles to play—the only hitch so far seemed to be the frightened horse.

A distant shot rang out, followed by another and another.

The rider jumped out of the saddle on the gray gelding, holding on to the lead as firmly as he could, and quickly untied the rope from the cell door. The horse continued to nay and protest, but it quit bucking once the rider dismounted. Josiah didn't have the insight to a horse's mind that Scrap did—it was one of the reasons that Josiah had grown comfortable with riding with him.

Once the rope was untied from the gray gelding, another man rushed inside the open jail cell, glanced over his shoulder in a panic, then grabbed the mousy man and headed back for the horse. The mousy man offered no verbal complaints, but he didn't aid in the escape, either. It was almost like he had to be dragged to the waiting horse.

It was an odd sight for Josiah, seeing a man busted out of jail in such dramatic fashion, not showing any emotion, specifically joy, or relief. He wasn't sure if the behavior mattered, but it sure did register with him as odd.

"Trouble's a-comin'," someone just outside the hole in the wall shouted inside.

The rider pushed the man up on the horse and yelled back, signaling for the first time that he might be the leader of the gang. "You know what to do."

A heartbeat later, more shots rang in the air, sounding much like a July 4th celebration. There was no way for Josiah to know how many men were actually involved in the jailbreak—he couldn't see beyond the blast hole, but from the sound of the guns, there were at least five, maybe more.

The gray gelding was quickly backed out of the hole, and in another half minute, the gunshots were trailing away, the firing continuing but growing distant.

The only noise in the wake of the jailbreak was the disappointed screams and whistles of the prisoners left behind. If there had been more will and opportunity, Josiah was certain that a riot could have broken out at any moment, leaving him in a worse position than he was in when the jail wall exploded open.

"They're gone," Scrap said.

Josiah nodded. "Keep quiet. I need to go find Jones and Sheriff Farnsworth."

"Well, I ain't goin' anywhere."

"Don't worry, I'll get you out of here." Josiah pulled himself out of the corner and started to head away from Scrap's cell but stopped just at the farthest corner of it. "Unless you deserve to be in here."

"I didn't kill no one, Wolfe. I swear."

"All right, that's all I need to hear."

CHAPTER 9

———◆◇◆———

Sergeant Jones was lying facedown in the middle of the foyer, a pool of blood growing underneath him like a dam had been breached by a heavy spring rain; red rivulets trailed away from the body in all directions on the uneven floor. He'd been shot in the back at least four times and at least once right through the heart. His hand was outstretched, only a few feet from the gun locker. Perhaps he'd died valiantly, or perhaps not, there was no way to know. Either way, there was no question that there had been at least one death, a murder through and through, associated with the jailbreak. There might have been more, for all Josiah knew.

Noonday light pushed inside from the open front door of the jail. The rays stabbed at the dreariness of the foyer, cutting through the dust and dirt that seemed to hang woefully suspended in the air. The room smelled like a mix of gunpowder and blood, an all too familiar assault on the senses for Josiah—he could taste war on the tip of his tongue, and he unconsciously spit it out as he rushed to Jones and pulled the keys off the man's belt. There was no use checking to see if Jones was still alive; his eyes were fixed upward, frozen open for the very last time.

Josiah headed to the gun cabinet, unlocked it, and quickly found his Peacemaker and Bowie knife.

He quickly buckled his gun belt on his waist, slid his knife back in the sheath, then pulled his six-shooter from the holster and made his way to the door. He was reasonably certain that the outlaws were gone, quick on their getaway, but he wasn't taking any chances.

There was still a great deal of riotous noise coming from the cell block, but it was a different sound; the prisoners' hopes of escape and rescue had faded to anger, disappointment, and rage.

Just as he was about to approach the door and exit the foyer to the outside world, Josiah heard a different variety of screams, shouts, and footsteps approaching from the wing behind him, as well as from down the hallway that led to the sheriff's quarters. He stopped and turned around.

"Put your hands up and drop the gun!" a man yelled, pushing through the hallway door, aiming a rifle directly at Josiah's head.

The man was a deputy that Josiah didn't recognize, but he quickly realized the situation he'd put himself in and what it must look like. He was an unknown man, with a gun, heading out the door just after a jailbreak. Luckily, Rory Farnsworth appeared right behind the deputy.

Josiah put his hands up automatically, still holding his Peacemaker.

"It's all right, he's one of us," Farnsworth shouted at the deputy. "Put your hands down, Wolfe."

The deputy didn't seem entirely convinced but stepped out of the way as a line of armed deputies pushed by him, rushing into the cell block and out the front door, weapons drawn—their reaction to the jailbreak certain if not swift.

Upon the deputies' entrance into the cell block, the noise

elevated to an unbearable level—it almost sounded like another explosion had gone off. Boos and hisses were followed by a string of antagonizing and hateful words.

Josiah knew Scrap was not one of the hecklers, that he was sitting silently in his cell, waiting for Josiah to return—and Josiah also knew that he was glad that there were bars separating the men from the deputies, or there would have been another melee, a riot of unimaginable consequences.

The deputy who'd pointed his gun at Josiah stepped away at the silent behest of a hard nod from Farnsworth, leaving the two men, along with Jones's body, alone in the foyer.

"Damn it, they've killed Jones," Farnsworth said. He walked over to the man, kneeled down, and felt for a pulse at the side of his neck. "Deader than dead. Now I'm going to have to go tell Matilda. That will be another entirely unpleasant event that I must face today. Can matters get any worse?"

"I suppose they could," Josiah said.

"How so?"

"Not sure, Rory. But I imagine they could."

"Jones was the best desk sergeant I ever had."

"He did his job, stripped me of all my weapons when I came in."

Farnsworth stood up and faced Josiah. "What are you doing here, Wolfe? I assumed you weren't involved in this mess. I am right, aren't I?"

"You are."

"Good to hear." It was hard to tell whether the sheriff believed what Josiah said or not; his face was as expressionless as a possum—and nearly as mean-looking—from a distance. "What were you doing here, anyway?"

"A friend told me Scrap Elliot had been brought in on a murder charge, and I came to see for myself."

There was no need to tell Farnsworth that the friend was Juan Carlos. The sheriff and Juan Carlos knew each other, but Josiah didn't know the depth of their relationship, and now was not the time to find out if it was a healthy friendship or not. Juan Carlos had many enemies in Austin. For all Josiah knew, Juan Carlos could have acted as a spy for the sheriff, just like he had done for Captain McNelly and the Texas Rangers.

"Your friend told you correctly," Farnsworth said.

"I haven't had much of a chance to speak to Elliot about the charge. The explosion went off just as I reached his cell."

"Now, that's a coincidence."

"What else would it be, Rory?" Josiah asked, with a cocked eyebrow.

The deputies were intent on quieting down the prisoners, yelling back, ordering them all to their bunks. All told there were twelve deputies swarming about, one for each man, trying to restore some kind of order to the Travis County jail.

Farnsworth didn't seem to notice or care; he was completely focused on Josiah. The noise level had been quickly reduced to about half of what it was before the deputies arrived. The smell of death and gunpowder persisted.

"I don't know, Wolfe, your reputation precedes you everywhere you go in this town. You ought to know that by now. I know you better than most folks in Austin, but I don't hardly know you at all. The newspapers have painted you as a renegade, a lawless Ranger harkening back to the State Police days."

"I'm well aware of what the newspapers have to say about me. They're wrong. And you know that."

"Do I? I saw you strolling down the street with Pearl Fikes yesterday. Do you know nothing of appearances or social graces?"

"Obviously not. I suspect that sentiment applies to you as well?" Josiah asked, remembering fully the same day Farnsworth spoke of. Only instead of being socially unaware, Blanche Dumont had publicly spit on the sheriff, for reasons unknown. "I came here with no other knowledge or intention than to see my fellow Ranger and to see for myself whether or not the charges are true."

"And are they?"

"I don't know the details of the crime, but Elliot says he is innocent. I take him at his word, and that's good enough for me."

"It's not good enough for me. Or the circuit judge who will be presiding over the trial. There has been a rash of killings on that side of town. Most folks would not normally take notice of the death of a single soiled dove at the hands of an unruly cowboy, but there have been too many within a short period of time. People are starting to ask questions. The boy literally had blood on his hands and just cause as far as I understand it."

"And what cause was that?" Josiah asked.

"Have you ever been rejected by a whore, Wolfe?"

"Can't say that I have."

"Me, either. I'm sure that'd be reason enough to drive some men to kill."

"We'll see about that."

"I'm sure we will." Farnsworth nodded, then stared harshly at Josiah. "I have a witness, Wolfe. Regardless of your question of motive or the boy's character, which I know you hold in high esteem, someone saw Scrap Elliot plunge a knife into the girl's belly and run away like a coward. A rope will end this story, you mark my words."

The air escaped Josiah's lungs. He could hardly breathe at the news, much less say anything in Scrap's defense.

"What did you see when the explosion occurred?" Farnsworth asked, changing the subject.

Josiah stared at the sheriff and then replied, not anxious to let go of the discussion about Scrap but sure that he had to for the moment. "Wasn't much to see, everybody was dressed in black, had their faces covered, and seemed well organized, rehearsed, like they knew what to do and when to do it. Only thing that stood out was a gray gelding that gave one of the men trouble for a minute or so."

"Would you recognize that horse again if you saw it?"

"I think I would."

"That's it? That's all you saw?"

Josiah scrunched his shoulders, frustrated. "Is there something else I should have seen, Rory, besides the prisoner that got heisted out of here?"

"I'm just asking. A man of your position should have keen powers of observation."

Before Josiah could say anything else, the first deputy, who'd entered the foyer with Farnsworth and aimed his gun at Josiah, hurried to the sheriff's side. He was a tall, thin-faced man with a thick upside-down V mustache streaked with wiry gray hairs. Sweat beaded on his exposed brow, and his felt Stetson was cocked back on his head. He still held the rifle, but casually, so it didn't look to Josiah like there was an immediate threat to be concerned about.

"They took Randalls, Sheriff," the deputy said, words rolling off his tongue hurriedly.

Farnsworth didn't flinch. "Who'd you expect they busted out, Milt, the two drunk cowboys we brought in for fighting last night?"

"Didn't expect it to be Randalls, Sheriff, that's all," the deputy said.

For the first time, Josiah noticed that the deputy, Milt somebody or other, was holding a piece of paper. He thrust the paper toward Farnsworth. "I found this under Randalls's pillow. It don't make no sense though, does it?"

Farnsworth took the paper and stared at it, then shook his head as if he didn't understand it, either. "Doesn't make an ounce of sense to me."

"What is it?" Josiah asked.

"Looks like a bunch of letters thrown together, but they don't make any sense," the sheriff said.

"Could I see it?" Josiah asked.

Farnsworth eyed Josiah cautiously, then shrugged. "I guess I don't see why not."

Josiah took the paper and stared at it for a second, immediately recognizing that it was a cipher of some kind.

XLICAMPPOMPPQIYRHIVXLISEOXVII.

There was nothing else but that line of letters on the paper.

"I looks to me like this Randalls fella knew someone was coming for him," Josiah said. "Now that I think of it, he didn't seem real happy, or helpful, about going. He left you a message, Rory—in code. It's the only explanation I can think of."

"In code? Are you sure?"

Josiah took a deep breath. "Yes, this kind of message was pretty common in the War Between the States. Most likely, this Randalls fella served with the Confederacy. It looks like a familiar formula to me."

Farnsworth shrugged his shoulders. "I know nothing of the man's past other than his crimes."

Josiah knew that the sheriff had not served in the war. He was hardly old enough to wear the badge, and it was only because of his highly connected father, Myron Farnsworth, a banker, and his own education, obtained at a highfalutin college out East, that he held the position at all.

"Who was this man, Randalls, anyway? Why was he in jail?" Josiah asked.

Farnsworth and Milt exchanged a quick set of glances, then each looked away from the other quickly.

"Abram Randalls worked as an accountant for a bank, Wolfe," the sheriff said. "He's a thief, an embezzler."

"Why would an embezzler be worried about being broke out of jail?"

"Who said he was worried?"

Josiah shrugged and eyed Milt the deputy at the same

time. The man unnerved him. Milt acted like he wasn't
paying attention, like he was waiting to be discharged, but
neither was hardly the truth. He was listening to every word
and watching every move Josiah made.

"I just made an assumption, that's all," Josiah said.

Farnsworth pointed to the note. "Do you think you can
figure out what it says?"

Josiah nodded. "I think I can, but it might take some
time. It's been a lot of years since I had to figure something
like this out."

"You were good at it, then, in the war?" the sheriff asked.

"Good enough," Josiah answered. "I've always had a
knack for letters, but it wasn't my main duty."

"What was?"

"Whatever needed doing."

Farnsworth nodded. "Well, while you're figuring out
what that note says, I guess I better get these men out after
whoever took Randalls—and go face Matilda Jones to tell
her that her husband has left this world for another one. It'll
be a sad dinner for her on this night. The coldhearted bas-
tards shot the man in the back. Not sure I can tell Matilda
that."

The sheriff walked off then, with Milt the deputy following after him like a puppy, hungry for its milk.

Josiah stuffed the note in his pocket and turned back
toward the jail block. His most important cause for being at
the jail in the first place had not yet been satisfied.

He didn't know how Scrap Elliot had landed there in the
first place, and he wasn't leaving until he found out. Cipher
or no cipher. Jailbreak or no jailbreak.

CHAPTER 10

———◆·×◆×·◆———

Scrap was laying on his cot at the back of the cell, staring at the ceiling. A veil of silence had come over the jail as two deputies patrolled the hall, their weapons brandished firmly in wait for the slightest reason to use them.

The hole still gaped and would have to be protected until it was closed up. That wasn't Josiah's problem. It was Rory Farnsworth's—along with rounding up the men who had busted Abram Randalls out of jail in the first place.

What was Josiah's problem was Scrap and the situation at hand. Most importantly, whether or not the story Farnsworth had told him was true: Did Scrap stab a whore, run away, and did somebody see him do it? The sheriff seemed pretty confident that Scrap was as guilty as guilty can be.

"You come back with a key?" Scrap asked, hoisting himself up, spinning his legs over the side of the cot.

Josiah shook his head no. "Looks like you're stuck for the moment." He faced Scrap and dropped the volume of his voice to just above a soft whisper.

"I gotta get out of here, Wolfe."

"Why?"

"I got places to go, things to do. You know that. Besides, I ain't no killer, and you know that, too."

"I've seen you kill more than one man."

Scrap looked at Josiah like he had been slapped, then looked quickly away to the opposite wall. "Why would you go and say somethin' like that?"

"Because it's true."

"They said I killed a woman, Wolfe. You know that can't be true."

Josiah let a moment of silence fall between the two of them. He watched Scrap close, closer than he ever had, searching for a hint of a lie. Thankfully, he didn't see one.

"Sheriff says somebody saw you do it. Said you stabbed the girl in the belly and ran. Did you do that?"

"No." Scrap's voice quavered. "It was dark. I could hardly see in front of me. Ain't no way anybody saw anything."

"You're sure?"

"I'm absolutely sure, Wolfe. I was there. I was just tryin' to get a good look at the girl. I had no cause to stab her."

"She didn't turn you down?"

"Turn me down for what?"

"Spurn you? You know, for the business they're in? Tell you no?"

"I wasn't lookin' for entertainment, Wolfe."

Josiah breathed in a deep chestful of air. The dust had settled, but his tongue and his insides felt covered with the stuff from the blast.

"I'm not a woman killer," Scrap insisted. He punched the bed out of frustration.

"I know that," Josiah said, calmly. "But if you want me to help get you out of here, you're going to have to tell me everything that happened, exactly how it happened."

Scrap exhaled fully and gritted his teeth. "I don't rightly know what really happened, Wolfe. That's part of the problem."

"You don't remember?"

"Of course, I remember. It was just . . . I don't know, it's a mess of things, you know?"

Josiah shook his head. No, he didn't know or understand any of what was going on. At the moment, he was fully confused. "Start at the beginning. Why'd the company leave Corpus, and how'd you get to Austin?"

"General Steele and the governor want Captain McNelly to join up with the Frontier Battalion, double-flank Cortina, and put an end to him once and for all. They figured they'd need to do some restin' up and some trainin' in the camp before that happened. Once we got to Austin, we was free to blow off some steam, and that's all I was doin', at least until I saw . . ." Scrap stopped and didn't utter another word. It was like his tongue had locked up against the top of his mouth and he couldn't move it.

Josiah was glad to hear that McNelly was in town—assuming he was, based on Scrap's presence there. He had some business of his own to tend to with the captain—namely whether he was going to continue to ride with the company or not. But Scrap was acting odd. The whole situation, with Scrap behind bars and the jailbreak, which seemed like nothing more than coincidence at this point, was about as strange as strange could be.

"Saw who, Scrap?" Josiah asked.

"Damn it, Wolfe." Scrap's eyes were red like he was about to cry, and he bit his lip.

"Damn it, what?"

"I thought I saw Myra Lynn."

"Your sister? She's a nun in Dallas. Why would she be in Austin in a saloon?"

Scrap shook his head no. "She went to the convent but was never no nun."

"You said she was."

"I lied."

"Why? Why in the hell would you lie to me about something like that all this time?"

"Because I didn't want to tell you she was a whore, Wolfe. That's why. I was ashamed to tell you the truth. I still don't want it to be true, but it is, damn it. It's as true as the sky is blue, and my parents, God rest their broken souls, I'm sure they blame me for how she turned out, they surely do, even in heaven. Everything else was always my fault."

One of the deputies that was keeping watch on the prisoners walked within ten feet of Josiah, his boot crunching on the rubble that had yet to be cleaned up. The deputy, another one of Farnsworth's men that Josiah didn't know, stared at him and Scrap with disdain. He was a portly man, half again as round as he was tall, and his clothes, which couldn't hardly be called a uniform, were unkempt and dusty—and had most likely been that way before the blast occurred in the jail, judging from the looks of the shaggy man.

Outside, a team of horses clopped by pulling a wagon, and the first sounds of a gathering posse made its way just outside the jail.

Shouts and commands, along with the collection of guns, horses, and information, were all taking place about ten feet from the hole in the jailhouse wall. A crowd was growing on San Antonio Street, curious, scared, everyone wondering what was going to happen next. There was still a lingering aroma of gunpowder, but the everyday stink of the jail had returned as quickly as it had disappeared. No hole in the wall was big enough to clear out that smell.

"She was never a nun?" Josiah asked, his voice way down now. He didn't break eye contact with Scrap, who let a single tear escape his eye. It trailed down his cheek unattended to, ignored, just like the truth about his sister.

"No, sir," Scrap said, the quaver gone from his voice, replaced by a calm tone, sure and resigned to getting a secret off his chest. "She never was. Aunt Callie has been beside herself in her letters to me from Fort Worth. Worried about the girl's welfare and all, but she can't go on a hunt for her.

Besides, Myra Lynn is old enough to decide to live her life the way she wants to, I suppose. What good would it do to catch her and take her home? She'd just run away again. She's been doin' it all of her life. At least since Ma and Pa was killed, and I was supposed to look after her. It's my fault."

"What else did you lie to me about, Scrap?" Josiah's teeth were clenched. He was disappointed.

"Nothin', I swear."

Josiah let the answer settle to the ground just like the dust had, slowly and surely. As far as he knew, since everything about Scrap was starting to come into question, even the fact that the boy's parents had been killed in a Comanche raid was under suspicion. According to Scrap in previous conversations, he and Myra Lynn had been spared only by the boy's quick thinking, to hide under the house, hugging up next to the fireplace in the center.

Myra Lynn was a year younger than Scrap, fifteen when the raid occurred, and Scrap, with nothing left to do, along with his aunt in Fort Worth, thought the convent for the Ursuline nuns would be the best place for the girl to finish growing up. Obviously they were wrong—or there was more to the story. Either way, Josiah was more than a little steamed about being lied to.

He stiffened and tried to ignore the noise beyond the wall of the jail. He was accustomed to being in on a posse, and it was his inclination to offer his help, and gun, to find the men who'd busted out Abram Randalls. But he was sticking it out with Scrap, even though, at the moment, he wasn't exactly sure why.

"Tell me what happened as soon as you got to Austin," Josiah said.

Scrap stood up from the bunk and walked over to Josiah, so only the bars separated them. "I got a room, and . . ."

"Where?"

"Mrs. Bailey's. Same place as always when I'm in town.

I ain't got a house like you to go to, Wolfe." There was almost a sneer on Scrap's face when he said it.

"All right, what then?" Josiah asked, ignoring Scrap's attitude. He was used to the sneers and anger that erupted from Scrap's mouth on occasion. It was just the way he was—young and impetuous.

"I went over to the Easy Nickel."

"By yourself?"

"Yes, by myself. Why?"

"Just wondering why you didn't wait to go with the other boys."

Scrap exhaled deeply and looked away. "I was thinkin' Myra Lynn might be there, or at least in town, that's what Callie said in her last letter, that she thought maybe Myra Lynn was heading to Austin. I didn't want anybody to know that I was related to her, so I went alone."

"Related to a whore?"

Scrap nodded, then began to walk in a small circle inside the cell. He looked trapped, as if he was ready to go off in a rage but couldn't. "You gotta get me out of here, Wolfe."

"I think you're stuck here for a while." Josiah let a second of silence pass between them, as he heard a man, Milt he was pretty sure, call for the posse to move out. It was a muffled command but unmistakable, regardless.

Once the noise calmed down and the horses had ridden out, heading south, Josiah turned his attention back to Scrap. "What happened once you got to the saloon?"

"I got me a beer and started watchin' the doors. They got a line of little shacks out back, as well as rooms upstairs, for the pleasure business. It was pretty busy. The drives are heavy on the trail now . . ."

Josiah agreed silently. Spring was a busy time, getting cattle from the ranches in South Texas up to Abilene.

"Anyways," Scrap continued, "it was pretty dark, and there was this fella givin' one of the girls a hard time. A little blond thing that looked like a fawn tryin' to outrun a

wolf—no offense to you, Wolfe. About the time I thought
I'd help out, the bartender went after the fella with a three-
foot-long club. More like a big oak branch with the bark
whittled off, heavy. So I sat back down, and this fella, a
cowboy, got chased out of the saloon. I thought that was it.
The girl looked pretty shaken up. The fella was gettin' rough
with her, and she looked new to her duty, you know? Not
sure what to make of all the noise and people in the saloon,
and the gropin' hands comin' her way. She disappeared in
the crowd then, not comforted by the other girls, but looked
down on, mocked. She ran toward the back door, cryin'.

"It was about that time I thought I saw Myra Lynn. That girl
was headin' out the door, too, like maybe she's followin' after
the first one. So, of course, I go after her," Scrap said, looking down at the ground. "I guess that was my mistake. Always
has been. Goin' after Myra Lynn, fightin' her battles. It's a
bad habit that I would be glad to be rid of if the truth be told."

"Did anybody follow you or pay attention to you?"

"No. I just got a beer and was sittin' there all quiet-like,
until I thought about helpin' the girl. But I didn't do anything. Why are you askin' if somebody followed after me?"

"Sheriff says somebody saw you kill the girl."

"I didn't kill nobody."

"I'm just saying there's a witness, Scrap. If there's a trial,
you'll need to know who that person was. Think about it.
Are you sure there wasn't anybody around?"

"I don't know, I swear, Wolfe." Scrap stopped pacing the
circle he was wearing down and stared straight at Josiah.
"They're gonna hang me, aren't they?"

"Not if I have anything to say about it, you can trust that,
Scrap. I guess I got reason not to believe a word you say,
since you lied to me. But I can see your way of thinking,
wanting to hide the truth about Myra Lynn. I know you're
prideful. It's a curse you carry, but I can understand that,
too. I've ridden with you long enough to know you're no
woman killer. At least, not on purpose," Josiah said.

"Thanks, Wolfe, that means a lot. It surely does. I couldn't hurt no girl, ever."

"What happened next?"

"Well," Scrap said, "I got outside, and that cowboy fella jumped the blond girl. I never got much of a look at him. He could be right in the next cell and I wouldn't know it. Anyways, she screamed and fell to the ground almost right away. I yelled at the fella and started to pull my gun, but I flinched, lost my focus 'cause I saw Myra Lynn rush to the left, just out of the shadows. She saw me, too, about the same time I saw her. We ain't seen each other since I took her to the convent, so it's been some years, but I swear it was her. She didn't say anything, just looked at me like I was the worst thing on the bottom of her shoe, then she ran off into the darkness. I wanted to go after her, more than anything I did. But I couldn't."

"The girl needed your help."

Scrap nodded. "When I turned back to her, she had a knife stuck in her chest, and the cowboy ran off in between the shacks. Before I could pull my gun the rest of the way, he was gone. I thought the girl was still alive, so I went over to help her. I pulled the knife out, and she took her last gasp."

"You're sure you didn't get a good look at him?" Josiah asked.

Scrap shook his head. "I told you, Wolfe, no. It was dark, and he was wearin' dark clothes. I wasn't real worried about what he looked like, but I guess I should've been."

"Probably so. But you did have blood on your hands, like they say?"

Scrap nodded. "And a knife in my grip. The back door of the saloon busted open and the bartender rushed at me with that big stick. I ran, Wolfe. I knew how it looked. But I was running after Myra Lynn, too."

"She disappeared?"

"Yes. Again. I didn't kill that blond girl, I swear to you, Wolfe. I swear on my parents' graves and my sister's soul.

That cowboy did, I'm sure of it, but nobody believes my story."

"I'm sorry, Scrap. I really am."

"Can you help me, Wolfe?"

"I'll do everything I can," Josiah said. "I owe you that, and more."

CHAPTER 11

———◆◆✦◆◆———

The crowd was starting to break up as Josiah left the jail. There was no sign of the posse, Sheriff Farnsworth, or any of his men, outside of the two deputies standing guard at the new entryway created by the blast.

The Black Hole of Calcutta nickname was now a literal reference to the jail's structure. Josiah was surprised that there wasn't any more apparent damage to the building. It was obviously a fortress, durable with its brick and stone facade, but the interior of the building must have been stronger than normal to have survived the explosion, too.

In its entirety, the jailbreak had taken less than five minutes. It was a masterful undertaking, and from the look of the exterior, the crew behind it obviously had experience with detonations, which meant one of two things to Josiah: They were miners, or they had been in the military. Considering the note in his pocket and the cipher it had been written in, he suspected the latter. No matter the circumstance, everything always seemed to lead back to the war. Though the use of dynamite as a regular explosive was a more recent development, Josiah was betting the men who orchestrated the break were army men, through and through. He would have just about bet his life on it.

It was amazing how quickly life got back to normal on the streets of Austin after such a dramatic event.

A Butterfield stagecoach passed by. The boardwalks were full of people walking to and fro, chatting, laughing, not paying any attention to the world around them. The giddiness of a fine day was intoxicating, a tonic to wash away the worst events and darkest memories. If only it lasted.

A smell from a nearby restaurant greeted Josiah's nose. Simmering beans and a waft of fresh cooked beef made him realize that he had not eaten since breakfast.

Regardless of Scrap's dire circumstance, life for everyone else, including Josiah, was moving on.

With a mind full of questions, and an empty belly, Josiah headed toward home, sure that he needed to think things through before doing anything else. Searching out Captain McNelly would have to wait until tomorrow.

"Wolfe, wait!" a man yelled out, pushing out of the door of a barbershop, about a block and a half from Josiah's house.

Josiah recognized the man immediately, and had had more than one run-in with Paul Hoagland, a reporter for the *Austin Statesman*, since he had moved to the city.

Hoagland was a short bit of a man with a long, pointed rodent nose, bushy eyebrows, and a skittishness that was not immediately apparent but was always there nonetheless, whether in the tapping of his impatient foot or the darting of his eyes. It was like Hoagland was always on the lookout for a predator that was about to swoop down from the sky and eat him.

The reporter wore a tattered bowler, wire-frame glasses, and usually had an unlit, thin cigar dangling from his pale lips. His skin was the color of the white, salty ground in and around the San Saba River, and he smelled like he was slowly rotting from the inside out, like a piece of meat left out in the sun too long to dry. Josiah was surprised there weren't any maggots crawling all over the man. He was repulsed by him.

Josiah acted like he didn't hear the man, or see him for that matter, and kept on walking, picking up his pace just a bit, but knowing that unless he broke into a full run, the exercise of trying to escape the reporter was futile.

Hoagland was as persistent as a hungry rat, and, as expected, he chased after Josiah, with shaving cream globbed to the right side of his face and a white barber sheet still fastened to his neck, flying behind him like a gentleman's evening cape.

"Wolfe, stop. I've got a couple of questions for you."

Now people were staring at Josiah, perhaps recognizing him from his own recent troubles. His face reddened, and he clinched his fists as he came to a stop and turned to face the reporter.

Of course, most people knew Paul Hoagland, too. He had plenty of his own legendary tales, which he promoted continually around town to boost his image, and his access to anyone he might need a story from.

"What do you want, Hoagland?" Josiah asked.

Paul Hoagland stopped a few feet from Josiah, ripped off the sheet, and wiped away the shaving cream from his face as best he could.

"Another Ranger is in trouble for murder, care to comment?"

"There hasn't been a trial yet, Hoagland. Ranger Elliot is accused of murder, not guilty of committing a murder. I would hope that you would keep your facts straight before you go prematurely condemning a man and unnecessarily damaging his reputation."

Hoagland smiled, exposing a chipped front tooth. "Are you lecturing me on how to do my job, Wolfe?"

"I'm asking you to be a professional, sir, and not parade a man's guilt in front of the public until it has been determined. I've been a victim of your pen. I know its sting." Josiah swept his hand out, motioning to the people passing by. "These fine folks think I, myself, have no respect for the law, that I am nothing more than a renegade Ranger—thanks to you."

"It's just business, Wolfe. Nothing personal."

"Says you."

Hoagland scrunched his shoulders, signaling an end to the argument. "So you have no comment to make about the most recent string of murders of, how should we say this delicately, soiled doves?"

"What would you say just between two men?" Josiah asked.

"I doubt the topic would come up. The murders are of no consequence to most of the fine citizens in this town. One dead whore is one less scourge on society."

Josiah drew back a bit, having not expected Hoagland to reveal anything about himself, or how he felt about society as a whole.

"I'm only aware of the murder Ranger Elliot is accused of, and that only recently. There've been more?"

"Four in the last month, to be exact."

"Ranger Elliot has been riding with the Rangers in South Texas. He was nowhere near Austin, so he can't be linked to the other three. Is that what you're up to? Making this an issue because a Ranger's involved and now people will pay attention to what's happening in the back rooms of the saloons they wish didn't exist in the first place?"

"I'm just doing my job," Hoagland said. "Murder is murder no matter the state of the victim's social standing."

"Well, at least we can agree on that."

Hoagland didn't miss a beat, didn't seem interested in building a camaraderie with Josiah, and that was just fine by Josiah.

"How do you know Elliot was where he said he was?" Hoagland asked.

"I was riding with him, that's how. We spent a good deal of time together in Corpus and beyond, on a mission issued by Captain McNelly."

"You were with Ranger Elliot the whole time you were away from Austin?"

Josiah hesitated but had to answer truthfully, even if he was just talking to a newspaper reporter. "No."

"Then the question still remains open."

"What question?"

"Whether this Ranger killed one whore, or four."

People pushed by Josiah and Hoagland, paying them little mind now. Josiah felt like he had been trapped, outwitted by a much smarter man. No matter what he said, he was just making things worse for Scrap.

"We're done here, Hoagland," Josiah said. "Why don't you just leave me and my friends alone?"

The reporter smiled again, only this time it was just a feigned flash of cruddy teeth, a twisted sneer that was not hospitable or humorous. "I will leave you alone when you quit giving me so much to write about, Wolfe. And not until. Or, perhaps, you should learn to pick your friends better. Maybe I'll stop writing about you then."

The smell of a simmering stew greeted Josiah's nose as he walked into his house. He was so angry at Hoagland that he had forgotten he was hungry. It was a moment of comfort, a greeting that he longed for every minute of the day when he was away, whether it be on a trip into town, or on the trail with his company of Rangers. Scrap was right to be envious of his home, as far as Josiah was concerned.

It was the one constant in his life: a safe place, where all pretenses and threats were left at the door. Or so he hoped.

Ofelia was standing in the kitchen, her back to Josiah. Lyle was sitting at the table, waiting patiently, an empty bowl in front of him, a freshly baked loaf of uncut bread sitting on a platter just out of his reach.

The boy grinned when he saw Josiah walk in the door, but he did not jump down or run to him like normal. Instead, Lyle looked away and dropped his head.

There was no question that there was trouble in the air. Something was wrong.

Josiah hung his hat on the hook on the wall, then unbuckled his gun belt and hung it next to his hat—it was high enough that Lyle couldn't reach it.

"I was waiting on you, señor," Ofelia said, stirring a pot, still not turning around.

There was a slight spicy smell to the stew, but it would be a pleasure on Josiah's tongue. He had grown comfortable with Ofelia's flavor of cooking.

"I'm sorry I was longer than I planned. Is everything all right?"

"*Yo era malo*," Lyle said.

Josiah frowned at the boy. "What?"

"I was bad."

"What'd you do?"

"He ran off, Señor Josiah. Right out into the street. Vamoose. I look up, and he was gone," Ofelia said, turning around, a long wooden cooking spoon gripped tightly in her hand.

A long scratch ran down the side of her face, a red streak surrounded by a bruise the size of an apple that was not fully ripe. "I fall down trying to catch him."

It had been a long day, and the last thing Josiah had expected to encounter when he came home was this kind of trouble. He instantly felt a white-hot wave of anger dart up his neck and travel quickly to his hand. Without his realizing it, his hand immediately clinched into a hard fist.

Josiah took four quick, giant steps and was suddenly standing over Lyle, his arm raised, ready to strike the boy. "You hurt Ofelia."

Rage had taken hold of Josiah. The wounds on Ofelia's face struck a nerve deep within him. For a moment, Josiah didn't even know where he was.

"Stop!" Ofelia screamed. She had quickly inserted herself between Josiah and Lyle. One second she was across the room, and the next she was in between Lyle and Josiah, protecting the boy.

Lyle drew back, his blue eyes open wide, showing an ocean of fear and uncertainty.

Ofelia's movement and reaction startled Josiah. "He can't keep running off like that, damn it."

"Please do not swear, Señor Josiah, I know you are angry."

"I will swear, damn it, it's my house. The last time he ran off, he almost got sucked under a train and killed. He hurt you. He's going to hurt himself." Josiah looked into Ofelia's soft brown eyes. They were brimming with tears, pleading. He dropped his hand but did nothing to push away his anger.

Instead of hitting Lyle, Josiah yanked him out of his chair. The boy slumped to the floor, trying to keep his butt out of range. "Stand up," Josiah demanded, as he pulled Lyle to his feet.

"*Por favor, no,*" Ofelia whispered. A tear fell to the floor. "It is my fault, I should have paid closer attention."

"He's not a baby anymore, Ofelia. He needs to understand that there are consequences for acting bad, for hurting other people."

The look on Ofelia's face was a mixture of grief, fear, and pain.

Josiah had to look away or she was going to find a way into his better nature. "I'm sorry, Ofelia, he has to learn."

Before Ofelia could object, Josiah swatted Lyle on the behind.

As far as Josiah was concerned, it was not a hard hit, just hard enough to let Lyle know he meant business.

Lyle screamed like he had been hit upside the head by a rock.

Ofelia quickly kneeled down to comfort the boy, but it was Josiah's turn to intervene. "No," he said. "Lyle. Tell Ofelia you're sorry, and then you go on and take yourself to bed."

With red eyes, and tears rolling off his puffy cheeks, Lyle stood still, staring at Josiah like he didn't hear a word.

"To bed, now!" Josiah yelled.

Lyle took a deep breath. Bubbles popped out of his nose, and he wiped them away with the sleeve of his shirt. A look of resignation fell over his face. "Sorry, Ofelia. I din't mean to hurt you."

"*Està bien.* It is all right."

"To bed. Now," Josiah said, pointing to the bedroom.

Lyle nodded and trudged slowly to the door, looking back only once.

Josiah had not moved, was pointing like he was a statue. Rage still flowed through his veins, but the first hint of questioning and doubt was starting to rise from the back of his mind, wondering if he was creating fear, love, or respect in his son. But all he had to do was look at the marks on Ofelia's face, and that doubt was quickly erased from his mind.

There were consequences for not taking other people into consideration, for causing harm. There had to be. It was the way the world worked, even for a little boy.

CHAPTER 12

———◆◆◆———

The tiny flame in the hurricane lamp fluttered, casting a slow, dancing shadow on the wall. Night had fallen slowly, settling in like a dark prison outside the house. Inside, it was as quiet as a tomb. There was no ticking of a clock, or scratching of a mouse along on the floor; nothing, it seemed, wanted entrance into the house after Josiah's earlier outburst.

To kill time, since it was too early for him to go to sleep, Josiah sat at the table staring at the note left behind by Abram Randalls at the jail. If that were really the case. There was no sure way for Milt the deputy to know positively that Randalls had left the note there at all. It could have been left behind by the previous occupant of the cell for all Josiah knew, or the ten before him. It was hard to say. Milt seemed pretty sure the note had come from Randalls, but he never said how or why he was so certain.

Regardless, the cipher intrigued Josiah; his attention was drawn to the puzzle like a drunkard is drawn to beer or whiskey.

It had been a long time since he had engaged his mind in the matter of un-jumbling letters so they made sense, and it was a distraction that could not have come to him at any better time.

Not only the incident with Lyle was weighing heavily on his mind, but so was Scrap's situation, and of course, so, too, was his own relationship with Pearl Fikes. And then there was his ultimate status with the Rangers; his future was at stake in more ways than one, in more ways than just matters of the heart.

If he did not ride with Captain McNelly's company, then honestly, Josiah was not sure that he would continue to live in Austin. City life was like a new, odd-fitting suit that still did not feel comfortable on him. The only way to shed the suit was to leave it, if it came to that. And at the moment, leaving the city certainly was a consideration, but not one he wanted to dwell on.

The cipher would have to do as a distraction. *The future could wait*, he thought. But no matter how long or how deeply Josiah looked at the piece of paper, he could not focus on it, could not corral his thoughts on what the jumble of letters meant. His mind kept wandering to the recent past— he knew he was questioning himself, his actions, not only with his son, but with everybody he came into contact with. For some reason, he could not help himself; discipline was lost to him.

Lyle had not been allowed to whimper or beg for any undue attention after he was sent to bed without dinner. His punishment had been swift and certain, and Josiah knew no other way to be a father to the boy than to show him the error of his ways. Enforcement of the sentence, to bed without dinner, had to be strict and without waver. It was one of the ways Josiah had been taught right from wrong.

Ofelia had finished up her duties, remaining quiet throughout. When she left the house just before dark, she barely spoke a word to Josiah and avoided looking directly into his eyes. She scurried off without her normal promise of returning the next day, and the air and attitude she left behind in her wake was cold with disappointment and judgment.

Whether he'd handled the situation with Lyle correctly or not was yet to be seen.

The only thing that Josiah knew for certain was that it was not the last time he would have to confront his own rage and restrain himself from whipping the boy directly, and harshly. He had been shown that kind of correction, too, as a boy, and he wondered now if any kind of physical punishment was right and just, if the beatings he'd taken at the hand of his own father had had an effect on him that made it easier to pull the trigger when he was in danger, instead of looking for another outcome.

Still, discipline had to be enforced. Lyle could not be allowed to hurt anyone. And Ofelia, regardless of Josiah's need and respect for her, did not have the final say in how Lyle was raised.

There was no question that he needed Ofelia, that she was a big part of his life, and an even bigger part of Lyle's. His dependence on Ofelia was one of the reasons why he was courting Pearl. And the reasons were many, beyond his physical attraction to her and his need to have a normal life for himself and Lyle—but even that relationship looked precarious. He could not see a time in the immediate future when he would consider taking Pearl as his wife. Neither of them was ready for that. Maybe in a year . . . or longer.

Josiah stared at the paper again, thought about Randalls's lack of enthusiasm for the jailbreak, then stared upward at the ceiling.

No amount of focus could keep his mind occupied.

There was no apparent reward in deciphering the message left at the jail, other than gaining favor with Rory Farnsworth, and that in itself bore little currency. There would only be need to curry favor with the sheriff if it could help

Scrap. And at the moment, the jailbreak and the murders didn't seem to be related.

Now, as the darkness of the night deepened, and silence surrounded him even more fully, Josiah had nothing left to absorb his attention except the cipher.

It didn't matter if it belonged to Randalls or not. What mattered was finding a solution, a trail of wandering thoughts focused on a fixed point, notching off incorrect assumptions, one thing leading to another, until the emotion of the night was far behind him.

The joy of success would be minimal, a silent victory, if Josiah was able to determine what the note said. There would be no celebration of the promise of Scrap's freedom. The only glory would be the knowledge that an age-old skill had been revived and not forgotten. The haunting of the war came in many different forms.

Josiah picked up the pencil next to the note and fixed it securely between his fingers.

Mass production of lead pencils was a recent occurrence, beginning after the War Between the States had ended, with the convenience finding its way quickly into everyday life. Josiah now couldn't remember a time when pencils weren't close by even when pencils were rare. Reading and writing were a gift of his mother's patience and insistence that had seen him through the better part of his life—an offset to his father's stern and demanding nature.

Josiah was able to naturally understand the rhythm of words, the correct location of letters when paired with each other, without much effort at all. Reading and writing were a matter of survival to him and not a matter of education or being stuffy about such things, like he found Rory Farnsworth to be.

He stared at the letters with as much focus as he could muster, trying to make sense of them, trying to see some kind of pattern, trying to understand the foundation of the cipher:

XLICAMPPOMPPQIYRHIVXLISEOXVII.

Several different style codes had been used during the War
Between the States, and since Josiah's reading and writing
skills were apparent to everyone who encountered him, he
had been quickly set upon by the leading officers of the First
Texas Brigade to learn the art of writing and decoding
ciphers.

The cipher before him looked similar to the codes used
by all of the Confederacy to communicate between officers
and camps about troop movement, supply routes, and attack
plans. This one looked like a Vigenere cipher, which was a
pretty simple structure, for the most part; one letter stood
in place for another. An A was really a B, etc. But in reality,
the simplicity of the cipher was also what made it so difficult
to understand. Figuring out what letter stood in another's
place was far more difficult than it seemed.

The first part of the pattern that jumped out at Josiah was
the pair of double Ps.

There was no separation for words, so it was hard to say
where the double letters sat in the sentence. If he knew that,
it would be a great help. But whoever wrote the cipher was
not intent on making it an easy one to read.

The double Ps could have been any letter. Ts or Es or Ms.
Vowels or consonants. At this point, there was no way to
tell. He didn't think the double letters were the beginning
of a word. So, maybe they were at the end of a word. He
wrote down the letters and separated them:

XLICAMPP OMPP QIYRHIVXLISEOXVII.

Interestingly, as usually happened, a word appeared. Or he
assumed it was one, though he could have been wrong.
Double letters in the position they were placed in a single
four-letter word would have been rare. There was no diction-
ary to refer to.

Now Josiah noticed something else. An M was in the same place in comparison to the Ps in both instances. More of a pattern showing itself. The Ps weren't a vowel, so the M probably was.

All he needed was one more letter to help show him the way, a light at the end of the tunnel of ignorant darkness to shine on the solution.

As he fully focused now, the house around Josiah and the silence of it fell completely away, taking with it the confrontations, disappointments, and explosions of the day.

Josiah decided to mark the PPs as two Ls because it made sense to him that two words could possibly end that way. From there, he settled on an A to be the vowel. Words like "ball" and "call" came immediately to mind. Maybe they fit, maybe not—but nothing more jumped out at him. So he settled on the idea that the code was truly a Vigenere cipher and refocused on the LLs. If he moved the PPs back one letter, they would be OOs. Back two letters and they would be NNs. Three and they would be MMs, and finally, a break, four letters moved back would be LL.

Josiah could feel his heart racing. He knew he was close to solving the cipher. Now if his theory worked on the rest of the letters, he would have the answer in no time. So he worked the formula on the one word that he was fairly certain of, OMPP, and came up with KILL.

He sat back and breathed a sigh of relief, twirling the pencil among his fingers. That light at the end of the tunnel came rushing at him. Success for the sake of success was at hand.

It took Josiah less than a minute to work out the rest of the cipher, now that he knew with greater certainty that the formula was true. The note Milt the deputy claimed to have found in Abram Randalls's cell said:

THEY WILL KILL ME UNDER THE OAK TREE.

CHAPTER 13

Morning light cut softly inside the livery. There was a steady amount of activity going on; stalls were being cleaned out, and several horses were getting washed down and brushed out by a couple of familiar stable boys. On the other side of the stables, a wagon wheel was being repaired, the constant pounding out, metal against metal in perfect time, sounded like the beginning of a musical performance in an opera house somewhere. It wasn't like the livery was a beehive of activity; this was just a normal pace for a normal day. Urgency, as if in preparation for a battle, was nowhere to be seen.

As Josiah walked inside the livery, the odors of fresh straw, oils, and soap offered up plenty of reasons for a pleasant mood.

Lyle squeezed Josiah's hand, skipping a bit, mumbling happily, but not pulling on Josiah, not trying to get away, obviously glad to be in his father's company.

There had not been hide nor hair of Ofelia that morning, the lack of routine more than a little surprising to Josiah.

He'd been left little choice but to offer some warmed up beans and toasted bread to Lyle for his breakfast. The boy didn't complain about the food or ask for Ofelia.

Of course, Josiah was concerned about Ofelia's absence, but he had to get on with the day.

Tracking down McNelly was on his list, and so was stopping by the jail to see Scrap and give the decoded cipher to Rory Farnsworth to see if it meant anything to him. Neither of those trips seemed to lend themselves to Lyle's young and unpredictable presence, but Josiah might have no choice but to take the boy along if he was not able to find Ofelia in Little Mexico.

"Where's Chipper?" Lyle asked.

"Clipper," Josiah said.

"Chipper." Lyle smiled, sure that he'd gottten it right this time. "Where's Chipper?"

Josiah smiled and let it go. "In his stall. Let's go look."

Lyle nodded. "All right."

Josiah lead the boy to the stall, and Clipper, an Appaloosa that had been Josiah's mount for more years than he cared to count, looked up and greeted them with a snort, then pushed back a pile of freshly laid straw with his right hoof. Josiah reached into the stall, scratched the horse's nose, and hoisted Lyle up so he could do the same thing.

"Give him some oats," Josiah said. He leaned Lyle down so he could reach into a bucket that hung next to the gate.

Lyle scooped up a healthy portion of the dry oats and offered the treat to Clipper. The horse immediately obliged him with a munch, and Lyle started squirming and giggling. Oats fell to the floor like snowflakes fluttering from the sky, and Josiah let the boy down before he dropped him.

"What'd you do that for?" Josiah asked.

"Lips tickled. Don't like it."

"You'll get used to it."

Lyle shook his head no.

Clipper finished the oats, then looked at Josiah expectantly. Josiah shrugged. "Well, I guess we best get the saddle on him."

Lyle nodded yes, eagerly this time.

Josiah was about to open the gate and go inside the stall when he noticed a horse three stalls down. The gray gelding looked familiar. So familiar that Josiah stopped, grabbed Lyle's hand, and hurried down to the stall to make sure he was seeing what he thought he was.

He wasn't sure if it was the same horse he'd seen yesterday, the one he'd noticed at the jailbreak, but it sure looked like it.

The horse was dappled with darker gray against light, typical for a paint, and was a little over fifteen hands high. It had sweet black eyes, but it was the proud and calm way it held itself that had struck Josiah the first time he'd seen it, and this time, too. The horse acted battle-tested, like nothing could spook it or stir it out of its duty. That kind of horse always stood out to Josiah. It was a demeanor usually well earned, not bred.

This horse had been recently washed down and reshod, and there was no saddle in the stall. It must have been stored away in the tack room.

Perplexed, Josiah made his way to the front of the livery, looking for Jake Allred, the livery master.

It didn't take long to find the man. Allred was in the front office, yelling at one of the stable boys, a towheaded waif about four feet tall, twelve years old at the most, who looked like he was already a master himself—at being bawled out. The boy's eyes were distant, staring off in the opposite direction from Allred . . . and Josiah knew it was only a matter of years before Lyle reacted the same way to him when discipline was needed, like last night.

Jake Allred stopped in mid-sentence, looked up, and saw Josiah. "Now, go on, and don't miss another stitch, or that'll be the end of you, ya hear?" he said to the boy, shooing him off with a wave of the hand.

The stable boy nodded, looked up at Josiah, understandably relieved, then pushed by him and Lyle, disappearing quickly into the shadows of the livery.

"What's your need, Wolfe?" Jake Allred feigned a smile at Lyle, who promptly hid behind his father's legs.

Allred was a tall man with a beer keg for a belly, a heavy beard that was in serious need of trimming, and boots coated with mud and horse shit. He looked more like a smithy than a livery master, and for all Josiah knew, he had been one at one time in his life.

"Ain't no problem with that Appaloosa of yours, is it?" Allred asked. "I'll tell you, these boys are gettin' lazier by the day. I just don't know what I'm gonna do if I can't find some good help soon."

"I don't have any complaints."

Allred wiped his brow and stared back at Josiah. "Well, what is it then? Can't you see I'm a busy man?"

"I can see that. What can you tell me about the gray gelding a few stalls down from mine?"

The livery master narrowed his eyes, then looked Josiah up and down from head to toe.

There was never any question that Josiah was wearing a gun. He wore his Peacemaker in plain sight. Allred, on the other hand, didn't appear to be armed. But that would've been a stupid, and perhaps deadly, assumption on any man's part, to come to such a quick conclusion and threaten the man or his property.

Josiah hadn't known Jake Allred long, but he knew him to be a protective man as well as an honest one, and not inclined to hold back if he needed to shoot a man. He was of an age to have been in the war but carried no obvious scars, so the topic had never been broached in their short conversations. Most men kept that experience to themselves, unless a missing leg or arm spoke for them.

"What business is it of yours, Wolfe, who owns that horse? I don't get many questions like that."

"Just curious, I thought I recognized it."

Lyle had remained quiet, still as a mouse with a hawk circling overhead, peering out from behind Josiah's leg.

It was going to be a warm, sunny day, and the heat was already building inside the livery. There was no breeze, nothing to stir the tension that had suddenly found its way between Josiah and Allred and push it out the door.

"Is this Ranger business, Wolfe?"

"Might be business for Rory Farnsworth. Might not, I'm not sure."

"You workin' for the sheriff now? I don't see no badge."

"I don't wear a badge, and I don't work for Farnsworth."

"Good to know."

"Is there a reason for that?" Josiah asked.

"No reason that matters to you, I 'spect. Now, what's the question about this horse got to do with anything?"

"You hear about that jailbreak yesterday?"

Allred nodded. "Busted out Abram Randalls, I hear. A banker's thief and a whore's bookkeeper. The man must hold some powerful secrets in that mind of his."

"You know the man?"

"Nope."

"But you know his name."

"Every man who does business of any kind in this town knows his name. The man has a mind for numbers and names, unfortunately. If I was half as good with my money as the one he works for, then I wouldn't have to wade through horse piss and shit every day, would I?"

"Who do you think broke him out, this Abrams fella?"

"You're just full of questions, aren't you? First it was about that gray gelding down there, and now you're curious about Abram Randalls. What are you up to, Wolfe? Ain't like you at all to be stickin' your nose in other people's business. Usually, you just get your horse and go."

"You said it. I'm just curious."

"Sure you are." Allred shrugged. "Well, it makes no difference to me. I figure Randalls got broke out by the whore. She's got plenty of reason to have need of him keeping silent."

"She?"

Allred nodded. "Blanche Dumont. You know her?"

"I know of her."

"Sure, sure, I hear that a lot, too. But maybe you're tellin' the truth, not bein' from around here, and takin' up with that Fikes woman like you have."

"Careful now . . ."

"Not judgin', just statin' a fact, the way I see it. You denyin' that?"

Josiah just stared at the man and reached down to touch the top of Lyle's head. "Who's the gelding belong to? If you don't mind?" Bringing Pearl into the conversation would only make matters worse. Josiah was sensitive about her, even more so than he'd realized.

"No sweat off my back, I was just curious why you didn't know yourself."

"Why's that?"

"The gray gelding," Allred said, chewing on the corner of his lip, studying Josiah's face carefully, "belongs to Captain Leander McNelly. I figure one Ranger ought to know another Ranger's horse. But I guess I was wrong, just plum wrong, about that, now, wasn't I?"

CHAPTER 14

———◆◆◆———

Lyle was settled comfortably in the saddle in front of Josiah. It felt like summer had come early. The air was thick and humid, and the sun beat down from the sky with a vengeance. Sweat soaked Josiah's collar, and he could feel the heat rising under his felt Stetson, but the weather was of little concern.

The thought that the gray gelding belonged to Captain McNelly was unsettling to Josiah.

He questioned himself, replaying the explosion and jailbreak in his mind, trying to look closer at the horse and the man riding it. His memory was decent, but as the hours went by, the details started to fade, as they would in any normal person's mind. There was no way to tell if the man on the horse really had been McNelly. His face had been covered, and he was dressed in a black duster, his body all covered. It was impossible to know for sure who the man was. But at the time, Josiah would never have considered in a thousand years that the man could be Leander McNelly, and even now it was a difficult idea to swallow. But the horse sure did look like the same one.

The captain was a slight man, taken with consumption, determined to live a full life regardless of the illness. He was tough-minded, honest, and completely aboveboard as far as Josiah knew. So the idea that McNelly was somehow involved in a brazen jailbreak, conducted in the full light of day, was unimaginable. Almost unimaginable.

Pete Feders had been a Texas Ranger captain, too, and in the end, he had forged a relationship with Liam O'Reilly, an Irish outlaw, dead now, too, like Feders, and had been seeking to do some serious cattle rustling business with Juan Cortina. Still, Josiah just couldn't bring himself to believe McNelly was the same kind of man Feders was, driven by greed, avarice, and envy to do the unspeakable—betray his rank, the Rangers, and the state of Texas, as well.

"Where we going, Papa?" Lyle asked.

Josiah looked down at the boy, envious at the moment of his innocence and lack of responsibility. "Home to see if Ofelia is there. Is that all right?"

Lyle nodded his head yes.

Josiah eased Clipper down Sixth Street, not in a hurry, but hoping that Ofelia was at the house instead of in Little Mexico. There was no way he could take Lyle with him today, not with all he had to do and all of the places he had to go.

The information he'd gotten from Jake Allred about the gray gelding had changed everything.

The familiar smell of *menudo* greeted Josiah at the door. He breathed a heavy sigh of relief, seeing Ofelia standing over the stove, stirring a pot of the spicy stew made from leftovers, picking up where she'd left off the day before.

Ofelia looked over her shoulder when the door opened, and Lyle charged inside.

The bruises on her face were still apparent, but fading. He still winced at the sight, a sorrowful bit of guilt roiling in the pit of his stomach; the wounds were a reminder of his own failures, of how he was managing his life and the consequences to everyone involved. He had to look away and couldn't bring himself to say hello.

"*Hola*," Ofelia said, turning back to the stove.

"*Hola*, 'Felia," Lyle answered, rushing to Ofelia, wrapping himself around her leg, looking up at her expectantly.

Ofelia tapped Lyle's head. She did not smile, or otherwise change her expression, which bordered on stern. "*Vete a jugar*. Go play."

Disappointment slid down Lyle's face, but he did what he was told, pulling away from Ofelia and making his way to the bedroom without acknowledging Josiah.

"I'm glad to see you, Ofelia," Josiah said, standing in the middle of the room, his hands at his sides, unsure what to do next, leave or stay.

Ofelia turned and faced him, the wooden spoon in her hand. "You thought I was not coming today, señor?"

"I didn't know what to think."

"I will be here as long as you want me to be here," Ofelia said. "We have had this discussion many times. You do not need to worry. If I quit you, I will let you know plenty of days ahead of time so you can find someone else."

"No one could take your place."

"Someone will have to one day, señor."

Josiah exhaled heavily, knowing full well that what Ofelia said was true. "I would say I'm sorry . . ."

"There is no need to say you are sorry about anything. This is your *casa*. You are the *niño's papá*."

Josiah nodded. "But you are the closest thing he has to a mother."

"I'm not his momma."

"Maybe not. I'm not sure how that would work, if it ever could, you leaving Lyle. Us."

"You do not love Miss Pearl?"

Josiah stared at Ofelia blankly as a million memories rushed through his mind and heart. They had known each other a long time, before he had married Lily, before he had gone off to the war, and then after, when he returned a different man. There was not a living person in the world who knew as much about him, his way of thinking and feeling, and how and why he behaved the way he did, as Ofelia did. And Lyle had not known one day in his life without Ofelia. The loss of her presence was unthinkable for more reasons than Josiah could count.

"I don't know," Josiah said. "I don't know if I can allow myself to love her." Billie Webb had asked him the same question. Billie was a girl he'd helped a while back, and she had followed him to Austin. But once she figured out that there was no chance of a relationship with him, she left the city, disappeared as if she'd never existed.

"It has been long enough since Miss Lily died, Señor Josiah. The *niño* needs a *mamacita*, if that is possible. I am only Ofelia. There is not a woman's love in this house like there should be."

Josiah looked away from Ofelia, out the window. He wanted to tell her that he was afraid of losing Pearl, and that he was afraid of losing her, too, but couldn't bring himself to. Ofelia knew what he had lost, he didn't have to explain it to her.

"I'm sorry, Ofelia. I'll try not to yell or show my anger like that again," Josiah said.

"You're learning, too, and that is hard on you," Ofelia said, ignoring the apology. "Spending time here in the city is difficult for you. It makes Lyle happy when you sleep in your own bed, but you do not know which way the wind blows inside your own house. It is like you are a hundred miles from here. *Tomarà tiempo*. It will take time, just like all good things. I am sorry I was late this morning. My *hija*, my daughter, needed my help. All is well now. I had no way to get word to you."

"Good," Josiah said. "I have some things to take care of, I probably won't be back until this evening."

"That is fine, señor. We will be here, and your dinner will be on the stove."

CHAPTER 15

The adjunct general's office was on the second floor in the state capitol building. William Steele was a Yankee, a New Yorker who had been educated at the United States Military Academy, then come to Texas and served in the Confederate Army because of love. He'd married a Texas girl, put down stakes in the state, and put his life on the line valiantly more times than once wearing a gray uniform, just so he could return whole and alive to the woman he adored.

Steele's appointment to the position of adjunct general by the governor, Richard Coke, had come under some suspicion because of his origins, even with a rank of brigadier general attained in the war. But Steele was known as a hard task manager with little patience for nepotism, fraud, or any misdeeds performed by Texas Rangers or the militia he had been put in charge of. A consummate politician, he quickly won over the naysayers and the editorial pages of the *Austin Statesman*.

It had been Steele, in fact, who had ultimately decided Josiah's fate in the incident concerning Pete Feders. The proof had been laid out logically to the general, and in his wisdom, Steele saw that Josiah had had no choice but to defend his own life and kill Feders. Shooting to wound had never been an option.

Josiah could only hope that Scrap would receive the same kind of scrutiny and fair judgment from Steele that he had.

The inside of the office was luxurious. The walls were paneled with walnut, and the floors were covered with thick wool carpets, geometric in design, the colors rich, full of deep burgundies, greens, and golds.

Heavy scarlet draperies were pulled at the window, and bookshelves, full to the brim, lined half of the walls. Heavy furniture was scattered about in the office: a writing desk, bare of anything other than a pen-and-ink set, and several high-backed chairs that did not look the least bit inviting or comfortable. Hurricane lamps blazed brightly, lighting the room like it was late at night, and two fans swirled overhead, distributing the afternoon heat evenly, but still uncomfortably.

Another door stood behind the writing desk, and after being in the office prior to now, to answer for actions about killing Pete Feders, Josiah knew that Steele spent all of his time tucked away in that small office.

He walked to the door and knocked confidently. A little tap or a soft knock was a bad precedent to set when dealing with a man like Steele. A man's attitude had to be all bravado and strength, or the general would stomp his feet on you, then wave you off without a nod or a good-bye.

"Yes, what is it?" came from inside the small office in a deep voice, annoyed and curt.

"Josiah Wolfe to see you, sir," Josiah said, speaking directly into the door.

"What is it now, Wolfe?" Steele's voice grew closer.

"I am in need of an audience with Captain McNelly, sir, and this is the only place I know to look for him at the moment. I am hoping you know his whereabouts."

The door was flung open. "Does McNelly suck on my teat, Wolfe? I am not his nanny."

Steele was a tall, rangy man in his mid-fifties. Thin bits of gray streaked his thick brown hair and full beard. He had a strong Roman nose and carried himself regally: shoulders back, chin forward, always engaged fully in whatever came his way. His eyes were gray and penetrating, offering no sympathy for fools or ill-mannered human beings.

Josiah dared not look away from Steele. He held the man's gaze. "I don't mean to suggest that you are, sir."

Steele pulled open the door the rest of the way, offering a view into the office. Captain McNelly was seated in a chair in front of Steele's desk. "You are in luck, Wolfe. McNelly is here. Come in then, but make it quick. We have business to attend to."

Leander McNelly stood up as Josiah entered the room. "It is good to see you, Wolfe." He stuck his hand out, and they shook hands in a cold, professional way, not like they were old friends who had not seen each other for a long period of time. That was hardly the case.

"You, too, Captain." Josiah waited for Steele and McNelly to sit down in their chairs before he followed suit.

McNelly was a few years younger than Josiah, but he looked ten years older. His face was drawn in, and his skin was as pale as an onion pulled fresh out of the ground. His beard was not full from the ears like Steele's, but more of a long, bushy goatee; his jaws were freshly shaved. He was dressed in a black business suit, much like the one Rory Farnsworth had been sporting the day before, his riding clothes obviously put away, or getting cleaned for the next excursion, if there was to be one.

Steele settled into his chair. "Now, what brings you here, Wolfe? No more troubles, I hope? We're up to our necks in foibles of one kind or another."

McNelly eyed Josiah carefully but said nothing.

Josiah waited, then moved uncomfortably to the edge of

his own chair. "My status with the Rangers is uncertain, and I aim to clear that up with the captain, General Steele. If I may be so bold as to ask."

"Your last encounter with Cortina's bounty hunter garnered some undo attention, Wolfe," McNelly said. "But you have been cleared of any wrongdoing. The larger question is this: Do you still desire to ride with the Rangers?"

Josiah hesitated briefly, then nodded. "I do, sir."

"I am not convinced that your personal situation allows you to leave town without worry."

Josiah locked eyes with the captain. "I have seen to my situation, and I am able to come and go as I have in the past without worry or constraints, sir. There is nothing in my life that will stand in the way of performing my duty to the fullness of my capabilities."

"You're sure of that?"

"I wish to ride with the Rangers, sir. It is all I know how to do." Josiah hesitated and stared McNelly in the eye. "Are you still riding that gray gelding, Captain?"

"That's an odd question, Wolfe," McNelly said, drawing back, then scrutinizing Josiah head to toe.

"I thought I saw the horse."

"Without me? That's hardly likely."

Josiah was almost certain the captain's horse and the horse he saw at the jailbreak were one and the same. Still, he wasn't entirely positive. "Do you stable the horse at Allred's Livery?"

"Where I stable my horse is none of your concern, Wolfe. I assure you whatever you think you might have seen, you didn't."

"I beg your pardon, then," Josiah said. "I must have been mistaken."

McNelly nodded. "Very well then. As for your living situation in Austin, I am in no position to question a man of your character and skills on his personal life and restraints. Consider the matter behind us." He stood up, glancing quickly over to Steele, who dropped his chin, signaling approval.

Josiah followed suit and stood up, understanding clearly that he was being dismissed. "There's one more thing, sir."

"And what is that?" McNelly asked, breathing deeply.

Josiah wasn't sure if the captain was exasperated with him or if the difficulty he had catching a breath was caused by his ongoing battle with consumption. "I'm sure you're aware that Ranger Elliot has been arrested on the count of murder?" Josiah said.

"I am," McNelly said. "What do you know of this?"

"Very little actually. But I have spoken to Elliot, and he claims innocence of the crime."

"That is for the judge to decide and is out of our hands. The last thing the general public needs to be concerned about is a trial being meddled with by the Rangers or any other official of high office. Do you understand me on that, Wolfe? Do I make myself clear? We are not to interfere."

"I do understand, sir. But I believe Elliot's claim that he is innocent, and since we have ridden together, been partners so to speak, I'd like to help the boy. It's the least I can do. He has no one else to see him clear of this trouble that has found him."

McNelly coughed and shifted his weight. "The company leaves Austin in two days, Wolfe. If it is your plan to continue riding with the Rangers, then you will be there with us. If not, then we have no contract. Your service will be ended."

"Scrap needs our help, sir," Josiah insisted. "There is no way he killed one whore, much less four, if I understand correctly the magnitude of the current situation in Austin."

"The killings are a local matter, Wolfe. You know the law. We can't get involved until the sheriff asks for our assistance," McNelly said.

"Are you willing to let an innocent man hang?" Josiah asked.

William Steele stood up from behind the desk, pushing his chair out from behind him with a little extra effort to let Josiah know he was truly finished with the conversation.

"These are difficult times, Wolfe, as you know," Steele said. "Governor Coke is under pressure to dissolve the Rangers, and the public trust for the organization is shallow the way it is. The actions of this young Ranger have only made these matters worse. I would suggest that you leave the business of innocence and guilt to the courts. Return home and prepare for your next journey. Prove your value to the Rangers by serving the captain and his next assignment. Leave the law to those of us who know it best."

Josiah started to protest but took both men's hard gazes to mean that there would be no changing their decisions. He nodded, defeated, sad for Scrap, and started to back slowly out of the room, still facing both men.

"Two days, Wolfe," McNelly said. "Noon, in front of the old courthouse, packed and ready to go. I expect to see you there."

CHAPTER 16

Josiah stood on the steps of the capitol building, staring down Congress Avenue, certain of where he was going next.

The meeting had not gone quite as Josiah had hoped. He was glad to face McNelly and know what his place was within the Ranger organization, but he just couldn't shake the odd feeling he'd left Steele's office with.

There was no explanation for the horse being two places at once, and as Josiah looked out over the bustling city, he had to consider that maybe he was wrong, maybe it hadn't been McNelly's horse he saw during the jailbreak. Maybe he was making something out of nothing. That idea just didn't sit right with him, though. The horse looked exactly the same. But why would McNelly, of all people, be involved in busting an accountant and embezzler out of jail, especially considering the tenuous environment in Austin when it came to the Rangers? It made no sense.

Neither did the hands-off reaction of both men to Scrap's situation: leave the boy to his own fate, lost in the judicial system with no advocate, no one to help to see him to the right side of justice. Surely, if Josiah did as McNelly and Steele demanded of him, did nothing and went on with his life, then Scrap would be hanged. And Josiah would be on the trail, out with the company of Rangers, none the wiser but left with a guilty feeling eating away at his stomach for the rest of his life because he didn't do enough to save Scrap.

Doing nothing was unacceptable, regardless of the consequences.

Two days seemed like an impossible amount of time to offer Scrap any optimism, or to be able to keep him from dangling in the gallows, but Josiah knew he had no choice but to try.

He pushed his way down the steep collection of limestone steps at the capitol, lost in his thoughts, trying to figure out what he could do to make the situation better, barely paying attention to where he was walking. He was headed in the general direction of Clipper, who was tied to the long hitching post beyond the apron where the steps ended.

A hard bump to the shoulder brought his attention to the moment.

"Oh, pardon me," Josiah said, coming to a stop. He blinked, the sun catching his eyes, nearly blinding him, but he knew at once who he'd bumped into.

It was Paul Hoagland, the reporter from the *Statesman*.

"Are you following me?" Josiah demanded, anger rising from his toes upon full recognition of the man.

"Don't flatter yourself, Wolfe. You're interesting, but you're not that interesting."

It didn't appear that Hoagland had changed clothes from the last time Josiah had encountered him. The same cigar dangled from the corner of his mouth, unlit, and the pungent smell of ever-present burned and wet tobacco quickly reached Josiah's nose, causing him to recoil.

"Sorry, then," Josiah said, pushing on toward Clipper. Paul Hoagland was the last man he wanted to have a conversation with at the moment. At least, that's what he thought, trying to get downwind of the repulsive smell of the cigar. But he got about three steps past Hoagland, then came to an abrupt stop. "Hoagland," he called out. "Do you have a minute, now that I think about it?"

It had been the annoying reporter who gave Josiah the information about the four murders, broadening his knowledge of the crime Scrap was accused of. Maybe this was a fortuitous encounter after all. Maybe Hoagland could be an asset instead of an enemy. Time was short, and any opportunity that presented itself to help Scrap couldn't be overlooked, even if it meant dealing with a man like Hoagland to free him.

Hoagland had not moved up the steps but was staring at Josiah warily. "I have a minute. I'm not sure why, but I do."

Josiah stopped a few feet in front of Hoagland. The city moved on around them. A streetcar inched up Congress Avenue, the teamster hollering and snapping a whip, cracking along the strong back of a Springfield mule. A train was departing in the distance, steam rising over the rooftops to the west, dissipating into the cloudless blue sky, as the thump of its movement shook the ground, echoing off the buildings like a series of explosions in a canyon.

No one paid the pair much attention. People came and went from the statehouse on business of their own. The boardwalks were crowded with people strolling up and down the avenue, popping in and out of the shops and stores, solving the problems of their own daily needs and struggles. There was a rhythm of movement, almost like a heartbeat, around them, pronounced with each step of a passing horse or wagon, that was less than comforting to Josiah, but also growing less noticeable to him the more time he spent in the city.

"I need to know more about those killings," Josiah said.

Hoagland nodded. "Everything you need to know is written down in the paper. You don't need me for that information. You *can* read, can't you, Wolfe?"

It was a snide remark, and Josiah was tempted to not let it pass, but he did. He didn't have anything to prove to Paul Hoagland by arguing with the man out of the gate. "I'm short on time," he said.

"Why are the murders of four lowly whores suddenly a concern to you, Wolfe? It wouldn't have anything to do with the arrest of Ranger Elliot, would it?"

"It would."

"I figured as much."

"He's just a boy, and for whatever the reason, he's found himself in a bad situation. Besides that, he's my friend, and I aim to help him, if I can. There's no way he killed that girl, or the other three before her, and you, and everyone else that matters, know that to be true."

"Are you accusing me of scapegoating a Ranger, Wolfe? He literally had blood on his hands. He was running away from the saloon, like he was guilty and in fear of being caught. You can't protest the facts."

"I'm not accusing you of anything at the moment. But I am asking for your help. You know better than anyone that the facts are not always what they appear. Ask four different people what I just said, and you'll get four different answers."

Hoagland studied Josiah's face, eyeing him suspiciously. "It wasn't that long ago that you threatened me and demanded I stay out of your sight, and now you want my help?"

"I'm sure this isn't the first time that's happened."

"You're probably right." Hoagland relaxed a bit and chewed on the cigar, bobbing it up and down as he looked around him. He stepped in closer to Josiah. "I agree, there's no way that Elliot could have been involved in those murders. But I do think they were committed by the same person. I'd almost bet on it, and I, sir, am not a betting man. These are not simple murders. There are some high-level people trying to keep them on the q.t."

"Like who?"

"You name it, from the sheriff on up. Proper society dictates that the affairs of soiled doves not be mentioned. But when I put a piece in the paper, the sales go up exponentially."

Josiah exhaled deeply. Hoagland's cigar made his eyes burn. "Steele and McNelly basically told me that Elliot was on his own."

"And you accused me of scapegoating? The boy is a pariah. Proof, thanks in part to you, to the public that the government does not pull strings in favor of the Rangers. They will hang him as an example and nothing more."

It felt like there was no air in Josiah's lungs. In his mind's eye, he saw a glimpse of the future: Scrap screaming and kicking as they put the rope around his neck, pleading that the judge believe in his innocence—and then the deed, the trapdoor falling open, Scrap falling through, the rope snapping his neck, and the crowd rousing to a deafening cheer.

"I can't let that happen," Josiah said.

"I am not prone to interfering with justice, but I am opposed to the abuse of power. If one innocent man dies, then we're all in danger of the same thing happening to any one of us."

"So you think Farnsworth is involved in this manipulation of justice somehow?" Josiah asked.

Hoagland rolled his shoulders, then looked quickly about him, making sure, it seemed, that there was no one near enough to hear him speak. "I don't know. But the sheriff is under a lot of scrutiny at the moment. He's always been a loose fit in the job, elected as he was and supported by a group of men headed up by his father."

"Myron Farnsworth, the banker."

Hoagland nodded. "You know him?"

"No. Just of him. Saw him once at a dinner at the Fikes house."

"Oh yes, the coming out, so to speak, of the engagement that never happened because you killed the man."

"That's not what happened, and you know it."

"I wasn't there."

Josiah stared at Hoagland, instantly reminded of why he did not like, or trust, the man. Still, Scrap's neck was at stake. "Why is Farnsworth under scrutiny?"

"Surely you're aware of the blast that occurred at the jail?"

"I was there."

"Really?"

"I was visiting Scrap."

"Interesting. So you know they boosted an accountant and embezzler named Abram Randalls."

"I am. Farnsworth said he worked for a bank. I'm assuming his father's."

"You would be correct in that assumption, Wolfe. But Randalls worked for Blanche Dumont, too. He kept her books."

"Did he embezzle from her?"

Hoagland shrugged. "Can't say, you'll have to ask Blanche Dumont about that. I seriously doubt she'd go to the law with her problems." He watched Josiah closely, not taking his eyes off of him. "And you don't think that's odd?"

"I do." Josiah took a deep breath, trying to piece the information together. "Wait, what about the whores? Did any of them come from her house?"

"Ah, now you're on the right trail, Wolfe. The funny thing is, the answer is no. I can't find any connection between the girls that were killed and Blanche Dumont. Nothing. But I find the jailbreak too much of a coincidence not to be related somehow. What do you know about it?"

Josiah looked off in the distance, over Hoagland's shoulder. He had the cipher, and the solution to it, in his pocket. He still wasn't sure he could trust the reporter, so he chose to say nothing, at the moment. Instead, he recounted the entire jailbreak episode, including the assumed sighting of McNelly's horse.

"So did you accuse McNelly of being at the incident?" Hoagland asked.

"No. I didn't want to show my hand, if he was involved. I've had enough experience with men in command positions who turned out to be bad instead of good. I just asked where he stabled the horse. He took offense to the question, so I let it go."

"Probably best to be cautious."

"I think so."

Hoagland stepped back and switched the cigar from one side of his mouth to the other. "I would have never come to you for information, Wolfe, but I'm glad I ran into you."

"Why do you care about this so much?"

"It's my job."

Josiah shook his head no. "There's more to it than that."

"Let's just say, I have my reasons."

"I'll buy that."

"Doesn't matter. What does matter is that we don't let an innocent man hang."

"I have two days," Josiah said, abruptly.

"Two days for what?"

"Before I leave town with the Rangers on my next assignment."

"That complicates things."

"It does."

Hoagland dug into the front pocket of his jacket, pulled out a business card, and handed it to Josiah. "It's a lawyer. Woodrell Cranston. Go see him. Tell him I sent you, and tell him everything you know about Elliot and this entire episode. He may be the only man that can help you."

"I can't afford a lawyer, and I know Scrap can't, either."

"Go see him."

Before Josiah could say anything else, Hoagland bobbed his cigar, spun around, and hustled up the stairs. "I'll be in touch," he said, hollering over his shoulder, just before he disappeared inside the capitol building.

CHAPTER 17

It didn't take long to get to the jail. The hole in the wall had been boarded up, and the smell of gunpowder had long been whisked away on the strong, persistent spring breeze that continued to sweep through Austin.

Josiah took little notice of the fine weather that continued to visit the city. It was like background noise, a piano in a saloon, there but irrelevant to what was really happening. There was no threat of rain, or of a tornado, or destruction by any nature. The world seemed content with itself, and that was just fine with him. One less thing to deal with.

What concerned Josiah was the harm done by man in the name of greed, or another cause that he could not understand.

The death of four whores might not have been much of a concern to the general public, other than to reinforce their belief that the girls were less deserving of justice than an upstanding woman who might have met the same fate.

And to be honest, the murders, as they were, since Josiah

knew little of the details, were only of concern to him because of Scrap's involvement.

Somehow, the incidents had slipped by his notice, making him, in his own mind, no better than those who were unaware, the same general public he had condemned in his mind only seconds before.

The city was large. Crimes, of some sort, were continual— a daily occurrence, but mostly on a small scale. No man could be expected to know of every fallen dove. Still, the pull at Josiah's heart was there, only because he had known whores in his life who were good women, deserving of justice, and by far, more honest and innocent than any highbrow gentleman or gentlewoman could ever imagine.

The discussion with Paul Hoagland had been far more informative than he'd thought it would be.

He pushed through the heavy door of the jail, leaving the perfect day behind him, entering the fortress that seemed slightly weakened but not fatally harmed. There was still a darkness to the building that made even an innocent man reconsider any desire to enter.

Josiah recognized the deputy sitting at the door, Milt something-or-other. He hadn't caught the man's last name when he'd been at the jail the day before. There had been too much chaos for the niceties of a proper introduction at the time. The deputy recognized Josiah, too.

"What're you after, Wolfe?" Milt said, stroking his thick upside-down V mustache, not bothering to sit up straight or act the least bit surprised to see Josiah.

"I'll want to see Elliot before I leave, but I need to speak to the sheriff."

The foyer of the jail had been cleaned up of the rubble and dust from the explosion, and the gun locker was reinforced with a bar across the front and three different locks added to make it impossible to break into.

"Sheriff's busy," Milt said. He chewed at the corner of

his lip and reset his jaw, like it was some kind of tic or bad habit.

Josiah looked behind Milt and saw that the door to Farnsworth's office was closed. There was no sound coming from behind it. He looked back over his shoulder then, to the hitching post, which was empty of any horses except Clipper.

"I've got some information for him. Something he asked me to do for him," Josiah said.

Milt sat up straight, staring Josiah directly in the eyes. "Has to do with that note Randalls left in the cell, don't it?"

"There's nothing to say that Randalls left that note; it could've been any man that'd been there before."

"Sure, whatever you say, Wolfe. It was layin' right on top of the bunk. I think somebody woulda saw it before now. Seems to me that Randalls fella wanted it to be found, don't you think?"

"I suppose you could be right."

"Ain't no supposin' to it." The deputy's face was abnormally thin and his mustache extra bushy. When he inhaled and exhaled, the hairs puffed out, then drew deeply in, like he had a hard time breathing, almost like McNelly.

Josiah wondered if Milt had the consumption, too. He took a half step backward.

"What'd the posse find?" he asked.

"Not a lick of nothin'. Once the tracks hit the river, they disappeared. Must've had a barge of some kind ready, 'cause you know them banks are too high to ride any distance. Tried that myself once, chasin' after a loose horse."

"It seems to me," Josiah said, "this break was really well thought out."

"One of the most professional I ever seen. Them fellas had some military trainin'. Probably war vets. Along with the know-how of the explosives, they was precise and organized. They wanted Randalls and nothing else. The fact that they came when they did, when the sheriff and the deputies was all in the courthouse havin' a meetin', well, if'n you ask me . . ." Milt stopped, then leaned forward on the desk, motioning for Josiah to meet him halfway.

Josiah looked around quickly, then stooped down, steadying himself on the desk and one knee, so he and Milt were face-to-face.

"If'n you ask me," Milt repeated, lowering his voice almost to a whisper, "I think somebody on the inside gave them some 'portant information. It was all too easy to be dumb luck. Like I said, if'n you ask me. They killed Jones, but that don't look to be a surprise. He was the only one with a weapon and the only one who could stand in the way to stop them or slow them down."

"So you think they knew ahead of time the perfect moment to break Randalls out?" Josiah asked.

"That's what I said, ain't it?"

"I guess the bigger question is, who would want to bust Randalls out of jail in the first place? Who would be willing to take that risk? And why?"

"Can't answer that, Wolfe. But I'm tellin' you, there's a rat in the nest, that's for sure."

Josiah nodded, then stood up. "I still need to see the sheriff."

"Well, you're gonna have to wait, he's got some business to tend to, and he said he didn't want to be disturbed."

"All right, I guess I can go talk to Elliot."

"Nope, you can't do that, either. Sheriff said he didn't want you talkin' to the boy until after you talked to him."

"Why's that?"

"Hell if I know. I'm just the new desk sergeant since Jones got kilt, and Farnsworth don't tell me crap."

"What's so important that I have to wait is all I want to know?"

Milt waved Josiah back down to him and whispered, "He's in there with his father. They're arguin' about somethin'. I ain't seen Myron Farnsworth step foot in this place but once, and that was a long time ago, right after the sheriff won the election. It was a short celebration then, and this ain't one now, I can tell you that."

"Kind of odd, don't you think?"

"What?"

"That his father shows up here a day after one of his accountants has been busted out of the jail, Myron being one of the wealthiest bankers in the city."

"Ain't my place to know what's odd or not, but I can tell you this, things ain't been right around here for a couple of weeks, and they just keep gettin' more worrisome, if'n you ask me."

Josiah took a deep breath and stepped away from the desk, resigned to waiting for the sheriff and slightly confused, trying to sort out everything he'd learned from Milt and Paul Hoagland.

The door to the sheriff's office pushed open harshly, slamming off the wall and bouncing back with a loud thud as it crashed into place.

Myron Farnsworth walked out of the office. He was a tall man, with a full head of white hair, along with a short white beard that didn't fall too far over his chin. His clothes were impeccable, exactly what Josiah would expect a banker to wear. He guessed the man's tailored clothes cost more than a couple of months of his Ranger's salary.

"Like I said, take care of it, Rory," Myron Farnsworth bellowed. He marched forward to the door, staring right through Josiah like he didn't exist.

Sheriff Rory Farnsworth had stopped at the door to his office, his face red, either from embarrassment or anger, it was hard to tell which. He didn't say anything until his father was out of the building and his shadow gone from the walk leading up to the fortress. "And a good day to you, too, sir," he said.

Josiah stood back, unsure of what to do next.

"What do you want, Wolfe? Can't you see that I have

enough problems?" Farnsworth snapped, like he was talking to an annoying four-year-old boy.

Josiah nodded. "I have some information for you."

"You deciphered the note?"

"I did, but I'm not certain that the information will do you any good."

Rory Farnsworth stared past Josiah at Milt, then jerked his head. "Well, get in here then. I haven't got all day."

CHAPTER 18

———◆◈◆———

The inside of Rory Farnsworth's office was much smaller than Josiah remembered it.

A gun rack sat on the wall behind the desk, full of shotguns and rifles of various makes and vintages, as well as a gun cabinet below it that most likely held six-shooters and other sidearms. Between the locker out in the foyer and the guns in the office, it was obvious that the jail was well armed, not that all of the weapons in the world would have done much good during the jailbreak, with no one around to fire them. Josiah still found the timing of the incident more than curious.

"Have a seat," Farnsworth commanded, pointing to the spindly chair in front of the desk.

Josiah pulled the note out of his pocket, along with the solution to the cipher on a separate piece of paper, and placed them on the desk gently, then did as he was told. The seat was still warm from the previous occupant, Myron Farnsworth . . . or, at least, Josiah assumed it was Myron who had occupied the visitor's chair; for all he knew Rory might have been subservient and given up his normal position to his father. Surely, a man like Myron Farnsworth was more accustomed to sitting behind a desk rather than in front of it.

The sheriff plopped down in his chair, the effects of his father's visit still very much visible on his face and in his demeanor. "That man infuriates me," Farnsworth said, twisting his lip.

"I'm sorry?" Josiah said.

"Oh, never mind." Farnsworth picked up the solution that Josiah had worked out, and read it out loud. " 'They will kill me under the oak tree.' What the hell is that supposed to mean to me, Wolfe?"

"I was hoping you knew which oak tree Randalls was talking about."

"Well, how in the hell would I know that? Everybody thinks I'm the answer man today for some reason. Just because I have a star on my chest doesn't mean I know everything."

Josiah let the words fall away, just like his gaze to the sheriff. He stared at his boots for a long moment, not wanting to give credence to anything the sheriff had just said. Things were tense enough between them.

"I was just hoping you might know," Josiah finally said. "There seems to be a man's life at stake here. Why would Randalls be afraid of dying at the hands of his rescuers? Doesn't that seem odd to you? Especially considering he didn't protest when the cell door was torn off? The man showed no fear. Just resignation."

"You're concerned about a man who was busted out of jail? A criminal? What's become of you, Wolfe?" Farnsworth sneered.

"Why shouldn't I be concerned, Rory?"

"I don't know. I just don't know. Maybe because he's a criminal?" Farnsworth said, tossing the note on the desk. "This is no help. No help at all, Wolfe. If somebody hangs

Randalls, it will only save me the time and money of doing it myself. So be it, I say. So be it."

"I did what you asked," Josiah said, surprised by Farnsworth's reaction. "I can't make it say anything different than what it does."

Farnsworth's eyes were cold and hard, his lips twisted up like those of a spoiled child who had just been denied his favorite toy. "How can I be sure what you say is true, Wolfe? It's like asking a Mexican to translate what another one says."

Josiah shrugged. "Have someone else solve the cipher then. They'll come up with the same answer. I guarantee it."

The glare in the sheriff's eye was disconcerting. "I'll do that, Wolfe. I'll just damn well do that."

Josiah was growing extremely uncomfortable in Rory Farnsworth's presence, considering his attitude and agitation. There seemed to be a lot going on in both men's lives, though there was not a whole lot connecting them. The sheriff seemed to be overwhelmed by his job and by the expectations that came along with the privileges and title, but there was no way Josiah was going to show him any sympathy, or any other emotion, for that matter.

Instead, Josiah started to push himself forward, readying to leave. "I'd like to speak with Elliot, but Milt said I needed to see you first. What's the problem with Elliot?"

"He's caused us some trouble, getting the other prisoners all riled up and such. I had him put in the hole."

"I beg your pardon?"

"I said Elliot's in the hole, in the dungeon. Do I need to repeat myself again, Wolfe? What is the matter with you, this sudden soft spot for prisoners and wrongdoers? Have you lost your way as a Ranger?"

"Hardly, Rory. I think Elliot is falsely accused, and you know it."

"Perhaps you should become a lawyer."

"Perhaps I should get Elliot the best lawyer in Austin," Josiah snapped back.

"Is that a threat?"

Josiah shook his head no. "Just a consideration," he said, as he felt the tips of his fingers go numb. "Elliot is no outlaw, Rory. He's a Texas Ranger and nothing but a boy to boot. He doesn't deserve to be treated like the scum of the earth, and you know it."

"I had never met Ranger Elliot until the night he was brought to the jail, bloody and blabbering like a fool I might add. So I am unaware of his character, morals, or values. That he is a Ranger does not speak as highly of him as you think it does, Wolfe. Most of the population—the upstanding population, that is—think little of the organization, as nothing more than a troop of miscreants and thugs."

"I don't think that's a fair assessment."

"Doesn't matter what you think." Farnsworth leaned forward. "My jail, my rules, Wolfe. Elliot's down there for twenty-four hours. No visitors allowed. Not even you." There was a coldness to the sheriff's voice that Josiah found even more distant than the moment before, and the man's fingers were stiff on the desk, unyielding. The sheriff obviously meant what he said.

"That's not right, Rory, and you know it. Elliot is not that kind of boy." The thought of wasting twenty-four hours dawned on Josiah right away. McNelly had given him forty-eight hours to get ready to leave with the company of Rangers. It had been Josiah's plan to go along with McNelly, but he wanted to make sure that Scrap was with him when he joined up with the company, and at the moment that was looking impossible.

Farnsworth stood up so quickly and forcefully that he knocked his chair back into the gun cabinet.

The collision rattled the guns in the rack above it. "Don't test me, Wolfe. I'm in no mood to justify my rules or actions to you or to anybody else today. If you want to see Elliot, then you'll just have to come back tomorrow—unless you'd like to gather up some fellas and try to break him out, too."

Josiah took a couple of deep breaths. He held his teeth together, restraining his tongue so he couldn't speak, and say something he'd regret later.

He knew when he was up against a brick wall, and when to push and when not to. The last thing he wanted was to make an enemy out of the sheriff or do anything stupid that would get him thrown in the dungeon alongside Elliot. For his own sake, and for Scrap's, he needed to keep his head about him and his mouth shut.

As it was, he and Farnsworth weren't close friends, and it didn't look like a genial relationship was going to bloom any time soon.

"I'll be back tomorrow, Rory," Josiah said sternly, staring the sheriff hard in the eyes. "Bright and early."

"That's fine, Wolfe. Just fine. You come back then. I'll be right here." Rory Farnsworth cocked his head at the door, and without the sheriff saying another word, Josiah knew he'd been dismissed.

Clipper trotted away from the jail at an easy gait. Josiah sat stiffly in the saddle, looking over his shoulder at regular intervals, watching the Travis County jail disappear slowly behind him.

A low-hanging cloud passed between the sun and the ground, covering the building with a long, gray shadow, making the jail seem drearier and more foreboding than it normally did.

Josiah thought about going home; it was near time to grab a bite for lunch, but he couldn't get Scrap out of his mind.

The boy was alone, in the dark, fighting off who knew what kind of vermin—rats, snakes, or scorpions—and accused of a crime he didn't commit. Elliot would've been better off if he'd stayed in South Texas. But he hadn't.

It took little to imagine the terror of being stuffed in a dark hole with nothing but earth walls and a locked gate overhead. Josiah wasn't sure he could take the punishment himself without going mad.

He pushed away the thought, only to replace it with worry over the quick passage of time. Forty-eight hours began to tick away as he thought about Scrap. It felt like there was a brick sitting securely on the back of his neck. *How in the heck*, he wondered to himself, *am I going to get everything done I need to get done before I have to leave?*

The list was long: See and say good-bye to Pearl, with great hopes that she would understand his departure and his need to continue to ride with the Rangers. Then make sure that Lyle and Ofelia had everything they needed for his extended absence. And now see to it that Scrap had every possible chance of proving his innocence and avoiding a quick trip to the gallows. All before he left on an assignment to face Juan Cortina and put an end to that trouble, once and for all.

Instead of heading toward Sixth Street, Josiah guided Clipper toward the scene of the crime, the Easy Nickel Saloon. Pearl would have to wait.

If he couldn't see Elliot, then he could poke around, find out what he could, and see for himself if Scrap's sister, Myra Lynn, was really there or not. Scrap thought he had seen the girl. It was the only way Josiah could think of helping Scrap at the moment. That and go see the lawyer that Hoagland suggested, but he wasn't about to do that on an empty stomach.

The Easy Nickel was a short ride from the jail, and Josiah was glad for the Black Hole of Calcutta to be completely out of his sight. If he never had to go back to the jail, it would be too soon.

There were a few horses tied to the hitching post in front of the saloon, and since it wasn't quite noon, there was no piano music banging out of the open windows and doors, no rousing noise at all.

The street and the saloon were quiet, no obvious sign of cowboys just in off the trail looking for a good time regardless of the time of day.

Josiah knew little of the saloon's owner, Brogdon Caine, or how he treated the girls that worked for him, but regardless, having one of his moneymakers murdered must have been troubling. As it was, there didn't look to be any sign of concern about trouble, or mourning, as Josiah pushed through the batwing doors and stepped inside the Easy Nickel.

It was nearly as dark and dreary as the inside of the jail, except the smells were different. There was bacon frying in the kitchen, and it mixed with the yeasty smell of beer, making the interior of the saloon feel familiar, if not exactly welcoming. Lamps burned low overhead and sconces on the walls were at half light, the smell of burning coal oil slight but noticeable. Most of the light inside came from the open windows that faced out to the street.

The saloon was typical: floor dotted with tables and chairs, a couple of faro tables in the back, an upright piano that looked like it had been shipped from the East with less than gentle hands, and one entire wall fronted by a long, hand-carved bar.

A couple of men sitting with their backs to the door checked out Josiah in the mirror that hung over the bar.

As Josiah walked up to the bar, the barkeep, a broad-shouldered man who looked to be of German descent and demeanor, with light-colored hair, square jaw, and constant anger set deep in his chin, glanced up at him, then went back to sweeping the floor.

There was no sign of any whores, or of the violence that had recently occurred. It was like the murder had never happened, like the memory of it had been completely rejected, an unseen event that had happened somewhere else.

But it had happened at the Easy Nickel, and Scrap Elliot was doing time in the darkness, bound in a hole, for something he didn't do, as far as Josiah was concerned. Regardless of the time he had left before leaving Austin, he had to see to it that the real murderer was found and Scrap set free.

He had no other choice. Scrap Elliot was his friend.

CHAPTER 19

———◆◆◆———

"I'll have a whiskey," Josiah said as he settled onto a stool at the end of the bar. From his vantage point, and with the help of the mirror, he could see both the front door and the back door leading into the kitchen.

There had been a time when Josiah would have never sat down in a saloon and ordered a whiskey just to drink it by himself. But he'd spent several months in Corpus Christi over the past winter, sitting in a cantina, acting as a spy for Captain McNelly, trying to gain information about the cattle rustling. It had been a long, four-month assignment, born out of the desire of the adjunct general and Captain McNelly to get him out of Austin, to take the attention off of one Ranger killing another. Somewhere along the line, Josiah had developed a taste, if not a tolerance, for the warmth and comfort of a good sip of whiskey.

He'd found the numbing effect a welcome relief to the heartache he felt every second, missing his son and longing to be home in the city—which had come as a great surprise to him. The liquor had helped him sleep deeply, passing off his wartime nightmares and other angry encouragements, allowing for some true rest—as much as that was possible while he pretended to be someone else.

The barkeep looked up from his sweeping and growled, "Ain't got no whiskey for the likes of you."

"What're these fellas drinking?" Josiah was a little surprised at the reception. The Easy Nickel Saloon wasn't exactly a grand palace that didn't need every dime for one expense or the other. Just the opposite. The place looked to be on its last legs. Everything looked old and worn out . . . including the barkeep and the two regulars sitting at the end of the bar.

"Lemonade. These fellas are drinkin' lemonade, and we're fresh out."

Josiah nodded and felt a twinge of anger shoot up his back. "This isn't a drinking club. Doors are open. What gives?"

The barkeep stopped sweeping and walked to where Josiah was sitting. He leaned in face-to-face, so the only things between them were the bar and a wall of sour breath escaping from a mouthful of rotting teeth. Josiah could smell a hint of whiskey and tobacco clinging to the man's stained white apron, too. "We don't serve your kind here," the barkeep said.

"And what *kind* is that?" Josiah asked, glancing up to the mirror, checking out the two men at the other end of the bar. They were still as statues. For the moment. Both of them wore sidearms in open view. Colts much like Josiah's. The men didn't look wrung out by trail riding, just wrung out from living day to day. They looked to be about the same age as him, mid-thirties, with stubble on their faces, mixed with a nice thick coat of daily dirt. It had probably been a month since they'd seen the inside of a bathhouse. The twirling fan overhead helped spread their odor among the other fading rot in the saloon.

"Rangers," the barkeep said. "We don't serve no Rangers here. That clear enough for you?"

Josiah stiffened, sat up as straight as he could. "I suppose that's your right."

"Damn straight it is."

"How'd you know I'm a Ranger?"

"Most folks know who you are, Wolfe. You been in here before. I got a memory inside this thick head. Rangers ain't nothin' but trouble, you ask me and a load of other folks around these parts of town."

"All I asked you for was a whiskey."

"And I said we don't have none."

Josiah said nothing for a long second, just stared at the barkeep, unwavering. "I'll have the lemonade then."

"You got cotton in your ears, mister?"

"My duty doesn't start for two days. I'm no Ranger today."

"Once a Ranger, always a Ranger."

"So they say."

The barkeep leaned closer this time, so he was almost nose-to-nose with Josiah. "You need to leave here now." He glanced over to the men at the other end of the bar, then back to Josiah. "They work for me. Tossed out more cowboys on their asses than you've seen in your entire life. What they did with 'em after that was none of my business. But I ain't never seen none of those cowboys step foot back into this establishment, and I 'spect it'll be that way with you if it comes to that."

"So you're saying they're tough?" Josiah looked down to the men, smiled, and tapped the front brim of his Stetson. They glared back at him, still unmoving. One of them blinked, the skinnier of the two. The one with dark hair had a thick shadow across his face and a scar under his eye.

"Tough enough to do away with a stick of a man like you, killer or no killer," the barkeep said.

"I'm not a killer."

"You think I'm so stupid I can't read? Even if I can't, I can listen. You've killed two men in the last few months.

How many men you kill before that, all in the name of keepin' the peace? Law's on your side, or so's you think."

The barkeep was most certainly aware of who Josiah was and of the incident with Feders and the bounty hunter, Leathers, that Cortina had sent to Austin. "What's your beef with Rangers anyway?" Josiah asked.

"My beef? That other Ranger killed one of our best girls. What do you think my beef is? You gotta lot of nerve settin' foot in this place. You're lucky you're still breathin' the way it is."

"Scrap Elliot's innocent. He didn't kill that girl, and I aim to prove it."

With an amazing amount of speed, the barkeep reached out in an attempt to grab Josiah by the throat.

But Josiah was ready.

He had slid his hand down to his leg and opened his palm. When he saw the barkeep flinch, saw him signal that he was going to come at Josiah like he had expected him to, intentionally provoked him to if truth be told, Josiah parried his hand across his face, and his fast-moving wrist crashed into the barkeep's arm, knocking his grasping hands away from Josiah's throat.

Josiah didn't stop there. He quickly grasped the big man's wrist with a hearty grip, then twisted the wrist under, straightened the arm, and pulled the barkeep forward. One wrong move, since Josiah had swung up his other arm to meet the man's elbow, and he would snap the barkeep's arm like it was a weak piece of kindling.

"You move another inch," Josiah sneered, "and I'll break your arm, then I'll feed your mouth my elbow for lunch, mister. Now, what's it going to be? Lemonade, or I knock your teeth out? I got just as much of a right to a drink here as any other man. Maybe more, since I find your hatred of Rangers distasteful."

Josiah could feel his heart racing, could feel the adrenaline pushing through his veins, numbing his body and focusing his mind directly on the threat before him . . . and at the other end of the bar. He hadn't lost sight of the two men sitting at the bar. They were now on their feet, hands reaching for their guns.

He only had seconds to succeed at restraining the barkeep and getting him to see things his way.

The barkeep's face was beet red, and sweat beaded on his forehead. Rage was building up from the man's toes, along with the pain as Josiah pressured the weakest part of the barkeep's arm.

Any hold he had on the man was only going to last a second or two longer. The barkeep was a big man, a stronger man than Josiah could ever hope to be, and when that volcano of fury erupted, there wasn't going to be any place to run or hide.

The cock of a gun can get a man's attention real quick, along with a snarling bull barely held back by a weaker man.

Josiah had no choice but to act, to save his own hide.

He thrust his one arm forward, and with as much force as he could pulled the barkeep's arm back with the other, snapping the man's forearm cleanly as he struggled against the pressure of Josiah's elbow. The barkeep's own attempt to escape the grasp and position Josiah had him in had worked against him as he tried to escape.

The skills of hand-to-hand combat revisited Josiah like a comfortable ghost that had lingered in a cemetery, awaiting a visit from a loved one. His time in the Texas Brigade and the War Between the States, and the skills he gained there, never left him, even though sometimes he wished they would.

The snap of the bone was ten times louder than the cock of the man's gun at the other end of the bar and was quickly followed by an agonizing scream as Josiah let go of the barkeep and followed up with his promise.

He flung his elbow into the big German man's mouth with as much force and rage as he could muster.

Teeth, soft and rotted, shot out the side of the barkeep's mouth like lead balls loaded with an extra tap of gunpowder, quickly followed by an explosion of sinewy blood.

The barkeep tumbled backward, crashing into a counter that held a thick inventory of liquor bottles. The mirror rattled and threatened to tip forward, but it was attached to the wall too securely for that to happen. Forethought on someone's part was obvious. Fights in saloons were as common as flies on a horse's ass.

Josiah spun around and gripped his Peacemaker, pointing it forward—one of the advantages of wearing a swivel rig was not having to unholster the gun when it was needed; there was a hole to fire through at the end of the swivel holster.

"You want to meet the same fate as this fella, or worse," Josiah yelled, "then go right ahead. One of you is going to fall before I do. Do we need to go any further with this conversation?"

Both men were standing at the other end of the bar, almost like twins, mirror images of each other, with their weapons drawn and Josiah in their sights, each with a finger on a trigger. Something behind Josiah caught the skinny man's attention.

If there was going to be a time to shoot, it would be now, but Josiah restrained himself. He'd already hurt the barkeep worse than he'd intended, let his anger get away from him. There was no way he could justify killing one of the two men, or both of them if it came to that, and he knew it. The previous two killings, and the trouble that followed, had put a hitch in his trigger finger, and at that moment, that second of hesitation would likely get him killed, and he knew it.

Josiah took half a breath, just as a gunshot exploded behind him.

CHAPTER 20

———◆•※•◆———

Out of instinct, Josiah spun around just enough to see who was behind him, all the while keeping the two men, with their guns trained on him, in his peripheral vision.

A tall man stood just outside the door that led into the kitchen. He was holding a rifle, with a thin whisp of smoke trailing upward.

Josiah glanced up at the ceiling, saw more than one bullet hole there, and focused back on the man he knew to be Brogdon Caine.

He was wholly grateful that the bullet had found a place in the ceiling and not in his back, but he was certain that his troubles weren't over. Three guns to one didn't offer him any favors in unknown territory. Josiah was aware that every breath he took could be his last.

"Back it down, boys. Ain't gonna be no more killin' in this place," Caine demanded. He had a hint of a Yankee accent, enough for Josiah to know that the man wasn't a born-and-raised Texan, but hard and stern enough for any fool to take him seriously.

The barkeep staggered up from behind the bar, pulling himself up on the counter like a man who'd been pushed over a cliff. His face was twisted in pain, and he was hanging onto his arm in search of comfort, or release of pain. There was no way that he'd find either any time soon. The bones were completely snapped.

"That son-of-a-bitchin' Ranger broke my arm, Mr. Caine." The barkeep's words were a little slurred, and a spot of drool leaked out of the corner of his mouth as he bit and fidgeted his tongue, trying to ward off and stomach the pain as much as he could. His face was as pale as a white sheet soaked in lye.

"Boys, take William over to see Doc Handley. Lock the door behind you. Ain't gonna be no business to be had while you're gone."

The skinny man started to protest, but thought better of it. He broke Caine's gaze with a defeated exhale and put away his Colt. "Ain't right what he did there, Mr. Caine."

Brogdon Caine stood his ground, didn't act like he heard a word the man said.

Caine had a thick head of black hair and skin that didn't look like it had been touched by the sun in years. He looked Scottish to Josiah, and it was perhaps that accent he had heard in the man's voice, a hint of the Highlands and not the East, like he'd originally thought. Or it could have been both for all he knew. Caine's eyes were dark, too, and he was just as faded and worn as the rest of the Easy Nickel was. Maybe more. The pants he wore were stitched and patched in a few places, and both legs rose off his scruffy boots just a little higher than most men wore them. He kind of looked like a teenager who'd had a quick growing spurt and his ma couldn't keep up with the mending, but in reality Caine was an older man, maybe twenty years older than Josiah.

"You leave Ranger Wolfe to me. Go on now. Get," Brogdon Caine said. "I can handle myself better than most. You know that."

The two men didn't protest any further. Instead, they moved with quick obedience to William the barkeep's side and directed him out the door, one man on each side of him, giving support.

Josiah stood there facing Caine, his hand still gripped on his Peacemaker.

"They'll be no need for shootin', Wolfe. You can lower your weapon."

"How do I know I can trust you, Caine?"

"The fact that we're standin' here havin' this conversation should be a fine startin' point for you. I coulda just shot you dead, if I thought you was vermin. Would've had a right, too, considerin' the hurt you just put on William. The man's a bull. I'm surprised he didn't tear your head off."

"He tried."

"If it wasn't for that, I'da shot you. Good thing as it was I recognized you."

"You'd shoot a man in the back?" Josiah relaxed a bit. He didn't trust Caine, wasn't sure what the man was up to, or why he hadn't shot him when he'd more than had the chance.

"If I thought it necessary," Caine said as he set the rifle down, a Winchester '73, and propped it against the door-jamb. "There's a sign of trust for you."

Josiah took a deep breath and let go of his gun, spinning it downward.

The door locked behind him as the two men ushered William outside.

He eyed Caine curiously, still not sure what was going on or what the owner of the Easy Nickel was up to. "I didn't intend to break William's arm. He came at me pretty quick."

"I'm sure he had reason. You provoke him, Wolfe?"

Truth be told, the answer would have been yes. Josiah knew he'd provoked the man to attack him, but it had been easier than he'd thought it would be. The barkeep had been on tenderfoot standing more than Josiah had anticipated.

"Well, I suppose I might've taken a little more offense to not being served than I might normally have."

One of Caine's eyes, the left one, was a little lazy, slower to catch up with the other one when he looked away or right at somebody. It kind of unnerved Josiah. He didn't want to stare, and he didn't know how to look the man straight in the eye . . . so he just focused on the right one.

Caine eased behind the bar and stopped to look at the mess William had made. When he'd stumbled back, the big barkeep had knocked a couple of bottles of good whiskey to the floor, shattering them.

"What're you doin' here, Wolfe? Don't you have Ranger business to tend to?"

"I'm looking for a girl."

"I can't tell you how many times I've heard a man say that."

"I'd be glad of it if I was you."

"You'd think, wouldn't you? But this is not as good a business as you might 'spect it to be. Who's the girl?"

Josiah's hand was still within a quick reach of the Peacemaker's trigger, and he wasn't about to sit down. He stood about a foot from the bar, plenty of room in between him and Caine.

He was uncomfortable. The danger, at least as far as he could tell, was past, unless there was a gun under the bar—and Josiah knew there was—or a man lurking in the shadows somewhere in the building that he didn't know about. That was possible, but didn't seem likely. Caine and his boys had had more than a clear chance to kill him if they'd wanted to.

His skin prickled, his every sense was open and alert, as he answered Caine's question. "Girl's name is Myra Lynn. Myra Lynn Elliot as far as I know. I don't know that that's the name she goes by, either, but it's all I got."

Caine shook his head no as he grabbed a bottle of whiskey and two glasses, putting them on the bar in between him and Josiah. "I don't know no girl named Myra Lynn. What she look like?"

Josiah took a deep breath. That was a good question. He'd never met Scrap's sister, and he hadn't thought to ask Scrap to describe her. He didn't know if she was tall or short, skinny or fat . . . Scrap was on the skinny side himself, all muscle no fat, but he was young, always on the move. There'd never been much discussion between them about the girl, other than the fact that she was a nun, and that had turned out to be a lie.

He looked at the empty glass, then shrugged. "I haven't got a clue what she looks like. I just know her kin. He's kind of rangy, black hair, but not as thick as yours. I don't suppose that helps much."

"Don't help at all. I only got six girls, and the one of them has black hair like you say, I've knowed her for a long time." Caine poured them each a finger of whiskey. "On the house."

"Thanks. What do I owe the pleasure?"

"Just call it a hunch that we're on the same side of things."

"You don't have a grudge against Rangers like William?"

"That boy killed his favorite girl."

"He didn't kill her."

"So you say. People saw what they saw."

"Sometimes people see what they want to see. What did you see?"

Caine shrugged. "I was in my office. We was pretty busy. Busier than I 'spect to be again for a while, if ever."

Josiah stiffened. Caine knew more about what happened the night Scrap came in. "And that's it, that's all you know?"

"Why should I answer your questions? Give me one good reason."

"If an innocent man hangs, it could be your turn next. Simple as that."

Caine studied Josiah for a long second without a blink. "I suppose you're right. I don't believe your boy's innocent, though."

"I guess it's my job to prove that."

Caine nodded. "The way William tells it, the Ranger was goin' around to the girls askin' questions. He finally met up with Lola, and they headed out back, probably up the back stairs to the private quarters, not to the business rooms, I tell you. Anyways, William didn't like the look of things, so he followed after Lola. He always kept a watchful eye on her. She was a real beauty. China doll face, happy eyes, and a body that didn't show no age or wear, if you know what I mean. Pert and happy, with skills that kept 'em comin' back."

Josiah feigned a smile.

"William heard a scream when he was about halfway through the kitchen. When he rushed out, he saw the Ranger leaning over Lola, blood on his hands and an odd look on his face. The boy took off runnin' and William tackled him, held him down till the sheriff's men came and took him away. Simple as that. There was no one else around. He gutted Lola deep. She died right away." Caine lowered his head.

"That's some story, if you believe every word William says," Josiah said.

"Why wouldn't I? I've knowed the man for nigh on seven years and he ain't never lied to me before. Least not that I know of."

"Elliot said there was another man, a cowboy, but he couldn't tell for sure. The man ran off. Maybe William didn't see everything."

"Maybe not. But I'd trust William long before I'd trust that Ranger. Or you for that matter. He never said nothin' about another man. That might just be a figment of Elliot's imagination. You ever think of that?"

"Nope. I got no reason to think Elliot's lying." That wasn't entirely true, but Josiah wasn't going to tell Caine that.

"Or you could be as much a liar as the boy. There's some that think little of you as it is."

Josiah knew he could do little to overcome his own reputation, and that of some of the Rangers. But it was a good outfit, with a higher purpose than any other he'd ever ridden with, including the State Police and the Rangers in their previous incarnation. Caine's attitude rankled him, made him angry all over, but it wouldn't be smart to show that anger, and Josiah knew it.

"However it went, it's a sad story," Josiah said.

Caine lifted the glass and downed the whiskey without a flinch. "I'll give you that," he said, settling his glass next to the bottle.

Josiah stared at the whiskey, then glanced to the half-full bottle. Without any further hesitation, he picked his glass up, let the sting of the aroma touch his nose, then followed suit and downed the whiskey in one gulp.

The burn felt good. Warmth and comfort came in a small dose quickly behind the burn. A few more fingers would be good, but it wasn't that kind of day. He didn't have time for comfort, or the hazy vision that drinking the day away tended to bring on.

"Good whiskey," Josiah said.

"Glad you like it. Who's this girl that you don't know anything about, and why are you lookin' for her here?"

"She's supposed to be working in town, just in from Fort Worth."

"I take it you mean she's whorin'?"

"That's what I mean."

"I'm out of that business."

"Really?"

"Girls don't feel safe here. And I ain't the kind to lock 'em down."

It was the practice of some saloon owners to chain down new girls. Break them down, so to speak, overpower them with such fear that any thought of running away never entered their minds. Josiah was glad Caine was not the kind of man who chained his girls . . . or so he said.

"So there are no girls here?" Josiah asked.

"That's what I said. Once Lola was killed, well that was that. Next mornin' the girls were all gone. Done with me, regardless of all I done for them. I wasn't no beater, either. Gave them a fair shake, a good bit of the money, food in their bellies, a roof over their heads. A doctor when they needed it, and as much laudanum as they wanted when the woman's curse struck. William was a kind enforcer, too. Wouldn't let no cowboy get a touch for free, or out of hand. I took good care of my girls, I tell you. And they left me for nothin' I could control."

"Four whores have been killed in the last month or so in this town. I can understand them being a bit nervous, can't you?" Josiah said.

"I'm well aware of the killin's goin' on in this town. But they got the right man, didn't they? That Ranger that you say didn't kill anybody. He's a friend of yours, isn't he?"

Josiah nodded. "Yes, he's my friend. And the brother of Myra Lynn Elliot. He was looking for her here—that's why he was questioning the girls. Says he saw her, too, but she ran off when the other girl was killed. He was trying to help the injured girl, not kill her. That's why he had blood on his hands."

Caine poured himself another finger of whiskey, then offered the bottle to Josiah.

He declined, waving his hand over the glass.

"You believe your friend." It wasn't a question, but a statement.

"I do."

"So you want to clear his name?" Caine asked.

"I'd like to, but I'm short on time." Josiah watched Caine down the second glass of whiskey. There was no comfort to be found on the man's face. "What do you want, Caine? You're obviously not a killer or I'd be a dead man right now."

"I'm a businessman. Or I thought I was. I want my girls back. I want cowboys crowdin' in the door so thick you can hardly breathe, but that doesn't look to happen any time soon. And now, thanks to you, I don't have the service of my barkeep. You're gonna have that debt to settle, you know? With me and with William."

"I was defending myself."

"It's business, Wolfe. You owe me."

Josiah nodded and silently agreed, but the debt to Brogdon Caine was the least of his worries at the moment.

"Your girls, where'd they go?" Josiah asked. "They didn't just disappear."

"Hell no, they didn't just disappear. They're all under one roof, not too far from here."

"And whose roof is that?"

"Whose do you think? Blanche Dumont's roof, that's whose . . ."

CHAPTER 21

———◆◈◆———

The day had turned dark. A bank of angry black storm clouds was rising high in the west, heading straight for Austin in a spring fury. The change of weather didn't surprise Josiah, not given the time of year, but it had made Clipper skittish, nervous. Though there was little time to waste, Josiah thought the best place to head next was the livery, to get the Appaloosa stabled before the storm hit.

He stared the horse in the eye, eased his hand out to its long neck, and touched Clipper as gently as possible. He trailed the palm of his hand up to the horn of the saddle, moving slowly, not saying a word, trying his best to relax Clipper and digest the whiskey and information he'd received inside the Easy Nickel.

Once he reached the saddle, Josiah climbed up and settled in on Clipper's back as gently as he could.

The first rumble of thunder broke over the horizon, causing Clipper to shake his head and snort heavily. It was unusual for the horse to react so dramatically to a coming storm.

Most of the time, Clipper was steady under the most extreme circumstances; lightning, thunder, rifle fire, even screaming Comanche didn't rile him or cause him to spook. Something was amiss, and Josiah wasn't going to ignore the horse's mood, all things considered.

He looked all about him, up and down the street, which was nearly vacant of any horse traffic, then up to the roof line, checking for shadows that didn't belong: gun barrels, men, anything out of the ordinary. Josiah had been ambushed from the rooftops before.

The air felt tense, full of energy, and the wind had suddenly picked up with so much force that it nearly flipped Josiah's hat completely off his head. He reached up and patted it down, catching the hat just in time. He cinched the drawstring up under his chin so he wouldn't have to worry about losing it again.

"Come on, fella, let's get you home." Josiah clicked his tongue a couple of times, easing Clipper away from the saloon, toward the livery. He looked behind him to make sure he wasn't being followed, and got a good dose of sand shooting straight at him from the heavy push of wind, up off the dry street. The grains of sand stung his eyes, but didn't blind him. He pushed the horse a little quicker then, and Clipper was glad to oblige, breaking into a trot, just short of a full-out run.

Josiah came up along a streetcar, mostly empty and heading for cover itself. He easily pushed past the newfangled mode of transportation. He wasn't sure how he felt about it, but that didn't really matter at the moment. Progress was progress. The city had changed tremendously in the short time Josiah had lived there. New buildings, homes, and now a new railroad coming straight down Cypress Avenue, though he had yet to see any of the actual transformation, the teardowns.

Thunder boomed again, closer this time, focusing Josiah's attention straight ahead. Clipper must have sensed their destination or held a desire of his own to outrun the impending storm and find refuge in the comfort of the livery—the horse picked up the pace and knew exactly where and when to turn.

The first spit of rain splashed off of Josiah's neck. It was cold, wakening his senses even further. The whiskey he'd had at the Easy Nickel had left him far from drunk, but he felt a little dazed by the events in the saloon.

He tried not to think about breaking the arm of the barkeep, William. Josiah knew he had reacted without thinking, that his body had taken over, skills and training erupting from somewhere deep in his soul, out of the darkness of the past, of the war, when every breath a man breathed could be his last. That fact still did not relieve him of a certain responsibility, and now, fleeing as he was, regret was starting to settle in. He hadn't meant to hurt the barkeep so severely. Josiah had been protecting himself, there was no doubt in that, but that last second, that last push might not have been necessary.

Questioning himself was always dangerous, especially when he realized he didn't have complete control over himself or his anger.

Maybe solving the Vigenere cipher had ignited something inside him, forcing the skills he'd learned in the war to come rushing back. Or maybe it was the frustration he felt, not being able to help Scrap. Or that time was running out, and there was so much to do—seeing to Lyle's needs, and saying good-bye to Pearl—all weighing heavily on his mind . . . and heart.

Caine had said Josiah owed him, and there was no denying that fact. He owed William the barkeep, too, even though neither of them had given him any new information that would be helpful to his cause: freeing Scrap from jail before he left with the Rangers. If Josiah had anything to do with it, Scrap would be with him, in his rightful place, doing what he did best, being a Ranger.

Clipper pushed harder toward the livery as the rain started to fall in buckets and the sky grew black and unpredictable. Thunder boomed. Lightning danced. The wind blew straight at Josiah's back, almost lifting him from the saddle. Both horse and man put their heads down and pushed forward. There was no place to take cover, and they were only a city block away from the livery.

Boom. Crack. Boom.

The storm and the suddenness of it were not lost on Josiah, but he could not help but think as much about what he had left as about what was before him.

The fact that Brogdon Caine hadn't really told him anything new frustrated him. Not about the night that Lola had been killed, anyway. The tale pretty much measured up with what Scrap had told him—with the exception of the sighting of the man. There had been no mention of that. Maybe he had run off before William had rushed out of the kitchen.

Josiah had been hoping that somebody had seen something, someone other than Scrap, but so far . . . there was nothing that would help him figure out what had happened.

He wasn't about to believe Scrap really was the killer. It would take far more evidence than what Brogdon Caine had told him to convince him of that.

It was strange to Josiah, however, that all of the whores under Caine's roof had sought refuge under Blanche Dumont's care after the killing.

Josiah wasn't sure what that meant, but considering the last time he'd seen Blanche Dumont, leading a funeral procession, then spitting on Rory Farnsworth's face, the information didn't surprise him.

Maybe she was the mother hen of all the whores in Austin, and her place was the only place they felt safe. He didn't know the inner workings of the flesh business well enough to know if that idea was true, or even possible, and he didn't want to know either.

If he was going to find Myra Lynn, and hopefully some

answers to what happened the night Lola was killed, Josiah knew where he'd have to go looking sooner rather than later. If Myra Lynn Elliot was anywhere in Austin, it only made sense she was at Blanche Dumont's house. And if what Scrap had told him was true, that he had followed Myra Lynn outside, then maybe she'd seen something . . . seen the real killer, seen what really happened to Lola. Either way, she was as close to an eyewitness as he had, and no matter what, he had to find her. But if he never saw the inside of another whorehouse, it would be too soon as far as he was concerned.

The cold rain on the back of Josiah's neck turned colder and harder. It had turned to ice, to hail.

Josiah kneed Clipper, urging him to run full out to the livery, which was now in sight. The Appaloosa responded with a snort and a shake of his head, protesting the sting of the ice pellets as they pinged down from the angry sky.

A quick glance over his shoulder told Josiah that the storm had gone from angry to downright mean. The black sky had suddenly turned green, and the wind had suddenly screeched to a stop. The hail was coming straight down, its impact hard and hurtful.

Muddy streets suddenly turned white and treacherous. Boardwalks were unnavigable, if anyone was foolish enough or unlucky enough to be caught out of doors.

Josiah had seen skies and weather like this a few times before in his life. They usually meant tornadoes could, or would, appear soon. Damaging winds and sudden floods, too. Nowhere was safe, not even the livery, but with a great amount of luck and effort both on his part and Clipper's, they made it inside the open double doors, just as a loud clap of thunder exploded over their heads and the hail ceased, leaving a breath of silence behind it and then the rush of wind and more pelting rain.

The green sky faded to gray at last look, a quick glance over the shoulder, as Josiah reined in Clipper, bringing the horse to a stop in the center of the barn.

He jumped off the horse, and one of the stable boys, the towheaded one Jake Allred was shouting at the last time Josiah was in the livery, appeared out of nowhere and grabbed Clipper's lead, taking him to his stall to calm him down and dry him off.

Josiah rushed to the doors and looked up at the sky, concerned by the threat, and by the direction that the storm was heading. As it was, the darkest, blackest cloud hung over the site of Josiah's house. He could only hope that Ofelia and Lyle were safe inside and not caught outdoors, as he had been.

Someone walked up behind Josiah, whose senses were still intact, and his nerves still on full alert. He spun around, expecting to see Jake Allred, the livery master, but instead he came face-to-face with Juan Carlos.

The old Mexican had a forlorn look on his face, sadness that could not be mistaken.

"You startled me," Josiah said, relaxing his hands, allowing the one to fall away from his six-shooter.

"I'm sorry, señor, I did not mean to frighten you."

Josiah forced a half smile, keeping one eye on the sky. "I should be used to it by now. You coming and going. It is good to see you."

"I wish I could say the same thing, señor."

The tone of Juan Carlos's voice sent a shiver up Josiah's spine. "What's the matter?"

"I have some bad news for you, Señor Josiah."

CHAPTER 22

———— ◆◆◆◆ ————

Josiah reached out for the livery door to brace himself. It had never been difficult to read Juan Carlos; his emotions and thoughts were usually apparent and forthright, and there was no mistaking that what he had just said was the truth. Bad news was coming, popped up like the spring storm that was now raging overhead.

"What is it?" Josiah asked.

"There is a woman who claims to have seen Señor Scrap kill that whore."

"A witness?" It was a breathless question, almost too difficult to say out loud. That wasn't the news Josiah had been expecting.

"Sí."

Hail battered the roof, and a straight wind pushed through from one end of the livery to the other. There was not a horse inside that wasn't pacing, nervous, or butting up against its stall. Whinnies and snorts mixed with the thundering downpour of ice pellets pinging above.

Josiah stood motionless, chilled, not sure he had heard

Juan Carlos correctly. Maybe he didn't want to hear what the Mexican said. Maybe it was impossible for him to consider that Scrap had actually killed the girl at the Easy Nickel Saloon. But the boy had lied to him before. Recently. Still, being ashamed of your sister and how she made a living was one thing; killing a whore was another. No matter the witness, Josiah just couldn't see it, couldn't see Scrap as the kind of man who was thoughtless and heartless enough to just stab a girl for no better reason than rejection or that she was just a whore in the wrong place at the wrong time. Scrap Elliot was a lot of things, but he wasn't a woman killer.

Josiah had been sure of that . . . up until a few seconds ago. "You're sure? A witness?" he repeated. "She saw Scrap stab the girl, Lola, to death?" He didn't know if that was the girl's real name or not, but it was the name Brogdon Caine had used, and Josiah had no other to put in its place. A lot of whores assumed different names so no one from their past would recognize them—or so they wouldn't recognize themselves. Shame was a common malady found in that trade.

"That is the word I hear," Juan Carlos said. "She is to appear before the judge and give her account of what happened."

There was no one else near, or in sight of them, inside the livery. Josiah could barely hear Juan Carlos himself over the roar of the storm, so he wasn't worried about being overheard.

Moisture clung to Josiah's face, and he wiped it away, brushing across the stubble of his beard, reminding him of the length of the day. A lot had happened since that morning. His stomach growled with hunger, and he made a mental note to check the saddlebag on Clipper's back to see if to tide him over there was some errant jerky about, leftover from a trail ride that he couldn't remember.

"Who is this girl, this new witness, do you know?" Josiah asked.

"No, señor, I don't know who she is. I have only come upon this information and thought it best I bring it to you right away."

"I'm glad you did. Thank you." Truth be told, Josiah was always glad to see Juan Carlos. There had been a time, recently, that their friendship had been strained, but there was no sign of that strain or distrust now.

"So you don't know if she is telling the truth or not, if she is credible?"

Juan Carlos shrugged.

Josiah kicked at the dirt just inside the door, tossing hail pellets, each about the size of a lead ball, back outside.

Thunder boomed overhead, clouds roiling into a murky stew. The storm was moving east. It had passed over his house and now was on the outskirts of town, trailing northeast, in the direction he always looked when he thought of home, of Tyler, and Seerville, the little town just outside of it where his family ranch sat vacant, left to the vermin and weeds.

Lightning danced down from the sky, white-hot bolts trailing after the hail like a jealous little brother left behind, running to catch up and join in the fun.

Josiah was glad the storm was past, glad that the hail had stopped and was being replaced with a steady rain that didn't look like it was going to let up any time soon. The rain fell in sheets, and the entire world, outside of the livery, looked like it had been drained of any color other than black, white, and gray.

The hail melted quickly, barely a memory after a minute or two on the ground. The street beyond the livery was now a muddy mess, with thin streams cutting ruts into what was once dry and hard-packed dirt. There was no traffic, not even a dog out scrounging for a bone or free bit of food.

Juan Carlos stood staring at Josiah, looking worried himself, a wisp of a man with leathery brown skin and pure white hair that poked out from underneath a hat that looked a little too large for him but was clearly large enough to shield his face from the sun, or recognition.

Scrap and Juan Carlos had never been friends, but the concern the Mexican bore on his face was real, and not out of necessity of respect, but from a growth of it. Regardless of what a man thought of Scrap Elliot's boisterous ways, prejudices, and general hotheadedness, there was no mistaking that he was a fine shot, an outstanding horseman, and a friend in a time of need. At least, he had been up until now.

"I'm leaving in two days," Josiah finally said. "McNelly is heading south again. I think he intends to put an end to Cortina and his cattle rustling operation once and for all."

"I know."

"I supposed you would. Are you riding along with us, in one capacity or another?"

"It is hard to say. I am old and tired these days. *Soy débil.* I am weak after the gut shot in Brackett, hardly myself on a good day. I cannot think about sitting on the porch of some *casa* for the rest of my life, but it is getting harder and harder to make the long journeys."

"I understand." Josiah turned away from the door, tired of worrying about the storm, relieved that it was passing without causing any damage, at least that he saw . . . or felt. "I have a lot to do before I leave. I fear if I don't muster with the company, my days as a Ranger are over. I've brought enough negative attention to myself, and to the organization, so I'm surprised that I am still welcome in the ranks."

"Captain McNelly is a loyal man. Maybe one of the most loyal men I have ever met. It is not luck that finds you in his good graces, but your contribution. You must realize that."

"I suppose I do. That doesn't stop the clock from ticking. I was hoping to be able to free Scrap so he could ride along with us, where he belongs, but that doesn't seem possible now."

"There is more bad news," Juan Carlos said. "This circuit court judge is not in favor of Rangers and does not see them in a good light. He is a relative of Captain Feders, an uncle. I fear he will *ser rencoroso*, um, hold a grudge against Señor Scrap."

Josiah felt his heart sink even deeper into despair than it already was.

Just when Josiah thought the shadow of his previous action had passed, just like the threat of the storm, it reared up again—only this time threatening Scrap, who had been there, near Laredo, with him when Feders had given Josiah no choice but to protect himself.

Kill or be killed. It seemed to be the way of his life.

"That's not good news." Josiah took a deep breath and looked up into the rafters of the livery, not focusing on any-thing, just feeling more and more frustrated and more than a little concerned about Scrap's welfare. Being in the hole in the jail might be the least of Scrap's worries at the moment.

"Do you think Scrap really killed that girl, Juan Carlos?" Josiah asked. "I can't bring myself to think of it, but I could be wrong, my judgment clouded by the good deeds Scrap has done in my presence. They surely outweigh the bad ones, even the lies that have circled around to bite him."

"I do not know what Elliot is capable of, Señor Josiah. There were no other witnesses that I know of to disprove what this girl might say."

"There is," Josiah said. "Or there might be. Scrap was chasing after his sister, Myra Lynn. At least that's what he said, when he stumbled on a man attacking the girl, Lola. But Myra Lynn ran off, disappeared into the night. Scrap lost her when he stopped to help the girl."

"What happened to the man?"

"He ran off, too, and Scrap didn't get a good look at him. At least that's what he said."

"Then we need to find his *hermana*, his sister."

"I was thinking the same thing. That and . . ."

"And what?"

"That maybe it's possible that I'm wrong. Maybe Scrap did kill Lola. I hate to think that, but it's possible, I guess, even though it doesn't settle right. Doesn't make sense. There've been four murders. Lola was the most recent of them. Scrap was nowhere near Austin when the others occurred."

"Why do you think the murders are all connected, señor?"

"I don't know. I just think they are, and so does the reporter, Paul Hoagland. Doesn't it seem a little strange that there have been four similar murders and that they would have been committed by four different killers?"

"It is possible, señor. Stranger things have happened in this city. You are new to it. A killing is big news in the town where you came up. Here? Not so much. There are thousands of people who live here. More coming every day. And even more will come when the new railroad comes in. Two trains instead of one coming and going. Imagine what that will mean."

"What does it mean now?"

Juan Carlos looked confused. "What are you saying?"

"The new railroad coming to town. Right down Cypress Avenue. Buildings are being torn down. Houses are being torn down. There's money being made and lost there, and surely anger, too, now that I think about it. I remember what happened in Tyler when the railroad came in. There were big winners and big losers. When the tracks turned the wrong way, Seerville up and died. Maybe there's more to these murders than we think. Maybe they aren't just happenstance."

"You think the new railroad is connected to the murders? That makes no sense," Juan Carlos said, twisting his face up in disbelief.

"Maybe it doesn't make sense. But when I was at the jail, Rory Farnsworth's father left in a huff, ordering him to 'Take care of it.' Now, I don't know what he was talking about, but Myron Farnsworth is a banker. Murder can't be good for business. You said it yourself, more people are coming and going. There's going to be more at stake, more investments being made, more at risk for the bank."

Juan Carlos nodded. "I can see that."

"Now, figure in Abram Randalls to all of that."

"Who is that?"

"Randalls is the man who was busted out of the Black Hole. He was an accountant and an embezzler." Josiah raised his eyebrow and caught his breath as he put two and two together. "*And* he kept the books for none other than Blanche Dumont. Now get this. When I was at the Easy Nickel poking around, Brogdon Caine told me all of his girls left and sought refuge at Blanche Dumont's house."

"That is interesting, but I see that it means very little."

"I don't know what it means. But there's a kettle of vultures circling over Blanche Dumont's house, pointing to something there that needs to be looked at. Besides, I think we might just find Myra Lynn there, too. But there's something even more important than that." Josiah's mind was running quickly now. "Do you know where there's a big oak tree that is used for hanging?"

Juan Carlos thought for a minute, then nodded yes. "*Sí*, I do. It's just on the other side of the river, just before you get to the Jensen Ranch off the cow trail."

"Good. We need to get there before we go to Blanche Dumont's . . . if it's not already too late," Josiah said, rushing to Clipper's stall.

CHAPTER 23

━━━◆━✕━◆━━━

An empty noose dangled from a lone live oak, standing in a vacant field like a sentinel, or the last man standing in battle. It was an old tree, at least seventy feet tall, with limbs curving and jutting out in every direction, almost as big around as it was tall. Live oaks stayed green in winter, so there was no spring tenderness to its leaves.

The tree reminded Josiah of a time not too long ago that he'd spent in a mott, what most Texans call a grove of live oaks, as he and Scrap ushered a whore, Maudie Mae Johnson, to a new life in Fort Worth. Mae, as she liked to be called, was a wildcat of a girl, who in the end took a shine to Josiah, but that shine could not be, and was not, fruitfully returned—Josiah had no interest in the girl, other than helping her get her life in order.

Scrap, on the other hand, was jealous as jealous could be about Mae's shine on Josiah. He later confessed to Josiah that he hadn't been with a woman in a biblical way yet. Somewhere since, Josiah was almost certain Scrap's predicament had corrected itself, but he wasn't exactly sure when.

Josiah remembered plenty about the time in the mott and didn't care for the memory at all. It showed Scrap in a bad light—impetuous, angry, and apt to go off half-cocked at the smallest of matters, all traits that added up to a boy who was able to let his emotions get away from him and end up killing somebody for no other reason than emotional rage.

Doubting Scrap made Josiah's heart ache, and he had to push away the memory, along with the memory of Mae who, in the end, had left Scrap's aunt Callie's boardinghouse, disappearing, as it was, Josiah assumed, back to the life from where she had been rescued. Once a whore, always a whore, as the saying went. Though the thought saddened Josiah immensely.

He stopped Clipper about twenty yards from the tree, taking in the view around him.

Juan Carlos stopped alongside him on his roan mare that looked nearly as haggard and old as the Mexican himself. "We are too late, señor," he said, staring at the empty noose, blowing to and fro in the breeze as if it were a child's swing instead of a vehicle of death.

"Looks that way," Josiah said. "Or too early."

"How did you know of this place, señor?" Juan Carlos asked, with a nod. "Many men have lost their lives here instead of on the gallows. *Los hombres buenos*, *hombres malos*. Good men, bad men. No law but that of the vigilante. Many Mexicans have dangled here, but Anglos, too. It is called the Tree of Death, *Árbol de la Muerte*."

"You know about the jailbreak?"

Juan Carlos nodded yes.

"The man they busted out left a note behind. It was a cipher, a Vigenere cipher. I was able to identify it and solve it because I had experience in the war with messages being sent back and forth. It was a skill I'd long forgotten about,

and didn't want to think about, until the deputy in the jail
brought the note to Farnsworth, who then handed it to me
to see if I could read it."

"It all goes back to that, the war, aye, señor?"

"It does. For good and bad. Anyway, this fella, Abram
Randalls, said they would kill him under the oak tree. He
must have served in the war, too, to know how to write a
note like that. I'm not sure that means anything. Most men
of a certain age fought in the war in one capacity or another.
Nobody wears the uniform or signs on their sleeves. But we
all know the minute we meet up. There's a look, a language,
for good or bad, that we all share. That much blood and
battle has an effect on a man."

"The note said nothing about hanging him?"

"I'm sorry?"

"This note, this cipher, it said they would kill him, not
hang him?"

Josiah stared at Juan Carlos for a moment, then slid off
Clipper's saddle, his eyes glued to the ground, looking for
any sign of disturbance: a gathering of hooves, or blood,
anything that would validate what Juan Carlos had said.

Juan Carlos dismounted, too, pulling his six-shooter, a
sheriff's model Colt, his eyes flittering around, scoping out
the area with a renewed concern. Josiah had noticed a
change in Juan Carlos since he had been shot and nearly
died in the ambush in Brackett. He was more wary, nervous,
not confident like Josiah remembered, always willing to
lead—now the Mexican let Josiah lead and make all of the
decisions . . . mostly.

The ground under the towering tree was soft from the
recent storm. They had ridden out of the rain as they headed
southwest. The temperature of the air had dropped noticeably and was cooler, less humid. A hard breeze, just short
of a wind, still pushed at them, but the sky was starting to
lighten over their heads and to the west. Clouds broke apart
showing hints of blue, the promise of a better day. But the

birds were silent, not set on rejoicing after a storm had passed like they usually did.

"There's no sign of anyone being here," Josiah said. "Not recently anyway."

Juan Carlos didn't respond right away. He had stopped and had his back turned to Josiah, looking out over the empty field, back toward Austin, the way they had come.

"There is movement on the hill, señor." Juan Carlos cocked his Colt, chambering a cartridge.

Josiah followed the Mexican's gaze but did not see anything. He didn't doubt the man's ability to see movement when none was apparent to anyone else. Juan Carlos had more skills than any man ought to rightly have, as far as Josiah was concerned.

"Move the horses behind the tree," Josiah said.

Juan Carlos hurried to Clipper, took up the lead, all the while keeping his eyes on the distant hill, then grabbed his mare's lead as well. "There is more than one of them, señor. At least two of them."

Josiah wanted to ask how he could know that but didn't take the time. Again, there was no use questioning Juan Carlos's talents; they simply existed, and had saved his life on more than one occasion.

As he spun back, intent on taking cover behind the tree, Josiah saw what Juan Carlos had seen: the silhouette of two horses just over the rise, and the wave of weeds moving in the opposite direction, as a pair of shooters crawled down the hill to get a better position.

Before Josiah could say another word, the first shot rang out. It pinged off the tree, peeling a bit of bark and sending it flying like a weapon itself.

Juan Carlos hurried both horses behind the tree, and Josiah joined him there, firing blindly into the side of the hill. He couldn't see the men, hiding in the saw grass as they were, but there was no way he wasn't going to return fire. They had made him a target, and returning in kind was his only option. There was no need to ask questions or wonder at the intent of the shooters.

Somebody had followed them out to the Tree of Death, intent on contributing to its namesake.

Josiah had no idea who the men were, but for some reason, considering what had happened at the Easy Nickel earlier in the day, he wasn't surprised that he'd made a new set of enemies.

The hidden shooters returned fire.

It was a good thing that the trunk of the live oak tree was as broad as it was and that there was a bit of bramble to hide behind. Josiah and Juan Carlos could comfortably take up positions on either side of the tree. The horses were about ten feet beyond the bramble, hopefully hidden well enough so they wouldn't be targets, too.

Josiah grabbed his Winchester '73 from the scabbard, and Juan Carlos had pulled a Henry rifle off the roan mare's saddle. They both returned fire, shooting off enough rounds to drain a water tank.

The shooters didn't return fire.

They must have realized that their gunsmoke was giving away their positions. There was nothing for them to hide behind—no trees, no rocks. The men were out in the open with nothing but grass to take cover in. Not a wise move as far as Josiah was concerned, but then most outlaws shot first and thought later . . . if they had the opportunity.

Josiah waited, as did Juan Carlos, searching the hillside for any kind of movement at all. He saw nothing. "I wish I had my field glasses with me."

"I have none with me, either, señor. We may have killed them. Do you have any idea who they might be, or what they are after, señor?"

Josiah shrugged. "I got into a scuffle at the Easy Nickel earlier today. Might be revenge from that. I broke a man's arm. Brogdon Caine didn't seem like he was that angry, or wanted me to pay a price for my actions, at least not right away, but that could've been a ruse."

Juan Carlos looked unmoved. "Who knows about this note, this cipher you solved for the sheriff?"

"Just the sheriff, and the desk sergeant, Milt I think his name was. That's it as far as I know. Why?"

"We are here, Señor Josiah, and now we are being shot at."

"You think the cipher was a setup to draw us out here?"

"No, no, I don't think that at all. We were followed, that much is true, I suspect, but there's more going on than your fight at the saloon."

They both watched the hillside for more movement, still nothing. For all Josiah knew, they had gotten lucky and killed the two shooters.

Still, it was better to wait, better to hold tight, than do something stupid like showing themselves, breaking cover. If they were killed, Scrap would have no chance at all of having his innocence proven . . . or his guilt. Either way, there'd be no one left to help him.

"Don't you think that it is odd that a man who was broke out of jail feared for his life—obviously from his rescuers? The cipher was a plea for help. But only from a man who could read the note. It makes little sense to me."

"I do think it's strange. But there's no sign that Abram Randalls is dead."

"Or alive."

Josiah saw Juan Carlos's deep brown eyes flinch. He focused on the hill then and saw the movement the Mexican had. He wrapped his finger around the trigger, taking a breath before he pulled on it, waiting to get a decent shot.

"Wait," Juan Carlos ordered. "They are retreating, moving back to their horses. Let them go. They will be easy to track now, just after the rain."

Josiah exhaled and flipped his finger off the trigger,

agreeing with Juan Carlos. They would leave an easy trail in the mud, and Juan Carlos was an expert tracker.

"I will shoot behind them, just so they think they are getting away," the Mexican said.

"Good idea." Josiah stood back and watched.

The grass swished and swayed up to the crest of the hill. It was hard to see, to decipher from the hard breeze that was continuing to blow even though the storm had passed. But the two men were climbing in the opposite direction, giving a clear clue of their position to any man who had experience watching an enemy from a distance. Once again, Josiah's skills from the war proved beneficial.

Finally, the men had to break free of the tall grass, and they scurried to their horses, shooting as they went, covering themselves in a rain of gunfire.

Juan Carlos did as he'd said and fired behind the shooters, urging them on but not hurting them.

The clouds broke overhead from the gray cover of the storm, pushing east, allowing a bright ray of sun to shine down on the top of the hill, making the sight of the shooters clearer, but not completely recognizable from a distance.

Josiah could see that they were dressed all in black, from boot to duster to hat, and their facial features were covered by black kerchiefs, as well, but it was one of their horses that got Josiah's attention as they rode away, under no cover and in the bright sunlight.

The horse was a gray gelding, just like he had seen at the jailbreak, just like the one Captain Leander McNelly rode.

CHAPTER 24

———◆◆◆◆◆———

Juan Carlos stared down at the ground, studying the hoofprints of the shooters' horses like they were a sacred text.

"Maybe it wasn't wise, letting them go," Josiah said.

Juan Carlos looked up, squinted his eyes. "They didn't have a well-thought-out plan. Somebody sent them after us, put them on our trail. They will be back."

"There'll be more of them, too."

"*Sí*, there will be if what you say about the jailbreak is true."

"It is. They're well organized, disciplined."

"Then they are off balance. You are onto something, señor. They fear you know something or will discover the truth of their actions. This is not about one man."

"You mean killing the whores?"

"I don't know about that. But the jailbreak. There are more men involved in that than what you saw. How, or if, the two are related, is another matter. You must simply watch your back, Señor Josiah. We are tracking coyotes, sneaking, mean beasts who are there one minute, then gone the next."

"It seems like I always am."

"The path you have chosen is not easy."

"I don't feel like I chose anything."

"That is usually the way it is, señor," Juan Carlos said. "'*La bondad no tiene lìmites.*' My mother used to say that. Goodness knows no bounds."

Josiah took a deep breath and looked down the hill, over the small valley with the Tree of Death situated almost squarely in the center—a lonely monument that had been used by man as something other than what it was intended for.

"I don't know that I'm in the business of goodness, but I sure feel the need to see to the truth about Scrap's situation. He would do the same for me," Josiah said.

"I was not aware that you were so fond of Scrap Elliot," Juan Carlos said wryly.

"He grows on you."

A slight chuckle escaped the Mexican's lips. "That he does. Like bindweed that cannot be killed."

Gray clouds struggled to hold their shape as the west wind pushed at them, broke them apart, ate at them like termites on a fresh piece of wood. They almost looked like smoke, but there was no smell in the air that indicated anything was on fire. Just the opposite. Spring was in full bloom. The hill was covered with a quilt of bluebonnets, the color so deep that it looked like the sky had fallen to the ground, instead of a long patch of flowers that had sprung up to celebrate the season. There seemed to be a flock of butterflies tracking north, stopping frequently on the tall, spired blooms, to refuel themselves for a journey that was obviously not complete.

Josiah let the silence settle between him and Juan Carlos as his mind wandered away from Scrap, away from the present . . . just for a moment.

He knew the names of quite a few of the plants he was staring at thanks to Lily, his long-deceased wife.

Spring was her favorite time of the year, and there was always a moment of melancholy, of grief returned, when he thought about her, about their life that was gone forever. It all seemed so far away, like it was another person that the tragedy had happened to. But the hole in his heart told him that that was not the case. The grief belonged to him and no one else.

He stood still on the hillside, taking in the sights and smells, willing away his heartache, trying to be encouraged by the promise of the day, now that the storm had passed.

But in reality, Josiah knew there would be another storm. It was that season. Storms seemed to push through the hill country every other day. And no matter how much he wished against it, the troubles in Austin were growing deeper and darker as the clock ticked away, notching off seconds until he would have to leave with his company of Rangers, or leave the Rangers entirely and stay behind, trying on his own to see Scrap free of the murder charge. If that was even possible, now that there was a witness involved.

"The horse looked familiar," Josiah finally said.

"Which horse?"

"The gray gelding. McNelly rides one that looks just like it. The man in charge of the jailbreak rode one like it, too."

"Are you saying that they are the same horse, señor?"

"I can't be sure. But I keep seeing a gray gelding. It is a grand horse, hard to mistake, even from a distance."

"Why would Captain McNelly hide his face and break a whore's bookkeeper and a banker's embezzler out of jail? I do not believe he would do such a thing. Nor do I think he would track after you and shoot from a distance. If Leander McNelly wanted either of us dead, we would not be standing here, Señor Josiah. You must know that."

"I'm not saying any of it makes sense. All I'm saying is that I keep seeing the same horse."

"There is more than one gray gelding in Austin, señor."

"I don't doubt that. It just seems odd, that's all, a horse like that showing up in places connected to these incidents. I don't know McNelly's capabilities. But he is no Pete Feders, I am sure of that," Josiah said.

Juan Carlos looked away from Josiah then, studying the ground, eyeing the clear tracks in the mud. "They are heading back to town, back to report their failure. We must keep our wits about us on our return."

"Are you sure they meant to kill us?" Josiah asked.

Juan Carlos drew in a deep breath. "You are right, señor, it may have been nothing more than a warning. We had little to cover ourselves, and if they were serious about killing us, just as McNelly would see us dead if he were behind it, so would any outlaw worth his spit. Especially a gang as disciplined as those that you speak of, those that conducted the jailbreak."

"Seems risky."

"There is obviously a lot at stake."

Josiah nodded. "We should split up. Why don't you head back and let Ofelia know of the situation. I don't think she's in danger, Lyle either, but I can't be sure. My enemies have gone after my family before. And tell her I plan on riding with the company when they leave in two days' time. I will prepare her as much as possible. It may be late when I return this evening. The day is getting away from me, and there's still a lot of ground to cover."

"I fear you may not be able to follow the trail. I will track them, but I suspect I will lose the trail at the river."

"Are you sure?"

"*Sí*, you should go another way back to the city, the long way."

Josiah nodded. He found it nearly impossible to leave Juan Carlos on his own. He looked weak, old, incapable of taking care of himself. But that was hardly the case. Even in a diminished capacity, the effects of the gunshot wound to the gut still showing themselves, Juan Carlos was as lethal as a rattlesnake curled up under a rock. The snake just needed stirring to strike.

"It is a good plan, Señor Josiah," Juan Carlos said. "Where will you go now?"

"I have a lawyer to see—if it's not too late. And a witness to talk to—if I can find her."

"I think you know where to start looking."

"I do. But I'm not looking forward to knocking on Blanche Dumont's door any time soon."

The wetness had not left the air. It was humid, the air thick enough to make any man have trouble breathing, no less one with consumption, like Leander McNelly.

Josiah could not get the captain out of his mind as he tried to reason out the sighting of the gray gelding and all that had happened since he'd learned of Scrap's arrest. He still could not bring himself to believe the captain was involved in the jailbreak or the murders in any way, and there was no doubt that it would be heartbreaking if that were truly the case. McNelly was a legend, one of the most upright Texans Josiah had ever encountered.

Still, there was something nagging him about McNelly and the entire situation, like a splinter under the skin that just goes in deeper when any attempt to remove it is applied.

Josiah rode back toward Austin cautiously, keeping his eyes out for any sign of the shooters. Juan Carlos was on their trail, tracking them with the skill of the greatest of all hunters that Josiah knew. If anyone could find the two shooters, or their tracks, Juan Carlos could.

The sun was hanging effortlessly in the cloudless sky as Josiah rode back toward Austin. The storm was just a memory, and those smoky-looking clouds that had been overhead not so long ago were only dots on the horizon, pushing past the city. They looked like a mountain range in the distance instead of a fleeing storm.

Hints of the wind still existed but only in a softening breeze. It looked like it was going to turn out to be a pleasant day, after all. At least, weather wise.

If there was any benefit to the change in the weather and the unbearable humidity that followed the storm, it was that the bright shining sun made it easier to see shadows on the rocky cliffs of the limestone outcroppings that lined the trail Josiah had chosen to take. Of course, it was the most difficult route back to Austin, but hopefully also the most unlikely when it came to encountering trouble. If the shooters had somehow circled back, then Juan Carlos would be wise to that, providing backup to Josiah. He was sure of it, confident that the Mexican could handle whatever he encountered.

Clipper stepped cautiously forward, climbing to the top of the cliffs as carefully as possible.

Josiah sat stiffly in the saddle, every inch of his being on alert, the Winchester situated across his lap, his hand not far from the trigger.

He fully expected to be ambushed, and he was not about to ride full out—at least not until the city was completely in sight—and give the two shooters any undue opportunity to put an end to his journey, or his life.

A bird fluttered off ahead of him, a blue jay shrieking from a pecan tree, grabbing his attention, causing him to take his Winchester fully in hand and train the barrel on the low shrubs at the base of the tree.

He was at the tightest point of the trip up to the top of the outcropping, and if there was going to be an ambush, this would be the spot he would pick if he was the ambusher. It was too perfect to resist.

But life went on normally. Nothing jumped out at him, no shots were fired. Any birds or creatures that laid claim to the spot as home remained quiet, hidden, as Josiah crested the outcropping, easing Clipper onto the flat land that swept outward, offering a wide vista that included the city of Austin.

The answers to his search were right in front of him, but hidden from view, only because of the distance, Josiah was sure of it. Just as he was sure that the sun was hanging right over his head, beating down on the back of his neck like it was inches from his skin.

CHAPTER 25

———◆◆◆———

Woodrell Cranston's office was not hard to find. It was on the third floor of a building just off of Hickory Street and Congress Avenue. An alley cut through the center of the block, and entrance to the office was gained by climbing up a rickety set of steps that were precariously attached to the back of the building. A landing led into a thin hallway, capturing the humidity of the day and transforming it into mold and mildew, to be added to a well-established population of spores that smelled like they had been in the building since the beginning of time.

Josiah quickly found the door marked "Woodrell S. Cranston, Esq., Attorney at Law." The paint was fresh, but the door looked like it had served a long line of tenants. There was no telling how old the building was, but lawyers and the like came and went from the capital city like flies to shit, always moving in and moving out, depending on the political climate and the state of daily affairs.

A distorted reflection of himself on the frosted glass-paned door caught Josiah's attention, but he was only momentarily conscious of his own physical being. He had ridden out of town hard, exchanged gunfire with two unknown shooters, then rode straight, albeit nervously, back to where he'd started from. Whether he was of proper dress or not, whether he smelled of horse lather and sweat should not and did not matter to him when it came to the reason he was there in the first place: Scrap's guilt or innocence. The boy's life was in his hands, and if this attorney was worth his salt, then that's all that would matter. Proper dress and manners were better left for the governor's mansion and highfalutin functions that he hoped never to have to attend again.

Josiah pushed the door open without knocking. It was still working hours, sometime after noon, and the door was unlocked. That seemed to be enough protocol to enter.

The room was small, about three times as big as a wash closet. A desk was jammed up against the back wall with just enough room on one side for a man to scoot around and sit down. A fan swirled overhead, powered by water and a small turbine. Even at a low speed, the wind from the fan threatened to blow all of the papers off the desk. There was no window, but a sconce on each wall burned brightly with a coal oil flame, providing more than enough light in the tiny room.

A very young man was sitting behind the desk.

Josiah's entrance startled the man, or boy, as he looked no older than Scrap. The man's face was free of whiskers and showed no hint that he could even get any to grow. His cheeks were permanently flushed pink, making his face look like a baby's bottom touched with a rash. He wore a pair of round spectacles that made him look studious and did nothing to make him look mature. The man had flinched noticeably, almost knocking over an inkwell he had been dipping out of, like he was afraid of something.

"I'm sorry," Josiah said, "I'm looking for Woodrell Cranston."

"Well, you've found him. And who, may I ask, are you?" Cranston said, his eyes searching up, then down, resting squarely on Josiah's Peacemaker. Beyond that, he didn't move. He looked wide-eyed, bordering on afraid.

"Josiah Wolfe." It was almost a surprised stutter. The man before him barely looked old enough to be away from home, much less be a graduate of some university handing out law degrees. "You're Woodrell Cranston?"

"I take it you're not here to kill me?"

"Are you expecting someone?"

"Not necessarily, but in my line of work, one just never knows."

"No, I'm not here to kill you. I hoped to hire you, but you're not exactly . . ."

Cranston exhaled heavily. "Let me guess, you were expecting someone older, more refined maybe? Perhaps a tall man with an expensive black suit, long white beard, and oh, maybe a cane, or a smoking pipe to add to the effect?"

"Something like that."

"Sorry to disappoint you. What's your business with me, Mr. Wolfe? I know we have never met. How is it that you've come to this office in search of help with the law?"

Josiah shook his head no. "We haven't met." He stared at Cranston, who in return was staring at him expectantly. It was tempting to walk out, just leave the boy sitting there dumbfounded and fearful of who walked in next, but the fact was, Josiah didn't know where else to go, or who else to go to, for legal help. "Paul Hoagland sent me. He said you'd be my best bet with my problem."

"Hoagland, you say? The newspaper reporter?"

"One and the same."

"I should have guessed, actually. I have little reputation in Austin as it is, and Hoagland has been my champion in recent weeks. We're fraternity brothers, you see. Phi Beta Kappa."

Josiah had never heard of Phi Beta Kappa and hardly knew what a college fraternity was, so he said nothing, tried not to move. He suddenly felt like he'd not only worn the wrong kind of clothes but was also less educated than the man-boy before him.

"Well, come on in, Mr. Wolfe, and close the door behind you. If Hoagland sent you, then I expect that you're on the up-and-up and, indeed, are in need of my help."

"Up and up from what?"

"Just a manner of speech, good man. Just a manner of speech." Cranston glared at him, then removed his spectacles, waiting for Josiah to do as he'd been asked.

Josiah hadn't realized that he hadn't closed the door. His mouth must have gaped open, just like the door, at the sight of Cranston. He did as he was asked, then removed his hat and sat down in a simple wood chair that sat squarely in front of the desk. His knees butted against the desk when he sat down.

"What do you know of freeing a man innocent of a murder charge?" Josiah asked.

"More than you might expect, Mr. Wolfe."

"I'm sorry, I don't mean to doubt you so openly, it's just that . . ."

". . . I appear so young. Yes, you've made your point already. I am twenty-nine years old, Mr. Wolfe, and I'm a recent graduate of Harvard University. Have you heard of Harvard?"

"From back East?"

"Yes, of course."

"I don't know much about universities, but yes, I've heard of Harvard. I'm surprised that Hoagland is from there, too. I would've never known it."

"Perhaps that is not such a bad thing."

"Maybe not."

Silence settled between the two men. The building had its own set of noises rising up through the three floors: murmurs of other voices, groaning fans, the constant drip of water—all adding to Josiah's discomfort.

Cranston nodded. "I am cursed with my mother's fair skin and my father's brains. All of my family looks much younger than we are. It is a curse I bear. The diploma on the wall should appease any concerns you have."

Josiah glanced to the wall on the right of Cranston. There were two frames there, one with the diploma in it, the letters so fancy and loopy that he could barely read it. The other frame a picture of Abraham Lincoln.

Josiah had seen the picture before. It was of Lincoln sitting in a high-backed chair, his elbow resting comfortably on a round table. If memory served Josiah correctly, the picture had been taken in February of 1864, just two months before John Wilkes Booth assassinated the Union president.

"Brave of you," Josiah said.

"I'm sorry?" Cranston said, oblivious to Josiah's reference.

"Displaying the picture of Lincoln here, in Texas. Some folks won't take kindly to the presence of a Yankee in the midst of their troubles."

"The war has been over for a long time, Mr. Wolfe."

"Not for everyone."

"That very well may be, but Mr. Lincoln was the president of these United States, and I shall exercise the right of freedom of speech no matter in what state I live. You do believe Texas is a state in the union now, don't you, Mr. Wolfe?"

"I do."

"Then that should quell all of your concerns. My family supplied the Union with uniforms, Mr. Wolfe. Textiles are a common business in Massachusetts. But those days are long behind me. I have a new life. The factory wasn't for me. Books, and helping people, are my lifeblood."

"I would be cautious of sharing your lineage with just anyone, sir."

"I understand, but I refuse to dishonor our fallen president. He has been quite the inspiration to me, Mr. Wolfe."

"Josiah. People usually call me Josiah, or Ranger Wolfe."

Cranston sat back in his chair and clasped his hands together, making a steeple with his index fingers. "You're a Ranger? A Texas Ranger?"

"Yes. Does that matter?"

"It might. And then again, it might not." Cranston relaxed his hands, put them on his desk, and leaned forward. "Tell me of this murder. Is it the young Ranger recently accused and arrested?"

"Yes. He's my friend. He claims he's innocent, and I believe him."

"But you would."

"I've questioned whether he's telling me the truth or not, but I really think he's incapable of what they are accusing him of. Besides, there have been four murders, and he was in South Texas at the time of three of them, so there's no way he was involved in all of them."

"Ah, a scapegoat. Just what the sheriff needs!"

"I beg your pardon?"

"The sheriff needs a scapegoat. Surely you must be aware of the pressure he is under at the moment?"

"I haven't been paying close attention to the newspapers."

Cranston groaned and fought off a judging look. "Are you aware of the new railroad coming into town?"

"Yes, I'm aware of that."

"Murder is bad for business, Mr. Wolfe, um, Josiah. Even murders of a population of women the rest of society wishes did not exist. Paul Hoagland has been at the forefront of telling these girls' stories, but even he is getting pressure from the owners of the *Statesman* to back off. There is a cabal of sorts, a collection of businessmen trying to end the notoriety that these murders have brought forth on the city. Your friend is the answer to their needs. I fear they will stop at nothing to render swift justice."

Josiah was sitting on the edge of his chair. "I saw the sheriff's father . . ."

"Myron Farnsworth, president of the First Bank of Austin."

"Yes, that very Myron Farnsworth, I saw him storm out of the sheriff's office, demanding that he 'Take care of it.' I believe you're right. There's little time to waste to free Scrap of this mess he's gotten himself into."

"Scrap?"

"Robert Earl Elliot. Everybody calls him Scrap. You will, too, after you meet him."

Cranston exhaled loudly. "I'm not sure I'm the right man for this fight. I have little in the way of resources and even fewer connections in the city. I will be seen as an interloper. So you see, Josiah, I am very well aware of my place as a Yankee."

"They have thrown Scrap into the hole. He's unable to communicate with anyone, and now a witness has come forth."

"His fate is sealed then."

"I fear it is, unless you help him," Josiah said, studying the young lawyer's face for any sign that he was up to a fight that he would most likely lose.

CHAPTER 26

———◆·◆·◆———

Josiah stood on the landing of the three-storey building after leaving the cramped office, relieved as he caught a deep breath of air.

Cranston was going to see what he could do for Scrap and send word of any success or failure to the house on Sixth Street. The young lawyer had made no promises, and the mention of money never came up, but Josiah was certain that it would at some point. It always did. Besides, the lawyer had to make a living just like everyone else, whether he was a proud Yankee or not.

A chuckle came to Josiah then, unbridled, and a surprise to himself, considering the dire circumstances surrounding Scrap's fate. He couldn't help but think of the irony, and of Scrap's reaction to Woodrell Cranston if he got a chance to meet the lawyer any time soon and discover his origins. Of course, after hearing one or two words escape from Cranston's mouth, the Rs hard, and the As long, it wouldn't take a genius to figure out where the lawyer hailed from. Boston would be an obvious nickname for Cranston. The meeting between the two would be a priceless moment, but Josiah was certain he wouldn't be there to witness it. On the other hand, thinking about Scrap stuck in the hole was not amusing. It was downright disheartening and frightening.

Josiah had been in a lot of situations in his life that had seemed hopeless, but solitary confinement had never been one of them.

Hopefully, the boy wouldn't be so foolish as to anger and repel one of the few men who had the capability to help him—though Josiah had warned Cranston that Scrap might not be too receptive to his presence at first. Cranston had said he was accustomed to the rejection and felt certain he could handle Scrap. Josiah hoped so.

He squared his Stetson at the thought and made his way down the rickety stairs. He didn't feel overly hopeful, but there was a bounce in his step, a general feeling that he was on the right track, not alone now in his attempt to free Scrap, or at the worst, to discover the truth about Lola's murder, however it might fall. He still couldn't imagine Scrap Elliot as a cold-blooded killer, no matter that a witness was said to have come forward. The lawyer was certain there was a bigger plan afoot. He'd called Scrap a scapegoat—a term which Josiah was sure Scrap would take offense to if Cranston said it to him. All Scrap would hear would be "goat" and that would be that, he'd go off fully cocked like an angry tyrant. Josiah was sure of it.

Another thing came to mind. He would have never thought in a thousand years that Paul Hoagland would turn out to be an ally, a man with connections to turn to in a time of need. But that's exactly what had happened, or appeared to have happened. He was still leery of Hoagland, and of Cranston, too, for that matter. The two men seemed to have had a long history together, had attended Harvard, though most likely at very different times. Hoagland was notably older than Cranston. Still, fraternity brothers spanned the ages. It was not a family structure that Josiah fully understood, but he knew from his time out of Texas, his time back East, during the war, that it ran as deep as blood.

The late afternoon air was still humid and uncomfortable, and Josiah was glad to be free of the small office.

There were still times when he felt confined in the city, boxed in, and longed to be on the trail. But he was in no hurry to leave now. Not without Scrap. It would be the hour soon enough to depart, and even under normal circumstances, two days would be little time to prepare for the journey—even for a man with Josiah's experience. Leaving was an act he was well trained in.

A wafting smell of sizzling beef touched his nose, an enticing aroma coming from a café around the corner from Cranston's office. Josiah left Clipper hitched at the post and gave in to his hunger.

The café, noted as Grace's Fine Dinner Eats by a small, hand-painted sign in the window, was about five times larger than the office from which he had just come.

There were eight or nine white cloth–covered tables in the café, and only one was empty. It sat in the farthest corner, making it difficult to get to, but Josiah decided that he needed to eat and there was no use going anywhere else. He rarely ate in restaurants and knew little about their reputations or quality. All he cared about at the moment was gaining sustenance, filling a physical need so he could continue on with the day.

The noise inside the small café was loud, bouncing off the pressed tin ceiling overhead, confined as the sound was, with no place to go. Laughs, coughs, and booming voices made it nearly impossible to think.

Finally, Josiah pushed to the open table and took a seat, navigating through the crowd of men and women as gingerly and respectfully as possible.

The crowd was mostly workingmen, but there were a few bowlers and ties in the mix, too. This close to the capitol there was always a chance a decent establishment would draw professionals and cowboys alike. It was a good sign that the food would be good, at least edible.

To Josiah's great relief, there was no one in the room that he recognized, or that seemed to recognize him, and he hoped it would stay that way so he could eat in peace.

The waitress showed up, appearing almost as soon as Josiah had settled into the plain wood chair. Sweat beaded on the woman's forehead, and she sported a less than enthusiastic look on her pouty face. She was barely twenty, but droopy-eyed and tired-looking, and skinny enough that a good gust of wind would snap her in half.

In an odd way, the girl reminded Josiah of Pearl. It might have just been the blond hair, and the fact that Pearl was on his mind, too, since he had yet to tell her that he was leaving.

"Dinner, mister?"

Josiah nodded, trying not to think anymore about Pearl. "Steak and beans are fine," he said, eyeing the menu just over the waitress's head on the wall that separated the dining room from the kitchen, written in the same handwriting as the sign he'd seen when he entered.

The choices for dinner were few: chicken, stew, or steak, all with the same side dishes of beans and boiled potatoes or stewed greens, and each meal served with a biscuit for a penny extra.

"Might be a little while, Cookie's backed up a bit," the waitress said. Her lip curled unconsciously, exposing frustration and anger. Josiah hoped she wouldn't take her mood out on him, or his food.

"I'll wait." Josiah wondered if the girl was Grace, the owner, since she hadn't offered her name when she took his order; then he decided she probably wasn't. She was too young to be a business owner. And in the end, it didn't matter anyway. He wasn't up for any pointless small talk. He just wanted his dinner.

It might have been just as easy to have gone home. Ofelia would have surely had something on the stove for him to eat. But Josiah knew that once he was home, it would be hard to leave again. He'd want every second he could steal with Lyle—and that would leave Scrap in the hole. Or dead.

"Suit yourself." The waitress spun around and disappeared into the kitchen. He heard her shouting the order as the door swung open and closed so furiously that Josiah was certain it was going to come unhinged and fly unfettered through the café.

The smell of food inside the café made him even more hungry. The day had been long, and it was catching up with him. He felt tired and weak, but he knew he had to push on. He would need his strength for what he had planned for the rest of the day. Not going home was the right decision. Time was of the utmost importance since he seemed to have so little of it. The grains of sand were piling up, counting down to the moment he left with the company of Rangers . . . or the moment Scrap Elliot dangled from a hangman's noose. He shuddered at the thought, closed off his mind from Scrap's fate as best he could.

All of the banter and conversation around him melded into one loud voice, with words floating about in partial form, almost like waves crashing into the rocks at the seashore. There was nothing to concentrate on, nothing Josiah wanted to know or overhear; eavesdropping was of no interest to him.

He continued to close off his mind, shutting his eyes briefly, exhaling, trying his best to relax. It was hard, packed in the café like he was, but he managed to imagine he was the only man there—but only for a second. He felt a presence before him, like he was being stared at.

When he opened his eyes, there was a man standing at the opposite end of the table. "I thought that was you that came in, Wolfe."

It was Milt, the desk sergeant from the jail. Josiah felt his heart sink. He'd really hoped to avoid seeing anyone he knew in the café and was surprised he'd overlooked the deputy.

Josiah stood up and offered his hand for a shake. "Milt, right?"

The man nodded. "Yup, Milt Fulsum." He shook Josiah's hand with a limp, almost wet handshake.

"What can I do for you, Milt?" Josiah recoiled unconsciously, withdrawing his hand, dropping it to his side.

"Nothin'. Nothin'. Just saw you. Thought it'd be rude not to come over and say hello."

Josiah sat down and waved out his hand with an offer for Milt to join him at the table. He didn't really want company, but he didn't want to be rude, either.

"No, no, thanks, I was just headin' out," Milt said, glancing quickly to the right, then back to Josiah like he hoped not to be caught looking away. Milt seemed nervous about something.

But Josiah had seen the glance, and he followed it over to a table on the other side of the room. Three men sat at it, with one place empty. Nothing stuck out to him about the men. He didn't know them, assumed they were deputy friends of Milt's. One of them, though, wore a black canvas shirt, a black hat, and a black handkerchief. Nothing unusual about that, either . . . except that the men who had conducted the jailbreak were wearing black, just like the men who'd followed Josiah and Juan Carlos out to the Tree of Death and taken a few shots at them.

Josiah took a deep breath. Just like gray geldings, there were a lot of men in Austin who wore black. It was probably nothing, just a coincidence. So he sat there and stared at Milt expectantly. He was the one who'd approached Josiah in the first place.

"Well, that's all," Milt finally said. "I just wanted to say hello, and say I was sorry about the fate of your friend." The desk sergeant turned to leave then.

"Wait," Josiah called out, bringing more attention to himself in the small café than he wanted to. A few people turned around, craned their necks, and stared at Josiah, annoyed that he'd distracted them from their food and conversation.

Milt stopped and faced Josiah. His face was pale white, like fear had struck him straight in the middle of his spine and worked its way up to his glassy blue eyes. "What?"

"What's happened to Scrap that you have to be sorry for?"

"Nothin'. Not yet anyway. But his fate don't look good with a witness comin' forward and all. Be a quick trial and a quicker hangin' from the way I hear it. Judge wants to see things through purty fast. Your Rangers, too. They want an end to all the notoriety. But I 'spect you know all about that."

Josiah tried to keep his wits about him. Neither Milt nor the sheriff knew there was a lawyer involved. Not that Cranston had the power to stop the fast-moving train of vengeful justice, but he might help. Sad that innocence or guilt was a matter of money and influence, but that was the way it stood, whether a simple man liked it or not.

"You know who this witness is?" Josiah asked.

Milt shrugged. "Not for certain. Some whore, that's all I know. Sheriff Farnsworth's bein' pretty tight-lipped about all this. He's under a lot of pressure to clean up this mess, make a mark for himself, I guess, and he's taken the death of Emery Jones pretty hard, too. The old sergeant was a staple, a mainstay, who was in that chair long before Rory Farnsworth returned from school back East. Sheriff's blamin' himself purty hard."

Something ticked inside Josiah's mind. A connection. Another piece of a pattern showing itself, just like it had with the Vigenere cipher.

Schools back East.

First Cranston, then Hoagland, both educated in universities outside of Texas, and now Farnsworth, too.

Josiah had known that Farnsworth was formally educated, but had somehow forgotten, or thought that it wasn't important enough to remember.

Rory Farnsworth hung on to his school education like it was a war medal that made him special, and rarely did he let the uneducated around him forget that he had something they did not. What being educated had to do with four dead whores, a jailbreak that ended up taking the life of Emery Jones, and Scrap's guilt or innocence was not clear, if it had anything to do with it at all. But there might be something there. Josiah sensed it. Just as with the cipher, he might just need the right letter in the right place to get him started on the solution.

"You know what school Farnsworth was at, Milt?"

"That's a funny question, Wolfe."

"Just curious."

"Nope, can't say that I do, then." Milt shifted his weight nervously. He was about to say something else, but the waitress pushed in front of him with Josiah's plate of sizzling steak and beans.

The waitress slid the plate in front of Josiah, glanced up at Milt, and then said, "Everything all right here?"

"I was just leavin', ma'am," Milt said.

"All right then," she said, carefully eyeing Milt, who backed away then walked straight out of the café, instead of joining the three men.

As if it was the most natural thing in the world, the waitress rested her hand gently on Josiah's shoulder. "You need anything else, mister, you holler, ya hear now?" she said, eyeing Milt Fulsum's shadow like she'd just run off some kind of varmint.

Josiah nodded, not taking his eyes off Milt, or the muddy heels of his boots, as he disappeared out of the café door.

CHAPTER 27

Josiah felt like he was being watched the entire time he ate, but the three men at Milt's table seemed not to pay him any mind. More to the opposite. They huddled together, their faces out of sight, hidden by their hats, other patrons' faces, and, perhaps, by a direct and intentional attempt to shield themselves from Josiah's line of sight.

The feeling of scrutiny came from the other patrons around him, looking over at him slyly every once in a while, secretively, furtively, like he had done something wrong or was a wanted man. He wondered if they knew who he was, if it was his notoriety that was still following after him, instead of curiosity and suspicion.

He looked up from his meal every once in a while, in between bites, not making eye contact with anyone but keeping a watchful eye on the three men.

It was still just as loud in the café as it had been when he entered, and he was too far from the men to hear any of their conversation. Now he *was* interested in eavesdropping.

The steak melted in his mouth. It was cooked perfectly,

pink in the center, just the way he liked it. The rest of the
plate was just as tasty.

Everything that had happened throughout the day had
left him famished. Still, the conversation with Milt Fulsum
lingered in his mind. There had been an odd tone to the new
desk sergeant's voice, a quaver that hadn't been there
before . . . at least not that Josiah had noticed, or remembered noticing. It was just odd, the whole confrontation, the
mention of Scrap causing the situation to seem even more
dire.

There was no doubt that Josiah was desperate to help
Scrap, to find out what had happened outside of the Easy
Nickel Saloon, but even he knew he was grasping at the air,
seeing things connect that actually might not be connected
at all.

Doubt was not something he was entirely accustomed to,
but right now it seemed like every turn led him to a dead
end, and his intuition, which was usually strong and reliable,
was less than functional, lost to him like a sense taken for
granted.

The food was restoring his strength, and the noise around
him seemed to have settled down, become more tolerable
the longer he sat there. He continued to shovel food into his
mouth, to take sustenance and restore much needed energy.
At the rate the food was disappearing from the plate, Josiah
wondered if there'd be enough to fill him up, if he needed
to order another plate. That would be rare for him, but not
unheard of.

Chairs scooted across the floor, drawing Josiah's attention away from the last bite of steak on the plate.

The three men in black stood in unison, their backs to
him. One of the men was taller than the other two, and it
was he who nodded toward the door. The other two obeyed,
headed right for the door, pushing through the crowded café.
The tall man lingered for a moment, then followed the other
men. There was no indication that they had any interest in

Josiah, and they made a restrained beeline for the front door, leaving without incident or indication that they had been there for anything but a meal, their business now done.

Their exit gave Josiah a chance to see two of the men's profiles clearly. There were no scars, nothing of note that stood out about their facial features, and they weren't men who looked familiar. He was almost certain that he'd never seen them before. Not that that was a surprise. Austin was a big city. Milt Fulsum probably had a lot of friends. For all Josiah knew, the men were deputies for Rory Farnsworth. It took a big company of men to keep the county peaceful, all things considered, and Josiah did not know them all. He hardly knew any of the deputies, as far as that went.

The last man walked out of the door, his shoulders squared, looking straight ahead.

There was, however, something in the pit of Josiah's stomach that gurgled with discomfort, and it wasn't a reaction to the cooking at Grace's Fine Dinner Eats. It was more than likely the same tried and true feeling that came along when something didn't add up, when something was wrong. Maybe his intuition wasn't as numb as he'd thought it was, or maybe he was just looking for something that wasn't there. Still, the three men were a notice he wouldn't forget too soon.

He was still staring at the door when the waitress appeared at his side. "You save yourself some room for dessert? Grace's berry pie is 'bout the best around."

Josiah was reluctant to look away from the door. He'd hoped to see the men ride by the window on their horses. "You know those men?"

"The ones that just left?"

"Yes, ma'am, the three of them?"

"No, can't rightly say that I do. Never seen them before today that I can recall. But they's men in and out of here like that all of the time. I got my regulars, and they ain't none of them."

"Men like what?" Josiah said, still staring out the window.

"Like they're on the other side of good, or at least lookin' for a dose of trouble. Most cowboys are. Don't ya think?"

"They're usually looking for something. Work, or a release, the way I see it."

"Well, like I said, I never seen them fellas before, but I don't figure that means much," the waitress said.

What it meant, Josiah thought, but didn't say, *is that the men with Milt Fulsum probably weren't deputies*. If that was the case, then who were they? And why did it seem to matter?

"You want that pie?" the waitress demanded, looking about the room, scanning for her next duty.

Josiah looked down at his plate, then up at the waitress. He wished she didn't remind him of Pearl. He longed to see her, but he had other places to go. "No, thanks, not this time around. Maybe next time," he said, forgetting about his less than sated feeling. It had been replaced by annoyance and frustration.

"I hear that a lot."

"I bet you do."

"You don't know what you're missin'."

"I've heard that a time or two myself. But I best pay and get on out of here."

"Suit yourself."

Josiah looked up to offer the waitress a smile, but she was gone, pushing off to the next customer. He envied her journey. It seemed routine, known, even when she faced strangers. Unlike his route, always walking into the darkness . . . alone more times than not, unsure of what was next: life or death, a rescue or a hanging.

Josiah stood outside the café, looking up and down the street. There was no sign of the three men, or of

Milt Fulsum. He decided to let go of the discomfort and questioning, knowing full well what lay ahead as he made his way to his next destination.

He returned to Clipper, his senses engaged as much as possible. The meal had reinvigorated him, and for that Josiah was glad. He would need all of his capacities in complete working order if he was going to find, and hopefully face, the witness who had claimed to see Scrap kill Lola.

The day had worn on, and there was no sign of the earlier storm. Just the opposite. The sky was clear as the sun arced west, driving toward the horizon at a slow decline. The humidity had gotten worse. There was no breeze or wind now. Just thick air with no place to go. The hope and opportunity of the spring season seemed to have stalled, faltered after the storm.

Josiah's shirt stuck to his skin, and his wool Stetson itched at the sides as sweat began to bead at his hairline. The temperature had soared upward; it was as hot as it had been in recent memory. It suddenly felt like deep summer instead of early spring.

Clipper snorted at Josiah's arrival, and he unhitched the Appaloosa with gentle care. He was well aware that he'd asked a lot of the horse, but that was usually the case. Generally, Clipper didn't complain, just complied, so Josiah was a little curious about the noticeable outburst.

"Wolfe," a familiar voice said from behind him.

Josiah turned around to face Paul Hoagland. "Do you ever just walk straight up on a man?" The man's sneaky arrival had obviously not gotten past Clipper.

"Not if I can help it." Hoagland stopped a few feet in front of Josiah, chewing on his ever-present cigar, smiling slightly. "I have some news."

"Good news, I hope?" Josiah rubbed Clipper's neck, and the horse flipped his tail in approval but never let Hoagland out of his sight.

"Depends. The judge postponed until tomorrow. Won't

hear from the witness till then. That's what Cranston tells me anyway."

"I didn't know the judge had arrived. That's good, right? Gives us more time to get things in order to help Scrap."

"Maybe not. There's pressure to get on with this, so the judge is going to hear arguments in the morning. That happened after Woodrell showed up and tried to talk to Elliot. But he's in the hole, and they wouldn't allow that."

"Happened to me, too," Josiah said. "You think Farnsworth is keeping him away from everybody on purpose?"

"Looks that way, doesn't it?"

Josiah let his hand drop from Clipper's neck. "When you say 'hear arguments,' you mean they're going to start the trial tomorrow?"

"That's exactly what I mean."

"So it's not good news."

Hoagland shook his head no. "Woodrell and I think they're nervous now that he's poking around. I don't think they counted on any representation, except what they planned to provide."

"They're set on hanging Scrap, aren't they?"

"Looks that way."

"As a scapegoat," Josiah said, echoing Cranston's take on the situation.

"It would silence the critics for a while. At least until it happened again."

"Until what happened again?"

"Until another whore gets murdered."

"Maybe . . ." Josiah thought it was an odd assumption that the killings would continue, but he supposed it made sense, as chilling as that was. "Do you know who this witness is?"

Hoagland shook his head no. "Wish I did."

Josiah drew a deep breath. "What's your interest in this, anyway?"

"What do you mean? It's a story, it's what's going on in the city. Nothing more than that."

"You're just doing your job?"

"I am. Why?"

"You seem personally invested in this, especially considering you're willing to help a Ranger, a group which, judging from the coverage in the paper, you have been less than favorable toward."

"I just report the news the way I see it. Trust me, Wolfe, I have my journalistic ethics to uphold, just like you have your laws to uphold."

"If you say so."

"I do," Hoagland said, backing away. "I'll be in touch, but I expect I'll see you at the courthouse tomorrow morning."

"You can count on it."

"I know I can." And with that, Hoagland spun around and hurried along Congress Avenue, in the opposite direction of Cranston's office, disappearing quickly down an alley, into the thick gray heat, not relenting for a moment.

CHAPTER 28

Josiah hitched Clipper up in front of the elaborate, three-storey house. It had been easy to find. The lots on both sides of the house were empty. The houses, or anything else, that had once stood there had recently been demolished. Spring weeds had taken advantage of the free soil and sprouted everywhere within sight.

Other signs of progress abounded on Cypress Avenue; piles of lumber and steel set to be constructed as soon as the road and the surrounding buildings were cleared. The coming of the Great Northern Railroad was evident everywhere. It looked like the scene of a great disaster to Josiah, like a tornado, a fierce storm, or even a fire had traveled down the street without reverence to anything man-made. But the destruction and apparent chaos hadn't been an act of the weather; what Josiah saw was certainly the work of man, of greed and commerce, of something he had no understanding of, or a desire to learn about. The price of progress was high, and though he hadn't known it until that very moment, Josiah quickly figured out that Blanche Dumont and her business were sitting directly in the middle of progress's path.

He would have to rethink his approach, reformulate his idea about what was going on in Austin with the murders, with Scrap's situation. He couldn't quite grasp the entirety of the situation before him, but something had changed, something important, even though he wasn't quite sure exactly what that was.

The house didn't look old enough to be condemned. It had a fresh coat of white paint on the clapboards and was as neat and clean as any pen Josiah had ever seen. Even in the gray light of the early evening, the windows sparkled like they were made of smoothed out diamonds.

There was a widow's walk above the third floor, and a pair of French doors was centered squarely in the middle of that floor, offering a view of the city that was unimaginable. The roof was curved at the top, a half circle, and the wrought iron railing around the widow's walk was ornately decorated. A blacksmith with the eye of an artisan had spent many hours pounding and molding the intricate leaves and flower petals that were distinguishable as finely detailed, even from the ground.

Josiah had passed the house several times but had never had the inclination, need, or desire to stop and pay a visit. He hesitated even now.

The last time Josiah had been in a whorehouse was a little over a year before. Crestfallen, grieving, not knowing where he was going, he'd allowed the deceased Captain Hiram Fikes's horse to take him wherever it wanted. And he ended up in the bad side of Austin, at least for an Anglo, in Little Mexico, at a place called the Paradise Hotel.

He was several blocks away from that hotel now, and as the wind wrapped around him, standing there, he was uncertain of whether to put one more foot in front of the other, as memories of that visit came rushing back to him.

He had tried to forget about Suzanne del Toro, or "Fat

Susie," as the captain called her, but he couldn't. She had
rescued him from himself, showed him a night of kindness,
and there was a promise of more, even though Josiah knew
nothing could come of the relationship. She was Mexican.
He was Anglo. She was a madam. He was a Texas Ranger.
Her former lover was Captain Hiram Fikes, Pearl's father.
These were more complications than any relationship could
survive. But they had had something that was more than
sex, if not quite love. Their grief met on a stormy night,
easing their pain and allowing each of them to move on with
life. Suzanne was the first woman Josiah allowed himself
to be intimate with after the death of his wife, Lily. It was
at that moment that he had realized that he had to leave Lily
behind so he could move forward, live life again, maybe
love again at the very least, feel alive.

Unfortunately, now Suzanne del Toro was dead, too.
Murdered by her brother for nothing more than money and
the desire for the full book of business at the Paradise Hotel,
or *El Paradiso* as she called it, which in the end cost him
his life, too. Scrap had fired the kill shot, saving Josiah from
serious injury and maybe death. One of the many reasons
Josiah couldn't turn his back on Scrap.

He took a deep breath and forced himself to stand in
place, not to leave.

Pearl didn't know about his night with Suzanne, and he
wasn't sure he would ever have the heart to tell her.

The incident had happened before they began courting,
just after they met. It shouldn't mean anything to her . . . but
he knew it would if she ever found out. Josiah had slept with
her father's mistress. It was a sticking point, a grasp on his
wrist that held him back from committing totally to Pearl,
though he was working his way toward that now that they
were courting formally and publicly.

There was nothing he could do about the past now. Just
like on the morning he'd left Suzanne's bed, he needed to

walk forward again, unsure of what lay ahead or how he would be received.

There were lamps burning in several of the windows, and there was no question that the house was open for business. From what Josiah understood, it was never closed; someone worked the door twenty-four hours a day. There was no stopping him now, and he knew that, just as he knew that he was not calling on the house for pleasure. He hoped to find the witness, and Myra Lynn, too, since the girls that had fled the Easy Nickel were said to be under Blanche Dumont's wing now.

He walked up to the door and pounded the brass knocker loudly three times.

There was a distant sound of music coming from inside the house. A piano playing low and mournful, not happy and inviting like in a saloon or dance hall. The sweet honey to draw customers into this house was found elsewhere; waiting in the parlors in sheer clothing, exposing hints of flesh and pleasure to be had for a price.

There was an air of proper business about the place, a sharp edge that noted any kind of rowdiness wouldn't be tolerated. That might have been an assumption on Josiah's part only because Blanche Dumont herself came across that way. Her reputation preceded her in every manner of the house. She was one of the most notorious women in Austin.

The door opened and Josiah found himself staring at an amazingly short Negro, four feet tall, if that, dressed in a bright red velvet frock coat and a black top hat. The Negro smiled, exposing a mouthful of white teeth that were so perfect they looked like they belonged on a piano instead of inside a human head. A .41 rimfire over-and-under derringer dangled from the little Negro's belt. The gun looked too big for the man's hands but perfect for a woman's.

"What's your pleasure, mister man? I got a golden-haired girl, a redheaded girl, and a dark one, too, if that be to your taste, but tell no one about that, though she sure has special skills for a man like you. Five dollars mo' for the whole night, and you never be same, I swear. So what is it? What's your pleasure, mister man? Gold? Red? Or black?"

Josiah stood on the stoop, the door open, his view unobstructed into the house, ignoring the Negro's offer the best he could.

The interior of the Dumont house was as perfect as he'd expected it to be: Long curtains, nearly the color of the Negro's coat, hid a doorway that he assumed led upstairs to the pleasure rooms. Several plush, high-backed sofas lined the wall, all covered in fancy upholstery, and the rugs on the floor looked too pretty to walk on. A couple of girls sat together on one of the sofas, a golden-haired one and a red-haired one, neither of them looking like they could be Scrap's sister, or what Josiah expected Myra Lynn would look like. The black one was nowhere to be seen. He assumed she was hidden, or didn't really exist.

"I need to speak to Blanche Dumont," Josiah said, staring down at the Negro.

The smile faded quickly from the little man's face, and his right hand automatically slipped down to the over-and-under, coming to rest on the grip. "She don't take customers or visitors with no reasons or appointments, mister man."

"I'm not a customer."

"Then what is you then?"

"I'm a Ranger. My name's Josiah Wolfe, and I'm looking for a girl that came in from the Easy Nickel."

The Negro's eyes grew wide, the whites of them shining like beacons in the graying twilight. He started to slam the door shut, but Josiah had anticipated that. He slid his boot in between the door and the wall, stopping the action.

"Tell Miss Dumont I'm an old friend of Suzanne del Toro's, Fat Susie's. I'm not here for trouble. I'm here to help her if she'll have it."

"She don't need no help from a Ranger."

Josiah cocked his head to the street. "Looks like she needs all the help she can get."

The little Negro studied Josiah for a second, looking him up and down more than once, checking behind him to see if he was alone.

"I mean you, or her, no harm. Go on now, you go tell her a friend of Fat Susie's is here to see her."

"You be lyin' to me, mister man, and I'll shoot you through and through for causin' me to bother the miss. Trouble be comin' my way 'cause of it. And I got a bad place in my mind for peoples that bring troubles on me."

"Tell her what I said. I'll wait."

The Negro shoved the door, trying to close it, pressuring Josiah's boot, but he shook his head no. "I'll wait right here," Josiah said.

"Suit yourself then." The Negro glared at Josiah then hurried away, disappearing behind the red velvet curtains. He walked like one leg was shorter than the other, teetering back and forth like each step took a great amount of effort to cover any ground at all.

Josiah stood there with the door cracked open far enough so he could still see the two girls. He had got their attention, but they looked a little fearful, concerned about his presence, not like they were anticipating a customer. Neither of the girls made eye contact with Josiah, and he was glad of that.

The piano played on in the back of the house. The air smelled like every hint of it had been sprayed with a flowery perfume, but it wasn't overwhelming. It was sweet and intoxicating, like honeysuckle on a breeze, inviting on a spring day—after a long and odorless winter.

Behind him, the street was silent, void of any traffic, and there were no horses hitched out front other than Clipper.

In other words, Blanche Dumont didn't look like she was making any money at the moment, and Josiah thought that was odd since Congress Avenue, and the café he'd left earlier, were bustling and filled with cowboys and businessmen.

The minutes ticked away. Josiah could hear voices, but couldn't decide whether the tone was tension-filled or pleasure-filled—it was just a murmur, too low and too far away to be understood.

After a few more minutes, the Negro appeared from behind the curtains and returned to the door, which he opened fully, sweeping his arms to the floor in a great, if physically small, welcoming gesture. "Miss Dumont will see you now, mister man. But I needs your weapon."

Josiah hesitated. The last time he'd given up his Peacemaker, he'd found himself in the midst of a jailbreak with no way to protect himself. He shook his head no. "I don't think so. I don't mean anyone any harm."

"Rules is rules, mister man."

Determined to see Blanche Dumont and hold on to his gun, Josiah stepped confidently inside the house, right past the Negro. It was a mistake, of course, not taking the little man seriously. He worked the door for a reason, and the little Negro was surely talented with the skills of crowd control and taking down men three times his size, or that job would've belonged to a boulder-sized man.

Josiah felt the first bit of pain explode in his side as the Negro punched him directly in the kidney.

The force of the punch took his breath away. But it was only a distraction.

The little man swept out his stubby leg, pushing Josiah in the opposite direction, sweeping him backward, knocking him completely off his feet. There was no time, no clarity, that allowed Josiah to reach for his gun—the pain was tremendous and the surprise of the sweep total.

In the blink of an eye, the negro was standing in front of Josiah with the derringer trained between his eyes. "Now, gives me the gun, mister man, and any other weapon you might be hidin', or you're not gonna see Miss Dumont. Do I make myself clear? Or would ya like to go another round wit me? I got somethin' special I be savin' just for you."

Stunned, Josiah thought for a second about lunging forward, tackling the little man, and taking the derringer away from him. But something warned him off that idea. His attacker was probably aware of what he was thinking, had fooled men even more skilled than Josiah in the art of hand-to-hand combat. He had underestimated his opponent, and now he was not fully in control of the situation. It was just a matter of luck, timing, and lack of a serious threat from him that he wasn't dead, or at least badly injured.

The curtains swept open and Blanche Dumont pushed through, her skin pure white and her pink eyes, void of any glasses, almost glowing red in the dim, flickering light from the lamps in the windows.

"That'll be enough, Rufous. Mr. Wolfe is our guest and he is to be treated as such."

The Negro, Rufous, nodded, and a look of disappointment crossed his face as he stepped away from Josiah, tucking the over-and-under back into his belt. "You heard the miss, stand up, mister man. She saved you a sweet ass kickin' from a little man." He laughed then. But only for a second. Blanche Dumont looked at Rufous scornfully, and he cowered away, stopping a few steps from the door.

Josiah groaned and sighed in relief. He stared up at Blanche Dumont. Never having been this close to her, he hadn't realized how small and fragile she looked. Rufous was most likely protective of her for more reasons than Josiah knew.

He stood then, weakly, clutching his side. "That was a fine punch, Rufous."

"It be Mr. Rufous to you, thank you."

"Rufous!" Blanche Dumont said, continuing to admonish the little man. "That is impolite."

"I beg your pardon, miss," Rufous said, apologizing with another sweep of the hand, this one not welcoming at all.

"It's all right." Josiah drew in another breath, the pain in his side dissipating slowly. "I suppose I deserved what I got."

"Rufous said you're here to help, Mr. Wolfe."

"I hope to."

"Are you sure you know what you're getting yourself into?"

Josiah was fully on his feet now, facing Blanche Dumont directly. "Probably not, ma'am," he said, "probably not."

CHAPTER 29

———◆◆◆◆◆———

Blanche Dumont's private study was simpler than Josiah had expected it to be. Three of the walls were lined with dark walnut bookshelves, loaded to the edge with books of every size, the spines muted in color—dark browns, dark reds, dark greens, all of the titles embossed with fancy gold lettering.

The lone bare wall housed a working fireplace, vacant of any fire at the moment, along with the door that Josiah had entered.

A portrait of Blanche Dumont hung over the mantel, her pure white hair piled up on top of her head, her skin as white and fragile as alabaster, and wearing a formal, full-length dress that was as red as blood. Her pink eyes were penetrating and angry. It was not a flattering portrait at all.

There was, however, a hint of beauty to Blanche Dumont's face in real life; all she lacked was color, hue, a complexion that suggested something other than death. Her body was shapely, well proportioned, and under normal circumstances, if a man could imagine it, she would have been a stunning woman of above average beauty. Age showed itself on her face. Even in the portrait, sunlight was her enemy, burning spots into her skin, highlighting every wrinkle and worry line.

Josiah turned his attention away from the picture. Piano music still played softly in the distance, and the voices had quieted. Once Blanche Dumont closed the door to the study, they were enveloped in a silent tomb.

A desk sat in the middle of the room with one chair in front of it. Actually, the room looked like what Josiah had expected Woodrell Cranston's office to look like.

"Have a seat," Blanche said. Her voice was guarded, and she eyed him like an enemy. There was no doubt that she was armed, had a gun or knife within a second's reach, most likely under one of the ruffles of her long skirt.

Josiah did as he was told, remaining silent, his eyes focused on the woman, trying to determine her intentions. He was in enemy territory, and he knew it.

Blanche walked past Josiah, close enough for him to smell her perfume. It was just as light and understated as the other aromas in the house. More honeysuckle. Spring. Nectar. Opportunity. His nostrils flared, even though he barely realized it. Her dress swished as she passed, white satin rubbing on more unseen satin, the mystery of female garments a matter of quick and sudden speculation. Again, his mind's wandering was much to Josiah's surprise. The environment provoked something deep from inside him that he tried to ignore, to keep at bay.

Desire and need were recent redevelopments in his life, and even then with Pearl's circumstances, they still had to be restrained, pushed away constantly. Some days, he felt like a schoolboy, unrepentant, needful, and uncaring about any consequences. He knew he would have to keep his wits about him.

Blanche sat down in front of Josiah. Other than her pink eyes, the only color apparent, since her white skin melded perfectly into her white dress, was an emerald necklace centered perfectly on her neck. A gold chain held it in place, and it was easy to see that the jewel sat atop a locket. The secret pendant was the only manner of jewelry that she adorned herself with. Her fingers were bare of rings.

The choice of a white floor-length dress struck Josiah as odd, since it almost made Blanche look nonexistent. But it really didn't. Her eyes stood out like a pair of fires in a snowy field. She was fully aware of her deficiencies and capitalized on them in a way that drew even more attention to herself.

"Now, why is it you wanted to see me, Mr. Wolfe?" Blanche Dumont's voice was equally as measured as everything else about her. There was a hint of an accent, European of some kind—not Italian, not English or German, but a mix—that gave her an air of power, of aristocracy. It was then that Josiah remembered that he had heard that she had been born a duchess of some type or another but was shunned by her family, sent away, abandoned at a young age because of her appearance. She was lucky she hadn't been killed, drowned as a baby or something worse. Whether or not there was any truth to the story was questionable. It may have all been nothing more than lore to add to the mystery that swirled around Blanche Dumont—created and populated by no one other than the woman herself.

"Josiah. You can call me Josiah."

"Relax," Blanche said, not losing the authoritarian edge to her voice, but allowing it to soften just a bit. "I know who you are. We don't need to play games, Mr. Wolfe. I read the papers. And I was good friends with Suzanne del Toro."

Josiah exhaled deeply, felt his face flush, then sat back in the chair staring straight into Blanche's riveting pink eyes. "I was sorry for her death."

"I'm sure you were. She failed, though, to see the threat Emilo, her brother, posed. You can trust no one in this business. Not even family. Especially not family."

"I wouldn't know."

"Surely you understand the need to be suspicious."

"I do."

"Good. Then we are united in that thought. And you must consider that I am not trustful at all of your intentions to help. I presume there's a self-serving reason why you think I must need your aid."

"I didn't realize you would until I came here."

"And saw the street?"

"Yes, and the path of the new railroad."

"Old news, Mr. Wolfe. I refuse to sell, but there is no stopping progress. That is what you see?"

"I would think you'd be successful no matter where you take your business," Josiah said. "So I guess I don't understand the holdout."

"I doubt you would." Blanche sat as still as a statue, her hands clasped at her waist, her long, thin fingers just in sight over the braided lip of the ornately carved desk. "Now, why don't you just tell me what you came here looking for, and we can put all of these paladin issues aside."

"I'm sorry, I don't understand."

"I don't need a hero to save me, Mr. Wolfe. I am quite capable of sorting out my own matters for myself. You are quite correct in your assumption that location will have no bearing on my success. But this is my home. One I have worked hard to hold on to. You have a home, I'm sure?"

"Yes."

"Then, again, we can unite on a thought. We are forging quite the relationship, Mr. Wolfe. Now," she said, leaning forward, unblinking, "what are you looking for?"

"I'm looking for a girl. Two girls, in fact."

A slight smile cracked at the right corner of Blanche's pursed lips. "You don't look the type, Mr. Wolfe."

"Pleasure is not what I seek."

"Pity. I have just the pair to host you."

Josiah ignored the offer as best he could. If he were a different kind of man, he might have queried her for further information—for future reference—but he was not the least bit interested in a moment of double pleasure. "You're aware of the Ranger that is accused of the most recent murder of one of Brogdon Caine's whores, Lola something or other?"

"She had a last name, Mr. Wolfe. Wellsley. Her name was Lola Wellsley. She was a working girl, forced to use only what she carried on her frame to make a living. You would be wise to realize that I do not know what a whore is, Mr. Wolfe. Are we united on that understanding? That that is an offensive word to me?"

Josiah drew in a breath, felt like he had been slapped across the knuckles. "Yes, ma'am. I apologize."

Blanche Dumont nodded, then said, "Of course, I am aware of the murder. Though I am surprised that you are aware of the string of murders. Most of the social monarchs and patrons of respectability in this pitiful town have turned a blind eye to the savagery suffered by these girls."

"Much to your . . ."

"Rage, Mr. Wolfe. I am enraged at the lack of concern or efforts by the sheriff and his men to put a stop to the fear and to the senseless killings. Would you expect me to be anything else? Or are you of the opinion that I mistreat those that I manage, or that I exploit them just for my own riches?"

"I have no clue how you run your business, ma'am."

"Hmm . . . You are a surprise, Mr. Wolfe."

Josiah shrugged. "So you applaud the arrest of the Ranger?"

Blanche flinched, brought her hands to the top of the desk. "He is your friend, I assume? A person you know well. And let me guess, you believe him to be innocent."

"Yes, I do."

"He is wrongly accused, then? Another pawn in a game of power?"

"Yes, I think so."

"Then we are united on that thought, too. Does that surprise you, Mr. Wolfe?"

Josiah nodded, relieved. "I'm looking for the witness who has stepped forward. I'm hoping she is here. I was at the Easy Nickel earlier. Brogdon Caine said all of his girls had taken refuge with you."

"His girls? That is what he called them? They are meat to him. He beats them during the day and chains them at night. Do not speak that man's name in my presence again, Mr. Wolfe, do you understand?"

"Yes, ma'am. I beg your pardon."

"No need. You wouldn't know my enemies, or my benefactors for that matter. Many would surprise you. Not everyone manages their business in the same way."

"There was no evidence of chains or abuse that I saw. Could he be the killer?" Josiah asked.

Blanche shook her head no. "He has no motive that I know of, other than to see me out of business. And even that would not serve him well. He lives off my flies. His rates are cheaper, his girls desperate because they have nowhere else to go. I have standards, Mr. Wolfe. My clientele expects a certain level of comfort. The girls here are clean and educated. Many go on to live happy, successful lives once they leave here. Without me, Caine has no one to undercut, to tear down. He needs me to stay in business so he can stay in business. Rats have need of a successful grocer, do they not?"

Josiah nodded yes, then shifted in the chair. His Peacemaker pressed tight against his side. "So, if Caine isn't the killer, do you know who is, or suspect who is?"

"Your past relationship with Suzanne de Toro allows for a small amount of respect, Mr. Wolfe. I am still uncertain of your intentions."

"The same as yours. To find out who killed Lola Wellsley so my friend can be freed."

"I care nothing about that young Ranger's fate. Only that the killings stop. I believe they are directed at me, an effort to fully run me and my business out of Austin."

"Because you won't sell your house?"

"They will take my house, tear it down at will, with me in it, if they have to. Let's just say this, Mr. Wolfe. I may know too many secrets for my own good. Men who visit my place of business usually do so under the cover of night, carrying a lie with them in their purse. They have families. Children. Respectable jobs and positions in the government. I have used what I must to stay here as long as I can, and to see what can be done to stop the killings. It has cost me greatly."

"You have blackmailed your clients?"

"Call it what you want. I call it negotiating power."

"With who?"

"Mr. Wolfe, really . . . you know I cannot tell you that."

Josiah then studied Blanche Dumont, who had now sat back in her chair, putting as much distance between them as possible. "Okay, I understand that, but I have a name I need some information about. Maybe you can help with this, too?"

Blanche popped up her right shoulder and turned her head away from Josiah, staring at the closest bookshelf. "You can ask, but I may not answer."

He stared at her hard, directly, even though she would not make eye contact with him. "Abram Randalls. Will you tell me why he was busted out of jail? Is he the killer, Miss Dumont? If anybody would know . . . you would."

CHAPTER 30

———◆◆◆———

Blanche Dumont stiffened in the chair, then turned her attention back to Josiah. Her eyes were on fire. "Abram Randalls is a lying, conniving little thief who deserves everything he gets."

"He stole from you?"

"In more ways than one."

Josiah remained silent, waiting for an explanation. The piano music played on, faintly, somewhere beyond the closed door. Other than that, there was no noise in the house that he could detect. He knew if he listened hard enough he could hear his heartbeat, Blanche Dumont's, too. Only hers was beating faster. Anger boiled on her face. She did not blush. She turned pink from the inside out.

Blanche finally exhaled, bit the corner of her lip. "Abram is not a killer, Mr. Wolfe. That is all I will say. He does not have it in him to physically hurt anyone or anything. He only has the capability to take. Take what is not his. He has no self-control when it comes to money or valuable objects. I learned that lesson too late."

Josiah let her words settle. He didn't want to push her, or shut her down from telling him more. But something about what she'd said struck him as odd. Josiah was certain that Randalls had fought in the War Between the States, had learned the ways of the Vigenere cipher there, just like he had. Maybe it was an assumption based only on the man's age. "Do you know if Abram Randalls served in the war?"

"That's a strange question, Mr. Wolfe."

"Humor me, if you know the answer. I have a knack for asking strange questions."

"He was a carpetbagger, an opportunist, a magician with numbers, not a killer. One spot of blood, and he would have dropped to the ground like a battered fly. I know of no service to the Union that he performed in the war. He was probably hiding under a bed somewhere, afraid to peer out until Lee surrendered. The coward."

"Lee or Abrams?"

"Assume what you want, Mr. Wolfe. I have never had any interest in the war."

"Randalls is a Yankee then?" Josiah knew the answer to the question, knew full well what the term "carpetbagger" meant: a Yankee who stole from Southern states or people, acting in his own best interest, under the guise of helping the afflicted during Reconstruction.

"Born and raised in Massachusetts."

"Really?"

"Yes." Blanche eyed Josiah curiously, as if he were playing a game with her. "Why is that odd? There are a lot of Yankees in Austin."

"More and more every day, I 'spect," Josiah said, finding the information disturbing. Another pattern was forming, and he didn't exactly like seeing it. Paul Hoagland and Woodrell Cranston were from Massachusetts. Now he learned that Abram Randalls was, too. Maybe it didn't mean anything. Or maybe it did. There was no indication that the three men knew one another, but Josiah made a mental note to find out if they were acquaintances.

"I'm sorry, I still find your question about Abram Randalls as a soldier more than a little curious," Blanche said.

"A note was found in his cell, written in a reasonably elaborate cipher. I was trained with the skill of deciphering codes very similar to the one Randalls left behind, so I assumed he'd served in the war in a similar capacity. My assumption may be wrong, judging from what you say."

"I know nothing of those skills. Maybe he didn't write the note."

"Maybe not."

"What did it say?" Blanche asked.

"That they would hang him at the oak tree. It didn't take long to figure out that he was speaking about the Tree of Death. Do you know of it?"

"I do." Blanche looked confused. "That makes no sense, though. Why would Abram fear his own death from men who went to a lot of trouble to free him?"

"I wondered the same thing."

"What did you do?"

"I rode out there, and was attacked, shot at."

"I think you may have been lured out there under false pretenses, Mr. Wolfe. You are lucky you weren't killed."

Josiah wasn't going to agree or disagree with that. She might be right. Maybe Abram Randalls didn't write the note like he'd assumed. "Why do you think Abram Randalls was busted out of jail?"

"I do not know for sure. Unless he knows who the killer really is. That would make some sort of sense."

"If the killer has an army of men."

"He just might, Mr. Wolfe. He just might."

Josiah settled back in the chair as far as he could, not sure what to think about what Blanche Dumont had told him about Abram Randalls, but that was not what he had come for. "What about the girls? The witness that has come forward? Is she here?"

"I am not harboring any witness, Mr. Wolfe, nor would I. I think the charade being played out in the court considering your Ranger friend is unjust and unconscionable."

"I was afraid you were going to say that. Now I just have to . . ."

"Believe me?"

"Yes, ma'am. I guess I'm sorry to agree with you on that."

"I would be disappointed otherwise, Mr. Wolfe. Now tell me of this other girl."

"She's Scrap's sister. He's the Ranger accused of killing Lola Wellsley. His sister is a . . ." Josiah stopped short of saying *whore*. "She works in the same business as you. He saw her at Brogdon Caine's, followed her out the back door. That's when he encountered the murdered girl, Lola. His sister ran off into the dark, fearful, I assume, of seeing Scrap and dealing with his anger. He's ashamed of her, of how she earns a living. He's been trying to rescue her for years, even though he lied to me, told me all along that she was a nun. Her name is Myra Lynn. Myra Lynn Elliot. I assume she's got dark hair, black, a fair complexion, and a skinny build like her brother."

"I know those stories, Mr. Wolfe. They're mostly all the same with families. Girls don't just show up at on my door with a smile, begging for a job. They are usually broken down, poor, beaten, and worse. The stories I have heard would make your toes curl. What men do to girls and get away with is criminal beyond belief. But it is a man's world that we live in."

"Their parents were killed by Comanche."

"I can't justify the choices of a stranger, Mr. Wolfe. But trauma comes in many forms. I'm sorry, I can't help you on either count. I know no girl named Myra Lynn, or anyone who looks like that. She could have changed her name. They usually do. It's easier to live through the rough nights if you think what's happening to you is really happening to someone else. I doubted from the beginning I could be of any help to you."

"Why'd you see me then?"

"Because I can use all of the help I can get. Girls being brutally murdered is bad for business. The sheriff is of no help. He's turning a blind eye to the troubles. Which is no great surprise, considering his father . . ." Blanche stopped, looked away from Josiah for a brief second.

"His father, Myron Farnsworth, the president of the First Bank of Austin?"

"Yes." Blanche lowered her eyes to the desk.

"He's a client?"

"Assume what you will, Mr. Wolfe. But Rory Farnsworth has many reasons to revel in my current financial troubles, between the loss of revenue and the eventual loss of my home. The sheriff has ambitions, but I assume you know that if you know him at all. He dreams of being governor, or even bigger, if I'm correct in my read of him. He thinks the sheriff's position is beneath his stature and abilities. But he is wrong about that. He can't even handle his own men, can't lead his way out of a wet potato sack. And his father's discreet habit, at least one of them, I am sure, would be an embarrassment to him and his plans for the future."

Josiah nodded. "I know Rory well enough to know his ambitions, but I didn't know he was after the governorship."

"Like I said, Mr. Wolfe, the sheriff is ambitious . . . with all of the trappings that come to a man with that kind of desire. His weaknesses are apparent to everyone but him. He is likely to lose the next election if he does nothing to change that perception. The explosion at the jail will make everyone more nervous about his capabilities. Trust me, he wants to find Abram Randalls as much as you do. But for very different reasons, I'm afraid."

Josiah stood up. It was time to go—he was not going to

get what he came for. "I'm glad you took the time to see me, ma'am. I appreciate it."

"Will you kill him?"

"Who?"

"Abram. Will you kill Abram Randalls?"

"Only if I'm forced to, ma'am."

Blanche nodded, understanding, and remained seated, though a softness crossed her face. "Truth be told, I only saw you because of Suzanne del Toro, Mr. Wolfe. She cared greatly about her captain, the dead captain you returned to Austin to be buried, but you stirred something inside of her. Broke her grief from that time and allowed her to feel alive again, hopeful."

"She did the same thing for me," Josiah whispered.

"I figured if you were that kind of man, then you'd be worth seeing, worth pinning a hope on. It's just a shame that Suzanne's life was cut short. We would have made a great team, a force to be reckoned with in all of Texas, not just Austin."

"You know ambition when you see it," Josiah said.

Blanche Dumont smiled. "Of course, I do."

"I hope I didn't disappoint you then."

The smile on her alabaster face faded. "We are united in our desire that the killer of these innocent girls is brought to a swift justice, and that the travesty of the legal inequality and lack of attention to this matter is put to an end, once and for all. I can hope for nothing else."

"We are, ma'am. We most certainly are united on that front," Josiah said, with a nod. Then he turned and walked out the door of her office and out of the house, without saying a word to another person.

CHAPTER 31

———◆※◆———

Night had fallen while Josiah was inside Blanche Dumont's house. The air was cooler, drier, the humidity sucked out of it somehow. There was no wind, and it was good to be outside, away from the intoxicating aromas that had followed him everywhere inside the house. His senses, and virtue, were still intact—not that he had ever really feared losing either, but it could have happened, under the right circumstances. He knew that better than anyone. It had happened before. But Blanche Dumont was all business; her own survival, and the survival of her girls, was her main concern. There didn't look to be one drop of grief to overcome, one hint that she had any desire other than making sure she maintained the only business she knew.

Josiah unhitched Clipper, his mind a jumble of information. Freeing Scrap still seemed like a remote possibility at best, and most likely next to impossible, if he was being honest with himself. All he had collected so far was a string of people who believed Scrap was innocent and a scapegoat for a series of larger crimes that Josiah knew very little about. He didn't know whether the killings could even have been perpetrated by one man, and what the motive was, if any. Four dead whores was just as much a pattern as learning in the same day of three men from Massachusetts who may have traveled in familiar circles. But none of that information mattered if it couldn't be connected or proven significant in a court of law—which was set to start considering Scrap's case in hours, instead of days.

Time was running out.

And as far as Josiah knew, Scrap Elliot was still deep in the confines of the Black Hole of Calcutta, trapped, scared, unsure of what tomorrow might bring—or if tomorrow would come for him at all.

Josiah shuddered at the thought as he climbed up on the saddle and angled Clipper away from the white three-storey house. A lamp lit every window, and the house seemed to glow in the dark, even though there was no moon to be seen. He could see how Blanche Dumont and her house could be a beacon to cowboys and men lonely for the company of women, but he didn't exactly see how it was possible that every room was vacant on this night. Maybe it was only his imagination, but it seemed like the word had been put out that Blanche's girls were diseased, or worse. Even a whisper of syphilis could destroy a house. Josiah knew enough about whoring to know that was the truth. If that were the case, if someone had put the word out on Blanche Dumont, then her concerns about her impending failure were well founded. Somebody was trying to destroy her, and that destruction couldn't come soon enough for whoever it was.

What Josiah needed, he decided, was a dose of reality. Not only did he feel the pressure to find something that would help Scrap, but he also knew that if he wanted to stay a Texas Ranger, he had two nights and one whole day to prepare to leave on another journey. He was sacrificing his time with Lyle, and with Pearl, who didn't know of the recent development and his impending departure.

He flinched at the notion of this sacrifice being undue, and immediately realized that Scrap would have made the same sacrifice for him. He was sure of it.

Still, he had no idea how long McNelly's company of Rangers would be away from Austin. The last time out, when he was in Corpus Christi, had been for over four months. An eternity when you're courting a woman like Pearl Fikes and your son is growing like a weed—without your presence and influence. The boy would be lucky to know he had a father. Truth was, Lyle was more Ofelia's son than Josiah's own. Things could be worse. More than once recently, Josiah had faced death and come out on the lucky side. Lyle could have been an orphan, more than he already was. Still, regret found its way into Josiah's heart, especially when the minutes ticked away. Instead of going home, he turned his trusted Appaloosa and headed in the opposite direction.

He needed to see Pearl, needed to tell her he was leaving . . . again. He hoped she understood his need to stay on as a Ranger, to continue what he had started.

Pearl's father had been a Ranger, been away more than he was home, though that might have been more by design than duty. Pearl's mother was intolerable to Josiah, and he could hardly imagine what being married to the woman had been like for Hiram Fikes. Josiah stopped short of thinking too ill of the woman. She was currently in a sanatorium, her health, physical and mental, in rapid decline. Caring for herself was no longer possible from what he understood. Still, Josiah had little pity for the woman. She had caused him a great amount of grief, pushing the papers, the *Austin Statesman* in particular, to run a campaign that nearly destroyed his reputation and ended his service with the Rangers after he'd killed Pete Feders. Not that he held a grudge, but he wouldn't exactly be sad the day that woman left this world. Until then, no matter her state, he was sure she would thoroughly disapprove of the courting that was now in progress.

At least they had Juan Carlos's good blessings.

With Pearl on his mind, Josiah pushed Clipper to run at a gallop as he headed for Miss Amelia Angle's Home for Girls. Beyond anything else that was going on, he felt a deep need to see Pearl, to smell the sweetness of her skin, to touch her, if that was possible.

It didn't take Josiah long to get to the house on Second Street. There was little horse traffic to contend with on the streets of Austin, and the streetcars didn't run after dark.

The house was similar to Blanche Dumont's but not as glowing white, bright, or freshly painted. Miss Angle's rules were clear: No suitors were allowed to call after the fall of night. One break of the rule, and the girl was out on the street, left to find other accommodations, regardless of her financial or family situation. Nobody knew this better than Josiah, but he had pinged Pearl's window with pebbles before, and it was his plan to do so again.

There was an alley that ran behind the house, and Josiah slowed Clipper, then walked the horse quietly to a stop, tying the Appaloosa's lead to a tree in an open yard across from the house, next to the carriage house.

The house was dark, all of the lights out. Pearl's window was on the third floor, and it took a couple of tries to tap the window gently with a small rock. The trick was to throw the rock as softly as possible so it didn't shatter the fragile window. That would be the end to everything, but both the risk and Josiah's need to see Pearl were great, worth it as far as he was concerned.

Josiah stood there waiting for a lamp to grow to life, to see Pearl's shadow. Darkness enveloped him, and even in the middle of the city, night sounds began to bubble around him. Frogs peeped. Bats chattered overhead. A dog barked in the distance. Wildlife existed in the city, and the notion of spring was evident to every creature that walked the earth, not just those that lived out and away.

Normally, music could be heard since Miss Angle's wasn't that far from a row of saloons. Perhaps it was too early in the night, or the wind was blowing in the opposite direction, because Josiah couldn't hear anything that sounded remotely like the tinkling of happy keys being plunked on a piano. The absence of music seemed odd, but not worthy of too much concern.

Still no light in the window.

Josiah tossed up another pebble, pinging the window perfectly. He waited a long minute before he began to entertain the idea that Pearl might not be in her room, that she might have other, unknown, engagements. She was fully entrenched now in her new life, studying diligently at the local normal school, her objective to become a schoolteacher quickly becoming a reality.

Josiah thought Pearl would make a good teacher and supported the idea that she have a pursuit of her own. If they were going to have a life together, Pearl would need something to do while he was away, riding with the Rangers. That was the thought at the moment, anyway. So she could have been anywhere. They didn't bind each other up with their comings and goings. They weren't at that place in their courting yet—and they might never have that much account of each other. Josiah didn't live like that.

He was about to turn and leave when he saw her familiar silhouette ease around the corner of the house.

Pearl rushed to Josiah, meeting him in an embrace, first burying her face over his heart, then angling her face up to greet him with a smile.

Josiah could not resist. He kissed her. Gently at first, waiting for a hint of welcome. He didn't have to wait too long, a second if that. Pearl responded passionately, pressing into Josiah as hard as she could, from her lips to her toes.

Their bodies melded together in a familiar way, but there was still restraint there. At least on Josiah's part.

The last time they had seen each other was when he'd seen her home, distraught from her trip into the mercantile where she had been declined an account of her own.

Josiah hadn't really known what to expect, but he was more than happy at the reception he received.

He pulled away, restraining his hands from going places they shouldn't in open view of anyone who might stumble by. His heart was beating fast, his breathing ramped up like he was starting a run, his physical desire growing, making his pants tighter, uncomfortable, and that only promised to get worse if he held on to Pearl for a second longer.

"What's the matter?" Pearl whispered, a rejected look crossing her face as Josiah stepped back.

"I might be a little too happy to see you."

"There's nothing the matter with that." Her blond hair flowed over her shoulders, and she wore a simple day dress. She was barefoot. The look of rejection faded from her face and was replaced by an odd look, a cock of the head, like she was trying to smell something close, or far away, Josiah couldn't tell which.

"Not standing out here in the middle of the world," he said.

"Oh, Josiah, relax. Everybody's asleep or too busy to pay attention to us."

"I don't want you to get in trouble with Miss Angle." The tone of his voice changed. Desire to concern.

Pearl scrunched her forehead. "What's the matter?"

They were standing about a foot apart now, and Pearl held on to Josiah's fingers with hers. Her touch was warm, and he could smell the hint of her flowery toilet water, worn down from the day, but still there, subtly, not like the strong aromas at Blanche Dumont's house.

"I have to leave," Josiah said. "The company is heading out."

"When?"

"Day after tomorrow."

Pearl exhaled and then catapulted herself back into Josiah's arms. He didn't resist her, but his desire had calmed, changed instantly to comfort.

"How long will you be gone?" Pearl asked after a long minute of embracing him.

"I don't know. I don't know where we're going, what the assignment is. I just know if I don't show up when we muster, my days as a Ranger are over." He could feel the hint of moisture from her tears melting through his shirt into his chest.

"Would that be so bad?"

"I don't know. It's all I know. What would I do?"

"Anything you wanted. The sheriff could use a good man like you."

"I don't think that would work for me. Besides, it's not just that I'm leaving. I have some things to take care of before I go."

"What's the matter, Josiah?"

"Scrap's in trouble. He's been accused of killing a girl. He's innocent, and I need to help him prove it. I need to get him out of jail so he can leave with me."

Pearl recoiled. "That's awful. Can't the Rangers help him?"

"They've washed their hands of it. The press is bad enough for them right now."

Pearl nodded. There was no need to explain the power of the *Austin Statesman* to her. She knew full well the power the paper held over people's lives. "Scrap's your friend. I understand."

"It may take more time than I have."

"Are you telling me good-bye now?"

"No. I don't know. Maybe. I just needed to see you." He stepped forward, pulled her to him, and kissed her again, more passionately and more deeply than the first time. "I want you," he whispered. "But I don't know when or how that can happen . . ."

It was almost like he had said something disturbing again, because Pearl pushed off from him, breaking away from his embrace, a flash of anger crossing her face that seemed to come out of nowhere.

"Where have you been?"

"What do you mean where have I been? I've been trying to help Scrap. I told you."

"You smell like you bathed in flowers, cheap toilet water. Where have you been?" Pearl demanded again. "Don't you think one woman can smell another?"

Josiah sighed. Lying to her was not an option. "I was at Blanche Dumont's. I had to get some answers." Before he could finish explaining, Pearl reared back and slapped him hard across the right cheek. The slap crackled and echoed in the alley like a crack of thunder.

"How dare you!" Pearl said, spinning and hurrying away.

Stunned and surprised, Josiah was momentarily frozen, until he realized that Pearl was almost out of range, and close to turning the corner, as she rushed away from him.

He quickly caught up with her, grabbing her, halting her escape.

"Pearl, wait, please, it's not what you think."

"Let me go," she said, through clenched teeth. "I will not tolerate a man who visits those kind of places. I saw what that did to my mother. Don't think that I don't know about my father's womanizing ways. I will not make the same mistakes as my mother, do you understand, Josiah Wolfe, I won't. I won't end up like her."

It seemed like all of the air had been sucked out of the world. Any words that had formed on the tip of Josiah's tongue fell back into his throat. He let his grasp fall away from Pearl's arm, and then he stepped back. He knew he had done nothing wrong, that he could explain himself to a rational human being who was willing to listen, but she was not right now.

And he knew at that very moment that there was no way she would ever forgive him for sleeping with Suzanne del Toro. It didn't matter that it had happened before they began courting, before they hardly knew each other at all. What would matter is that it happened at all—and he would have to tell her about it, all of it, at some point. He wasn't the kind of man to keep secrets from the woman he loved. He was never like that with Lily, and he had no plan on starting to lie now.

Pearl hesitated, like she wanted Josiah to stop her, but he didn't. He watched her turn away as she burst into tears and ran off into the shadows, disappearing, taking with her his heart, and his hope of ever starting a new life.

CHAPTER 32

———◆◆◆———

Josiah's cheek stung all of the way home. He didn't ride full out, but he didn't trot, either. Navigating through the city was easy now. The shops and mercantiles were closed, blinds down, along with the law offices and any office that served the capital in a professional capacity. Horse traffic was almost nil, though the street was fully lit with gas lamps, glowing at measured intervals, casting light and an odd chorus of dancing shadows that Josiah had yet to grow accustomed to.

The sky was thick with low-hanging clouds that had suddenly appeared just after Pearl ran off. The weather in Texas changed so quickly in the spring it made a calm man's head spin—not that Josiah needed any help in that department. Pearl's reaction, while understandable, had caught him unawares. He could barely defend himself, stand up for himself and his cause, because he had done nothing wrong. At least in the present. The past was another matter—depending on where you stood.

The day had been long, and the thought of home, of

sleeping in his own bed, was a welcoming thought. He'd be in a bedroll, sleeping on the hard ground, soon enough.

He made the familiar trek home pretty quickly.

A dim light shined in the front window of the house on Sixth Street, and a shadowy figure sat on the front steps.

Josiah didn't hesitate jumping off Clipper and hitching up the Appaloosa. He recognized the figure. Juan Carlos posed no threat. Not now.

"I didn't expect to see you here, Juan Carlos," Josiah said with a comfortable nod. His voice was soft, sure as he was that Lyle would be asleep inside the house. "Is everything all right?"

Juan Carlos arched his right eyebrow, his face heavy with concern. "I have found the girl, señor."

"The girl? The witness or Scrap's sister?"

"They are one and the same, señor."

Josiah stared at Juan Carlos, having not expected to hear the news that had just come out of his mouth.

The old Mexican's hair was white as snow, almost glowing, even in the muted light. There were no gas lamps near Josiah's house, so what light there was reflected from the window, allowing Juan Carlos's face to be seen but not easily read. He was emotionless, or hardened to Scrap's fate, one or the other.

There were no other sounds in the world that Josiah could hear. The crickets and frogs were sleeping or pulled back in fear of a human presence. It was like all of the air had been sucked out of Josiah's body, like he was standing in the desert all alone. He couldn't believe what he was hearing, hadn't thought it even possible that the witness could be Scrap's sister, Myra Lynn.

"You're certain?"

"*Sí*, there is no question that it is his *hermana*, his sister."

"Did you talk to her?" Josiah thought he heard footsteps in the house. It was probably Ofelia checking on the voices she heard outside. She had reason to be edgy and was always armed in one way or another when Josiah was away.

Juan Carlos shook his head no. "She is locked up, señor."

"Locked up?"

"In a room above the Easy Nickel Saloon."

"That son of a bitch Brogdon Caine lied to me. He said she wasn't there. Tried to gain my trust. How'd you find her?"

Juan Carlos shrugged, then looked away.

Josiah knew better than to expect an answer, but he hadn't been able to stop himself from asking. Now that the shock of it was over, his mind began turning with questions that neither of them had the answers to.

"Why would she testify against her own brother?" Josiah asked out loud, not necessarily of Juan Carlos.

"I do not know, señor. Maybe for her freedom. The man whose arm you broke . . ."

"William, the barkeep."

"*Sí*, William, he blames Señor Elliot for killing his favorite girl. He had taken a shine to this Lola that was brutally killed."

"Caine told me as much, but why would he hold Myra Lynn captive?"

"I really do not know, but Brogdon Caine has much to gain if Blanche Dumont is no longer in business, señor, and William has a score to settle with you and Señor Elliot. There is nothing to say that Caine is not behind all of this."

"The girl is locked up in his saloon."

"I did not see Caine. Only the barkeep and another man outside of the room, guarding it."

Josiah nodded. "I think Caine has to know what's going on; according to him he's got the short end of the stick with all of the construction in town. Blanche Dumont has her fair share of enemies, and Caine's one of them."

"*Es la guerra*. It is war. This is just a battle for territory. Much like the Anglo and the Comanche. The old ways are losing to the new, but nothing ever changes. War is always about money, power, and boundaries."

"And you think Caine is just a soldier?"

"*Sí*, señor, I do. He is not as powerful a man as he thinks he is. He just carries out orders."

"How do you know this? Who does Caine answer to?"

"That I do not know."

"If we find the man who's giving orders, then we'll most likely find the man behind the killings? Is that what you're saying? That's why they have Myra Lynn? To make sure Scrap gets hanged, and the killings get swept under the rug, and they can go on doing whatever it is they're up to?"

"I think that might be it. But it could be more, or less, than that. *Me he equivocado antes.* I have been wrong before."

It didn't take long for Josiah to decide what to do next. He exhaled heavily. "We have to rescue her. Find out what she saw. If she's being coerced, then we'll have to see her to the trial to tell the truth for what it is, not because she fears for her life."

"Or Señor Elliot's. It is hard telling what they have threatened her with, señor. There is nothing Caine is above doing to survive. You must know that."

"I do." Josiah stiffened, stood silent for a long second. "All right. I need to peek inside, make sure Lyle is all right and see if Ofelia needs anything before we make our plans."

"I understand, Señor Josiah, I understand. I think it is best if we do this in the dead of night. Rest for a few hours. I will wake you when it is the best time to catch them by surprise."

Before Josiah could object, or add to the plan, Juan Carlos slid back into the shadows of the small house and disappeared down the street.

Ofelia was sitting on a cot alongside the outside wall, close to the window. Josiah was sure she'd heard everything said between him and Juan Carlos.

A lamp burned with a low flame, providing enough light in the house for Josiah to see one foot in front of the other. He could find his way to the small bedroom blindfolded, but he appreciated Ofelia's consideration. She was such a big part of his life that he couldn't even begin to think of living in the city, or anywhere else for that matter, without her.

The sting on his face from Pearl's slap had long vanished, but the pain had just fallen to his heart. As comfortable as he was with Ofelia in his house, he was just as uncomfortable with Pearl in his life, and in his heart. If there was any pain to be felt, it was there. But now was not the time to worry about what might or might not be. He just hoped he could set things straight with Pearl, if that was even possible, before he left with the company of Rangers.

Josiah padded by Ofelia, neither of them speaking a word. The Mexican woman just nodded solemnly and laid down on the cot, pulling a thin blanket over her, not taking her eyes off him.

He stopped at the bedroom door and listened to Lyle breathing easily, letting his vision adjust to the darkness of the room.

The boy was stretched out on his bed, his own blankets tangled at his feet. Even in dim light, Josiah could see the resemblance of the boy's face to Lily's. A miniature reflection of a life lost, and a life missed. More heartache. More realization on Josiah's part that he would be leaving again soon, missing more of the boy's days.

He hated to admit it, but sometimes being away was easier on him, not seeing the resemblance, not being forced to remember what once was, and to consider what would not and could never be again. As much as he'd thought he'd pushed through the grief of losing his family, he knew deep down that that was not true. He'd never gotten over losing Lily and the girls. Never. Maybe Pearl knew that, too, felt it, saw it as a chasm between them. Maybe she knew he could never love her like he'd loved the woman before her. Maybe she was better off without him. Life for her would be easier if their relationship ended, just like it was easier for him being away from Lyle for long stretches at a time.

The boy shifted in the bed then, rolled over, still asleep, turning his back to Josiah.

Josiah walked inside the room as softly as he could and covered Lyle up with the blanket, then sat down on the edge of the bed and touched the boy's shoulder as gently as possible—not to stir him awake, but just to touch him, to make sure he was real, alive, something of himself to leave behind when he was gone.

Josiah let the minutes pass, not worried about rest, or sleep, or anything else that mattered in the world. He just wanted to see as much of Lyle as he could.

CHAPTER 33

The soft tap on the window didn't surprise Josiah, or wake him. He'd been lying in the bed for over an hour, waiting for Juan Carlos to signal him that it was time to go.

With as much ease and silence as possible, Josiah swung his feet to the floor. The smooth pine planks were cool to his bare feet. He took a deep breath, tapped on the window softly to let Juan Carlos know he'd be right out, then leaned over Lyle, who was sleeping peacefully. There was just enough light in the room for Josiah to see the boy, though dimly; his face looked like a foggy memory. It would have to be good enough—Josiah had no clue what he was getting himself into, but he knew one thing for sure: Brogdon Caine wasn't going to give up Myra Lynn Elliot easily, especially if he was in the thick of the killings and all that they entailed. It sure looked like that was the case, and the more Josiah thought about it, the less it surprised him.

Without hesitating, and knowing it might well be the last time, he leaned down and kissed Lyle quickly on the cheek. As his father pulled away, the boy stirred a bit, never waking, most likely playing and roughhousing in the happy dreamland that existed only in his sleep.

Josiah left the room without looking back. He had slept with his pants and undershirt on; his shirt and boots were right outside the door.

Ofelia stirred awake as Josiah sat down to put on his boots. He looked up and saw her staring at him. The last thing he wanted to do was wake Lyle, so he said nothing, just got up, walked to the pantry, and pulled out a shotgun. It looked like the one his father'd kept in the cabin in Seerville, only beside the front door, instead of hidden away, out of easy reach; it had been a compromise with Ofelia.

He padded over to the cot and offered the gun to Ofelia. She, too, had slept in her day clothes. She eased the thin blanket off her, exposing a thin-bladed boning knife she used to gut chickens, just within her grasp.

Ofelia sat up, took the shotgun, then laid back down, cuddling the gun, covering herself and the gun back up, as if it didn't exist.

Any man coming into the house who underestimated Ofelia and her preparedness would quickly find himself in deep, deep trouble, if not dead before he knew what hit him.

There was no question in Josiah's mind that Ofelia was prepared to die for Lyle. She had shown him as much more than once. But there was more to the knife's presence, and he knew it. His own actions had brought trouble, and death, to the house, and to Lyle, before. Ofelia had seen it, felt it, been held hostage herself. They had never spoken of the trauma, or any residual fears she might carry because of the violence bestowed on her by Josiah's choices. She had just come to Austin with him. No questions asked. To protect Lyle, to see him to adulthood. Josiah was sure of that.

"*Tenga cuidado.* Be careful," Ofelia whispered.

Josiah nodded, grabbed up his guns, his own knife, put himself together as quietly and quickly as possible, and walked out the door without saying another word.

* * *

Juan Carlos stood in between Clipper and the black gelding with a perfect white star on its nose. The whites of the black horse's eyes followed Josiah's every move, judging him cautiously. Josiah had never seen the horse before but thought little of it. There was never much concerning Juan Carlos that was continually the same except his mysteriousness, his lack of predictability. Patterns were the cause of death as far as Juan Carlos was concerned, and Josiah was in agreement with that sentiment, though he was never as good at changing things up as Juan Carlos was.

"We will need another man, señor," Juan Carlos said in a low voice. "This is too dangerous for just you and me."

Before Josiah could protest, he detected movement, a man's shadow moving toward him from behind the black horse. The man was Miguel Vargas, another Mexican that Josiah had dealt with previously.

Under the guise of a guitar player in Corpus Christi, Miguel had been a spy for McNelly, too, only Josiah hadn't known it at the time. He only became aware of the man's allegiances when he had been followed back to Austin by the bounty hunter Leathers, and Miguel had shown up after Josiah had killed the man. After that, Miguel disappeared, off on another mission, Josiah assumed, or doing whatever Juan Carlos did when he was away. There was no clear-cut line of duty for either Mexican. The fact that they were employed by the Texas Rangers from time to time was a closely held secret. There were far more men on the payroll than Josiah, or anyone else, knew about. He didn't question the reasons, or the missions, but understood the need for men like Juan Carlos and Miguel completely.

"It is good to see you again, Señor Wolfe." Miguel stuck out his hand to shake.

Miguel was younger than Juan Carlos by about twenty years, his skin darker, his solid black hair oilier; it seemed to glow in the night, like the surface of a deep pond in the moonlight.

There was no distrust between the two men, and Josiah was glad to see Miguel. The Mexican was a good shot and had plenty of experience in situations like the one they were about to face. Juan Carlos had chosen the third man well.

"It is good to see you, too, Miguel." Josiah shook the Mexican's hand with a broad smile.

"We always seem to meet under dire circumstances, señor."

"It is the life we have chosen, I suppose," Josiah said.

"*Sí*, señor, I believe you are right about that. Just think, I could be sitting in a cantina serenading the *senoritas*."

Josiah dropped his smile as a flash of Maria Villareal, a beautiful woman in her own right, who had been killed by a mistake on his part, flashed through his mind. He looked away to Juan Carlos. "You have a plan?"

Juan Carlos nodded. "There are more men than I originally thought. Something else is going on. There are four men in the saloon waiting for something to happen. I am not sure what."

"How many men are guarding Myra Lynn?" Josiah asked.

"Three that I am aware of."

"Seven to three. I guess that's a fair fight," Josiah said.

Miguel stood back and said nothing, obviously leaving the details to Juan Carlos.

Juan Carlos shook his head no. "Nine to three if you include Brogdon Caine and William, the barkeep. He might have a broken arm, but I am sure his trigger finger is just fine."

Josiah exhaled. "We'll need more weapons, more ammunition."

"I have already arranged that." Juan Carlos flicked his head to the left.

Following the old Mexican's directive, Josiah looked

down the street and saw a wagon waiting, its cargo covered by a large tarp. "You have thought of everything."

"As much as possible," Juan Carlos said.

Josiah said nothing; he let the silence and coolness of the night surround them. It was a couple of hours before dawn. He began to think of what Juan Carlos had told him, what lay ahead of the three men, as he untied Clipper's lead from the hitching post.

"Four men, you say?" Josiah asked.

"*Sí*," Juan Carlos answered, cocking an eyebrow at Josiah. "Does that concern you, señor?"

"I encountered a man in the café earlier today, Milt Fulsum, the new desk sergeant at the jail. He replaced Emery Jones, the old sergeant who was killed during the jailbreak. He was with three other riders. Riders who all wore black like those that were involved in the jailbreak and took shots at us under the Tree of Death. I'm just wondering if they are all one and the same."

"They are, Señor Josiah. One of the horses that fled from the Tree of Death had a notch in its back shoe. I tracked it into town but lost it. I found the horse itself waiting outside of the Easy Nickel Saloon."

"Then it looks like Milt Fulsum, who was pretty nervous at the café, is not what he seems. He's not just a deputy for Farnsworth, he's an outlaw playing both sides of the fence. He was involved in breaking Abram Randalls out of the jail and has something to do with Brogdon Caine."

"It looks that way, señor," Juan Carlos said.

"Why do you say that?" Josiah asked.

Juan Carlos hesitated. "Milt Fulsum is a Texas Ranger, señor. Or, at least, he was as recently as six months ago. Just like me, and you, and Miguel, he, too, has worked as a spy for Captain McNelly."

CHAPTER 34

━━━━◆━✕━◆━━━━

After making their plans, the men rode away from
the small house on Sixth Street as silently as possible.
Miguel was on the black horse, and Juan Carlos drove the
wagon gently, not in a hurry. Its contents were . . . fragile.

They had all agreed to keep Milt Fulsum out of their gun
sights, but if the man threatened them with certain death,
or the point of a rifle, then all bets were off. Texas Ranger
or not, all three would shoot to kill and ask questions later.
The thought, of course, gave Josiah reason to be a little more
nervous than he would have been otherwise. Killing another
Texas Ranger would be the end of everything for him, and
he knew it. He'd most certainly have to leave Austin. His
reputation would be soiled forever, no matter how justified
the act was. But he knew he'd do it, kill Fulsum if he had
to, no matter the consequences. Freeing Myra Lynn and
seeing Juan Carlos and Miguel safe out of the coming melee
was all that mattered—because in the end, it was the only
way Josiah could see of clearing Scrap Elliot.

It was less than an hour until dawn. The air was cool,

and the sky was void of any clouds. Any sign of impending weather had pushed out during the night, leaving a pure black blanket overhead, adorned with the communal throbbing of silvery, faraway stars. The edge of the horizon was fading to gray, a promise of coming light that had yet to wake the first bird. The moon waned, dropping to the horizon, a sliver of its true self, casting very little light on the road ahead.

As far as Josiah could tell, all of Austin slept peacefully, entombed in the normalcy of the clock, of the expectations of one day ended and another one starting. There was no rest for the weary, as far as Josiah was concerned, and most certainly no rest for Scrap Elliot, who at last word was still stowed away in the hole, restrained against the hint of the smallest shaft of light, or hope of escape.

The thought urged Josiah forward, and he brought Clipper easily up next to the slow-paced wagon.

The common silence of the deep night was as much a gift as a curse. Any man worth his salt would hear the wagon coming a mile away, no matter how quiet Juan Carlos tried to keep the drive.

They were still far enough away from the Easy Nickel Saloon to avoid detection there—unless Brogdon Caine had a radius of men set up on watch. Somehow, Josiah doubted that. Juan Carlos would have known, would have checked, would have included taking out the watch in their plans. It was an assumption, and knowingly a foolhardy act, not to question the Mexican, but Josiah felt safe in his decision, knowing full well what the Mexican's skills included. But still, a few things gnawed at him, beyond the question of Caine's watch.

"You're sure of this plan?" Josiah asked, the volume of his voice just above a whisper.

Juan Carlos had a light grip on the reins, and the single horse pulling the wagon, a big, old bay draft horse, acted like it knew where it was going on its own. "Trust me,

Miguel and I will create a distraction out front and draw the majority of attention away from the back of the building. You will have to deal with the one guard at the back door and make your way to the room."

"You're sure Myra Lynn is in the room."

"*Absolutamenta positivo.* The one marked *tres.* There is another man inside, maybe two. I do not know what the distraction will cause, if they are prepared for it. I feel like Caine will be ready for you, señor. But you know that already. If she is as important to their cause as I think she is, the guard will be willing to die rather than face the *consecuencias*, um, consequences. Are you?"

"You have to ask?"

"You have more to lose, señor. A home, a son, the promise of love and a new life on the horizon, as close as in your hand."

"Scrap Elliot would risk everything for me." Without realizing it, Josiah had spoken through gritted teeth.

"*Sì*, I believe that as much as you do, Señor Josiah. But if something happens to you, Scrap Elliot does not have to answer to Pearl—to my *sobrina*, my niece."

Josiah smiled then. "I'll do whatever it takes so you won't have to deal with that, my friend."

"Then you will be ready to kill again?"

"Yes." Josiah dropped his chin, hopefully calming Juan Carlos's fears. "The Ketchum grenades are too risky," he said after a brief pause, his eyes narrowing, as he cast a glance back to the covered load in the wagon.

"*Sì*, but I have worked with them before. I am no expert, but one good hit will suffice."

Josiah nodded. "I wouldn't count on luck, and you may be facing what you throw."

The grenades had been used in the War Between the States, in the major battles, like Vicksburg and Petersburg, and smaller skirmishes alike. The explosives looked like thin darts, a cast iron ball with stabilizing wood fins, and

came in varying weights. The most widely used weighed a
pound, but the impact and use was as small as the weight.
Larger grenades weighed five pounds. The tip was armed
with a plunger, and the casing contained the charge. The bad
thing was that the nose had to land directly on the ground,
or its target, to engage the plunger and explode.

Josiah had no clue which grenades Juan Carlos carried
and planned on using. It didn't matter. Damage was not the
intention. A distraction, causing panic and surprise, was the
hoped for outcome.

But using the explosives was a big risk. The Ketchum
grenade was a Union invention, and there had been times
during battle that Confederate soldiers had used blankets—
a straw-drawn duty—to catch the incoming grenades. The
soldiers threw the unexploded grenades back from where
they came. Kind of like stabbing a man with his own knife.
Josiah had seen it done more than once. It was a possibility
that Juan Carlos and Miguel could find themselves in the
same situation.

"Besides, you worry too much, Señor Josiah," Juan Carlos continued, with a wry smile. "Miguel and I will handle
seven men, while you only handle two or three."

"The bombs will wake all of Austin," Josiah said.

"That, too, is part of the plan, señor. We hope to draw
some goodwill to our aid, if we are in need. I've never
known a curiosity seeker who was not armed."

"That's all good and fine as long as they shoot at the right
person."

"That is another chance we must take, señor. Perhaps we
will be gone by then, our quarry safe, and the smoke and
bullets behind us."

Josiah parted company with Juan Carlos and
Miguel with a silent nod once they were two blocks from
the saloon.

He stayed close to the buildings and boardwalk, using the shadows as much as he could for cover. His pace was steady, but he held Clipper back, aiming to ease in behind the Easy Nickel as stealthily as possible.

If there were times when Josiah thought riding a black horse, like the one Miguel rode, was a good idea, now was one of those times. But he would not part with Clipper. They had been through too much together.

A known and agreed upon alleyway appeared about a block away from the saloon, and Josiah guided Clipper into it.

The alleyway sat between a milliner's shop and a lady's dress shop, both places Pearl had most likely frequented— in her previous life. He pushed the thought of her from his mind but found it hard since Juan Carlos had brought up what he was risking.

Still, he needed to focus, stay grounded on the task at hand: his life and everyone else who was involved in the rescue. Scrap depended on the success of it, without even knowing what was going on. There were troubles with Pearl that Juan Carlos was unaware of, matters of the heart that had taken a hard turn, a turn Josiah wasn't sure could be straightened out—even if he had the time to properly bring the spat about his presence in Blanche Dumont's house, and all it entailed, to a complete end.

He tied Clipper's reins to the back corner post of a small porch behind the milliner's and loaded up with his weapons.

He had a knife in his boot, and his Peacemaker, along with a full accompaniment of cartridges in his belt, and another thrown over his shoulder. He pulled his rifle, a Winchester '73, out of the scabbard, patted Clipper on the neck, and eased away along the dark alley, certain of his next destination.

It didn't take long for the back of the Easy Nickel to come into sight.

Another alleyway ran along the rear of the building, and

it was cloaked in as much darkness as the one Josiah had left Clipper in.

The building was dark, at least what Josiah could see of it. There were no windows in the back. Just a door on the bottom floor, crowded with empty beer kegs, and a stairway that led up three flights. From what he could see, there were no lamps burning.

He had positioned himself at the corner of another building about twenty feet across from the back door. He was close to the spot where Lola had been killed, where Scrap's fate changed in a moment, only because of his desire to seek out his sister, and nothing more. That one act had changed everything for the boy. His life might never be the same again.

There was nothing to do now but wait.

A breeze kicked up, snaking through the alleyways, between the buildings, bringing with it a chill; a chill that ran up and down Josiah's spine, goading him to be afraid. Going into battle was never easy, never a joy. There was no way that Brogdon Caine was going to give up Myra Lynn without a fight. Josiah knew what death smelled like, tasted like, and the memory of those senses came rushing back to him, reminding him of his past, and of his future. He hoped his skills would see him through. His trigger finger was cold and numb.

Josiah didn't have to wait too long.

Like they'd planned, Juan Carlos was in position and threw a grenade into the saloon's front window.

The blanket of silence was so great that the first sound of breaking glass was like standing on a frozen pond and having the ice crack and then explode, right under your feet.

The shattering of the window echoed up and down the street, sounding the alarm of an immediate attack.

Josiah took a deep breath and waited for the Ketchum grenade to explode. It didn't. The grenade had obviously not

landed on the plunger. He hoped Juan Carlos was prepared
for what came next.

A light blazed on inside the kitchen of the saloon, lighting all of the back of the building like a fire had been set
and allowed to flare. But it was no fire. The grenade had
woken up everyone in the saloon, set the men on watch to
do their job: protect whatever needed protecting, at any cost.
Josiah had underestimated the little Negro at Blanche
Dumont's house. It was not a mistake he cared to repeat this
time around. The outcome would be worse than a bruised
ego if he underestimated Brogdon Caine.

Another shatter of glass quickly followed the first, as
Juan Carlos threw another grenade. This time a *boom!* followed as the grenade exploded inside the saloon.

Josiah didn't hesitate. He rushed across the dark alleyway, his knife firmly in one hand and his Winchester firmly
in the other.

CHAPTER 35

———◆◆◆◆◆———

Josiah saw the first hint of movement at the bottom of the outside stairway; the shadow of a hulking man just becoming aware of Josiah's presence.

There was enough light shining out from the kitchen for Josiah to see the man, who looked like a boulder with arms and legs, reaching for his sidearm. He was dressed all in black, like the riders at the jailbreak and those at the café the day before. Josiah could only assume the man was a member of that crew, though he didn't look familiar. Not that Josiah had gotten a good look at any of the men either time.

"Drop it, friend," Josiah said, the Winchester raised to chest level, his finger on the trigger.

The man looked like he'd just stirred awake; he seemed slightly disoriented—but he ignored Josiah's command, raising a Colt with a seven-and-a-half-inch barrel in the direction of Josiah's head.

There was no time for second chances, no second requests. Josiah pulled the trigger, shooting the man in the shoulder, sending him stumbling backward, the Colt falling from his grip. Josiah followed up with another shot to the opposite arm. The man spiraled to the ground in a heavy thud, landing on his side.

There were no other weapons that Josiah could see. He was surprised that the watchman was not better armed, that Caine hadn't been expecting a rescue, but it didn't look like he had been.

The shots had been meant to maim, not to kill. It might have been a mistake, not killing the man outright, but there'd be time to deal with the consequences of that decision later—regardless of Juan Carlos's warning.

Josiah tucked his knife in the sheath and scooped up the boulder man's Colt, then looked down at him, writhing in pain. "You come after me, I'll kill you outright, you understand?"

The man said nothing; his eyes were filled with pain, his skin pasty and white, sweat beading on his brow, and his thin undershirt soaked with two undammed rivers of blood. Shock was setting in—Josiah had seen it a thousand times in the war. The man was going nowhere quick. He might even die. Still, there was no trusting a wounded man like you could a dead man.

Josiah aimed the rifle at the man's ankle, then thought better of hobbling him, crippling him for the rest of his life—if he lived. Instead, he shot the man just above the ankle, in the calf, as close to the bone as possible without shattering it.

The shot echoed, joined with a weak scream of sudden pain, overtaking the man so much that his eyes rolled back in his head, the whites of his eyes shining in the night like two miniature moons had crashed to the ground.

Josiah didn't stop to check and see if the man was dead or not; he sprinted up the stairs, not looking back, armed with an extra gun now that the man's Colt had become his.

Time was ticking away.

Another Ketchum grenade exploded. A bigger one. There was a noticeable reverberation from inside the building, a shake of the foundation, like a thunderclap exploding inside the cellar instead of overhead. The whole building shook and threatened to collapse, but somehow it stayed standing.

Yells and screams came from inside the saloon. Gunfire rang out from the front, coming from both directions as Miguel returned fire. The fight was fully engaged now, and Josiah hoped Juan Carlos and Miguel could handle the attack from the hornet's nest they'd just intentionally kicked open.

The air smelled of gunpowder, blood, and the ghosts of war. Thinking or regret no longer mattered; only the mission was of any importance.

Josiah reached the top floor quickly, barely breathing hard. Adrenaline numbed his entire body. He felt nothing. He couldn't even hear his heart beating, but he could feel it throbbing in his chest.

Another grenade exploded, and the smell of a growing fire quickly met Josiah's nose. He pushed open the third-floor door cautiously, the Winchester in one hand, the Colt in the other. He'd sheathed the knife once he decided that any hand-to-hand fighting was out of the question.

The hallway was dark, no sconces burning, no light visible other than what came in behind him from the graying dawn. All he could smell was the fire and battle raging below him. The chaotic noise drowned everything else out, including any fears that might have followed him up the stairs.

Josiah took his chances and eased inside the hallway, his finger on the trigger of each gun he carried.

He focused his eyes, searching for shadows, anything that moved. A rat would have died an instant death if it had dared to show itself. But there was nothing, just an endless hallway bathed in darkness, the number 3 beckoning him.

He could only hope that Juan Carlos was right, that Myra

Lynn was safe inside, held captive for the moment in court when she would betray her brother and send him to the gallows. It was a thought Josiah had a hard time stomaching, but it was easy to figure; Myra Lynn's life for Scrap's was a simple whore's deal, one thing for another, a trade in flesh, only of a different kind.

The third door was easy to find. Josiah put his ear to it hoping to hear something, a clue of what, or who, might be waiting on the other side. There was nothing. Or at least nothing that he could decipher over the noise and racket below.

Smoke wafted up through the floor, a gray cloud followed by the first flicker of fire at the front of the building. There was no time to plan, or to wait for the most appropriate moment to rush in. The fire was hungry, already out of control.

Another grenade exploded, rattling his legs, shaking him all the way to the tips of his sweaty hair. His ears were deafened for a long moment; they tingled. He feared the floor underneath his feet would give way, fall out from underneath him, but it didn't.

Josiah took a deep breath, regained his footing, and kicked in the door, prepared to shoot at the first thing that moved.

Smoke wrapped around his ankles like a silent snake certain of its next meal, but he paid it no mind as his eyes adjusted to a stronger bit of light: A hurricane lamp burned a low flame at the far end of the small room.

A figure came clear before him, bound in a chair facing the door, arms tied to the side—no way out, no way to escape. It wasn't Myra Lynn, like Josiah had expected, like Juan Carlos had assured him it would be.

Instead, he was staring at the panicked face of a familiar man, Abram Randalls. The last time Josiah had seen the mousy little man, he was being carted out of the jail through a hole blown in the wall. Now he was captive on the burning floor of a three-storey saloon.

Randalls didn't appear to recognize Josiah. Only fear showed on his face; it was as white with shock as the man's at the bottom of the stairs.

There was no one else in the room that Josiah could see, but the door blocked half of his view. A guard was somewhere close, unless Juan Carlos had been wrong about that, too.

Blanche Dumont's bookkeeper and Myron Farnsworth's embezzler had no gag in his mouth, and without the blink of an eye, with sweat pouring from his forehead, he shouted, "They've taken her to the train!"

They were the last words Abram Randalls would ever speak.

A hail of bullets erupted from the opposite side of the door. The first one caught Abrams in the chin, ending any chance for a confession, or spouting any more revelations about Brogdon Caine's plans. Blood splattered outward, silencing the man. The impact of the bullet was so severe it nearly toppled over the chair. The second bullet sent shattered teeth flying into the air, along with muscle and sinew, while the third pierced the man's right eye, sending it completely to the back of his skull. Three more bullets followed, all directed at Randalls's head. There was nothing left but a fountain of blood exiting the holes; any skill with numbers, keeping secrets, or anything else was long gone, never to be seen or heard from again. He was dead before the echo of his last spoken word fell to the floor.

Josiah didn't wait, didn't breathe. He kept his promise to himself, asked no questions, and fired through the door, emptying the Colt, tossing it to the side, then firing the Winchester as blindly through the door as he had the pistol. A quick thump to the floor followed as the unseen guard met the same fate as Abram Randalls.

With a quick peek around the door, and a hearty dose of caution, Josiah made sure the guard was, in fact, dead, and that there was not another. He *was* dead, and the only man in the room. Josiah didn't recognize the man, but he was dressed all in black. Another rider, dead in Caine's whorehouse. It looked to him like the commander of the riders and the man behind the jailbreak was Caine, but at this point, he couldn't be one hundred percent certain. And there was still the question of what Caine was after in the first place.

Fire fully burst through the floor at the far end of the hallway. Flames reached hungrily upward, then outward, reaching out to any place there was dry wood to consume.

Smoke filled the hallway, and over the shouts and gunfire that now came from the street, Josiah heard the first blow of the morning train whistle, rising in the distance, calling all riders to it . . . before it was too late to board, or save Myra Lynn Elliot.

CHAPTER 36

———◆◇◆◇◆———

There was only one way out of the top floor of the Easy Nickel Saloon for Josiah: the same way he had come in. Any hesitation or fear was un–thought of; he knew the morning train left the station at sunrise. The scream of the train's loud whistle, and the rattle of the house, woke him every morning he slept in his own bed. A place he longed to be now, but could not be. If Myra Lynn really was on the early train out of town, he had no choice but to try and stop her from leaving, even though he had no reason to trust Abram Randalls. He didn't have any reason to distrust the man, either.

Josiah hugged the wall down to the door, keeping as low to the floor and in as much fresh air as possible.

Smoke from the fire below had filled the hallway, making it nearly impossible to see his way out. His eyes burned, and he quickly pulled his handkerchief up over his nose. It didn't help. His lungs burned like they were on fire, too. By the time he reached the door, Josiah could feel the heat biting at his back and toasting the bottoms of his feet through his boots. He didn't care what was waiting on the other side of the door. Once he reached it, he busted out, desperate for a breath of clean, breathable air.

Barely escaping the hallway before another flame reached out for him, Josiah coughed, choked, and yanked the handkerchief from his face.

Luckily, there hadn't been anyone waiting for him, either outside the door or hidden in a sniper's position somewhere on one of the roofs of the surrounding buildings. The well-planned troop of men who had executed a flawless jailbreak seemed to have faltered in their planning for a rescue attempt, if there had been a plan at all.

Josiah would have taken cover at the back door, but judging from the sound of the gunfire and screams and shouts from the front of the building, every available man was there, fighting off Miguel and Juan Carlos. He hoped the grenades had evened the count.

There was no time to join in and help. Josiah needed to get to the train. It was hard telling how many men Brogdon Caine had put on Myra Lynn's escort out of town, but it was clear that the saloon owner considered the girl valuable—or else he had been planning on getting her out of town all along, though that made little sense to Josiah at the moment. He was still trying to digest it all. Without Myra Lynn, there was no witness to Lola's murder, nothing other than hearsay to frame Scrap as the killer. And all that was left in Scrap's defense was his story of another man, the obscure cowboy, leaning over Lola, killing her outright, then running off.

Josiah still had no clue who the killer was, but he had a good idea that the man was no cowboy just passing through town, like Scrap had assumed.

It seemed to Josiah that the same man had killed all four whores, not just Lola, and that meant the murderer been in town for some time. Probably close. Even out in the open. Like behind the bar of the Easy Nickel Saloon. William, the barkeep, was as good a suspect in the murders as any, now that Josiah thought about it . . . now that everything had led back to the saloon.

Caine had said that William was upset with the Rangers because Scrap had killed his favorite girl. And there had been no mention of the cowboy or man Scrap had insisted he saw. Maybe that man was William himself. Or maybe nothing Caine said was true; it seemed likely now that it looked like he'd been the one behind the jailbreak.

The idea was worth noting, especially if Josiah was able to head off the train and get Myra Lynn to the trial, to speak *for* Scrap instead of against him. That was the new plan, but he had no way to communicate it with Juan Carlos and Miguel.

Once Josiah regained his breath, cleared his eyes, and was reasonably certain that he wasn't walking into a trap, he hurried down the stairs, keeping as close to the building as possible.

Flames poked out of the roof of the saloon and reached up to the sky, touching the coming dawn. Light was breaking on the horizon, gray turning to white, then a soft pink burning quickly to red. Thunderclouds towered in the distance, threatening the coming day with the promise of a storm. The air surrounding the saloon was like being in the midst of a fully engaged war; there was little time to notice or care about any impending weather. Josiah felt like he was in the middle of hell, not in the throes of spring.

The fire crackled hungrily inside and out of the saloon, and a wave of heat had followed Josiah down the stairs. The dead men on the third floor would be incinerated, their final moments lost to everyone but Josiah.

The first guard he'd encountered and shot was where he'd left him, still on the ground, still breathing, but not easily. For all Josiah knew, the man was close to death, too. If the building crumbled down to the ground, the man would surely die. Josiah left him there. Saving the man was of little consequence to him at the moment.

He hurried away, back toward the alley he'd left Clipper in, fleeing the saloon and all that was going on. He couldn't be certain what was happening, if Juan Carlos and Miguel were holding their own. There hadn't been an explosion for a long stretch of time, but there was plenty of back-and-forth gunfire. Either way, the only thing Josiah could do was hope they'd been as prepared as possible for what was to come once the first grenade exploded inside the saloon. That and hope that aid would come in the form of deputies or backup of some kind. Not knowing who to trust had prevented Juan Carlos and Josiah from alerting the Rangers or Rory Farnsworth to their plan.

A fire bell clanged in the distance as the black cloud of smoke wafted away from the saloon and over the city and was met by three short toots, almost in unison, from the departing train's whistle.

Josiah hurried his pace, then broke into a full run. It was still dark enough for the shadows to be of use to him, but he remained an easy target for any good shooter.

Clipper was right where he'd left him, standing sentinel, like a statue, like he had not moved a muscle since Josiah left.

Josiah slammed the Winchester into the scabbard, then untied and mounted the horse in a leap. He kneed Clipper, yanking the horse's head in the opposite direction. Clipper responded knowingly to the urgency. The horse broke into a full run, heading out of the alley at great speed, giving Josiah every ounce of energy it had.

The smell of smoke coated Josiah's tongue so densely that it felt like he'd licked the bottom of an ash can. Gunshots echoed up into the sky, carried on the same breeze that had spread the black cloud rising up from the Easy Nickel Saloon across the eastern side of Austin. Along with the noise, and his single-minded focus, the smoke made it almost impossible for Josiah to keep a clear eye out for any danger of his own as he made his way onto the street. He was so eager to reach the train, he nearly overlooked the troop of men on horseback heading straight for him.

Josiah pulled back on the reins, bringing Clipper to a quick stop. Dust kicked up behind him and the horse, and Clipper protested at the hard yank of the bit.

It only took Josiah a quick second to figure out whether the troop of men were friend or foe.

Captain Leander McNelly and the company of Rangers swept up around Josiah, surrounding him with curious eyes and an eagerness and nervousness of their own about what was going on.

"Boy, am I glad to see you, Captain," Josiah said.

"I should have figured you were in the middle of this mess, Wolfe."

The train whistled in the distance, taking Josiah's attention from the captain. "We haven't much time, Captain. Caine is carting a witness to the murders out of town as we speak. Juan Carlos and Miguel are engaged in a firefight at the Easy Nickel Saloon. I don't know what's become of them, but if I'm to catch that train before it leaves Austin, I need to go now!" Josiah was almost panting, he had spoken so quickly. "If you don't mind, sir," he added after catching his breath.

"You're certain about this, Wolfe?"

Josiah nodded. "Yes. I have to go, sir. The train is leaving," he said, feeling the first rumble of the train vibrating up through the street. He angled the horse's head toward a path that he could see his way clear of.

McNelly nodded. "Take the right flank with you," he ordered. "I'll take the rest of the men to the saloon and shore up Juan Carlos's fight."

Josiah didn't take time to answer or agree. He urged Clipper on again, only this time, ten well-armed men fell in behind him.

CHAPTER 37

The sky continued to lighten, and the threat of the coming storm was about to become a full-blown reality.

Thunderclouds reached high in the sky on the horizon. Streaks of lightning flashed far and wide, then buzzed to the ground with resounding booms. Overhead, the clouds were gray, mixed with the black smoke from the fire and the steam pushing up out of the locomotive.

The train had left the station and was slowly picking up speed, unconcerned about the weather it was driving into or the troop of Rangers who were trying to stop it from leaving Austin.

Josiah led the ten Rangers up along the south side of the train. He could hardly hear himself think, the train was so loud. Every ounce of his body shook from the rumble of the wheels banging forward on the tracks. Any closely held fear was not a consideration. His only focus was saving Myra Lynn and, ultimately, saving Scrap from the hangman's noose. It was a risk, going after Scrap's sister, but it was the only thing Josiah knew to do at this point.

The first passenger car behind the coal tender looked empty, until Josiah saw a shadow of movement at the farthest window, as a rifle barrel pointed out and fired in his direction.

The muzzle flash burned orange for a long second, and the crack of the shot echoed, but the sound was lost to the train's roar and the rising storm. Still, there was no mistaking the intent. Another silhouette appeared in the next window, a cowboy, black hat on his head, his face covered and unrecognizable, his rifle stuck out the window in the direction of the Rangers. He fired, too, into the troop.

Josiah immediately put up his hand and pulled back the reins, slowing Clipper, then called out over his shoulder, "Don't shoot back! We don't know where the girl is."

The truth was that Josiah didn't know for sure if Myra Lynn was really on the train or not. But he had taken Abram Randalls's last words to be true. The man had no reason to lie to him, to lead Josiah into harm. Perhaps it was a moment of redemption for the embezzler, or maybe it was a trick.

Josiah was betting on redemption. Either way, he'd find out soon enough.

He didn't wait for the troop behind to accept the order. Instead, he grabbed the Winchester out of his scabbard, then took a deep breath and a long second of concentration to gain a precise aim.

The two men inside the passenger car took advantage of that long second and continued to fire, hitting one of the Rangers behind Josiah.

The man, a Ranger whose name Josiah didn't know, screamed out and grabbed his arm in sudden pain.

Josiah returned fire, hitting the first shooter squarely in the forehead, sending him spiraling backward, out of sight. The second shooter pulled his rifle out of the window and retreated into the darkness of the car. Blood dripped down the side of the passenger car, glowing scarlet in the stormy morning light.

"Five of you sweep around to the other side of the train once it passes and take the car," Josiah shouted out.

The Ranger who was hit was still mounted on his horse, holding his arm. "It's just a flesh wound, Sergeant Wolfe. I'm fine," the man yelled out.

Josiah nodded. "The rest of you follow me. We'll take the car from this side. Two of you ride up to the engineer and get the brakeman to stop the train."

The first two men next to Josiah peeled off after the locomotive. The train was picking up speed even quicker, most likely because the engineer feared a robbery was in progress, instead of a rescue. With all of the noise, there was no way for Josiah to identify himself, or the men with him, as Texas Rangers, to the engineer. The man was likely to ignore the request anyway, fearing any variance to the schedule.

A clap of thunder boomed overhead. The ground shook, a joining of nature's force and the train's unrelenting power, making it hard for Josiah to consider anything else.

He urged Clipper forward, catching up to the train. He didn't need to look behind him to see if the other Rangers were following his lead, he could feel their presence, knew that their commitment to see the task through was strong, even though he was sure they didn't have the personal reasons that he did for putting their lives at risk. Blind fulfillment of duty carried its own beauty and dangers.

In a matter of seconds, Clipper was running full out, breathing heavily, his muscular white and black neck starting to lather with sweat. Josiah slid the Winchester back into the scabbard as he eyed the rear of the passenger car, gauging the speed of the train and Clipper's forward motion. He prepared himself to jump, knew what was at stake if he missed. Being severed by rushing train wheels would be a horrible way to die. Losing a leg or an arm and surviving the ordeal would be no way to live the rest of his life. Or he could be shot at any second . . .

Without thinking, tucking his fear away into the back of his mind, where it belonged, Josiah stood up in the stirrups, pulled his outside leg up on the saddle, then reached out for the speeding train and jumped.

It was like time stood still.

Lightning danced overhead. A steady stream of smoke and steam pushed up over the passenger car. It almost looked like night, like Josiah had fallen into the depths of hell again. A gunshot crackled behind him, and a zip of a bullet whizzed by his ear as he fell to the platform of the moving car. He landed squarely on his knees. One of the Rangers had taken a shot, had seen something Josiah didn't, maybe even saved his life.

Josiah rolled to the far corner of the passenger car platform, only the handrails stopping him from tumbling off the other side. His vision was still blurred, but his sense of survival wasn't; he reached for his Peacemaker immediately, ripping it out of the holster before he had stopped moving.

Clipper swerved away from the train, jumping and bucking forward. Josiah thought he heard the horse scream and bray, but he wasn't sure.

After a quick moment of gathering himself, he edged to the door of the passenger car and peeked inside as quickly as possible. He wasn't accustomed to the movement of the train, hadn't counterbalanced himself in anticipation of the sway of the passenger car as the train sped west out of Austin.

Josiah found himself standing in the middle of the window, an easy target. The glass shattered, and the shock of the explosion and the wobble of the train tossed him out of the way of the bullet that had come his way. It whizzed past his ear. Death was so close he could taste it.

The remaining three Rangers had caught up with the train. The lone shooter inside turned his attention to them and returned fire, knocking one of the Rangers completely off his horse. He fell hard, leaving nothing but a cloud of dust, and a frightened horse without a rider to tell it what direction to go.

Josiah took it as his chance to gain entry into the passenger car.

He pushed to the edge of the window, unconcerned about the glass on the floor of the rear platform, the fate of his fellow Rangers, the storm, or the train's speed.

Rain splashed down to the ground in big drops, and the unrelenting wind pushed the rain sideways. Lightning flashed and reflected off the train, temporarily blinding Josiah and every man on the chase. But now was not the time to quit or be deterred by elements out of his control.

Josiah peered inside the car quickly. There was only one shooter, and he had his rifle pointed out the window, more concerned with the Rangers riding up alongside the train. The other shooter lay on the floor, not moving. Josiah's first shot looked to have been deadly. The remaining shooter was outmanned, and Josiah thought about shouting inside and offering the man the chance to surrender, but decided against it. Giving out second chances was an account empty of purpose.

With as quiet and as easy a motion as possible, Josiah aimed his Peacemaker through the broken glass and pulled the trigger.

The blast echoed and met with thunder overhead. A blink of the eye to clear his vision told Josiah he'd hit his target.

There was no sign of the last window shooter. The man had fallen to the floor. There was no sign of Myra Lynn, either.

The train had driven directly into the storm, and it looked more like dusk than early dawn, leaving the inside of the passenger car filled with nothing but rolling shadows.

Knowing full well that he could be walking into a trap, Josiah eased carefully inside the car.

Neither of the men that had crumpled to the floor were

moving. The second man had been shot in the head, just like the first.

Shoot to kill, not maim.

Just as Josiah was about to call out for Myra Lynn, metal hit metal, and the squeal of the brakes of the train caught, sending Josiah lurching forward, then backward. He stumbled forward again, bouncing off the seats, not able to bring himself to a complete stop until he was nearly at the front of the car, up with the dead men.

After he regained control, he took a breath, glad that there were no other shooters on the car. He heard a whimper and saw a ball of human limbs stuffed in the corner: a black-haired girl with her head down, surrendering, it looked like, to certain death.

"Myra Lynn? Myra Lynn Elliot, is that you?" Josiah said aloud, trying to overcome the outside noise of the storm and the train coming to a stop, without sounding like he was angry. He didn't want the girl to be afraid of him.

She lifted up her head, leaving no doubt that she was, in fact, Scrap's sister. She looked exactly like him, only with longer hair and softer features. Her right eye was blackened, and there was terror, mixed with curiosity, on the girl's face. "How'd you know my name? I ain't told no one in Austin my true name."

The train ground to a halt, sending Josiah lurching forward again, stumbling over the two men. He almost dropped his gun, but didn't. And he didn't break eye contact with Myra Lynn, either.

"I'm a friend of Scrap's," Josiah said, gaining his footing again.

"My brother?"

Josiah nodded. "Yes, your brother, Robert Earl. Scrap."

"He can rot in hell. Go straight there and get stabbed in the heart by the devil's pitchfork for all I give a damn."

A great release of steam erupted from the locomotive, as

the fireman tried to control the power of the train but not lose all of it at once.

Rain pushed inside the car through the open windows, bringing a cold chill along with it. There was no question the girl was scared.

"Scrap's in trouble," Josiah said. "You know that, don't you? He needs your help, Myra Lynn."

"They told me if I told the judge that I saw Robert Earl kill that girl, then they'd make sure I never had to spread my legs for money again, ever. I'd be free, and I'd be rich. You know what rich is to a girl like me, mister?"

Josiah shook his head no. "I don't."

"Bein' a wife, a mother. Havin' a normal life. That's what they promised me. I'd be able to have a normal life."

"How'd you get the black eye?" Josiah asked. Whoever told her that she would have a normal life had lied to her, and he knew it.

"They showed me what they'd do if I didn't do what they wanted. This is the only thing you can see that they done," Myra Lynn said pointing to her eye.

"Who is they? The men that did this to you?"

Myra Lynn stared up at Josiah, her eyes hard. "What's it matter to you? Robert Earl turned his back on me. You know that? He's ashamed of me. Ashamed of his own flesh and blood. It ain't my fault what happened to me, spoiled by Indians and all. What do I care what happens to him? He ain't family no more. Wasn't the day he left me, for all I was concerned."

Josiah sighed. There was more to her story than Scrap had ever told. That was no surprise, but if her community had known she was raped by the Comanche, even at a young age, she would have been seen as spoiled goods. Obviously one thing had led to the other. He felt sad for her, but how she got herself into the troubles she was in wasn't anything he could solve. Helping Scrap, on the other hand, was still in his control.

Josiah leaned down so that he was face-to-face with the girl. She smelled like she hadn't had a bath in a month. "Who did this to you?" he demanded again, pointing at her eye.

Myra Lynn recoiled, then looked away from Josiah. "Brogdon Caine and that bastard barkeep of his. He's a handy one with his fists. You think I don't believe him when he says there's worse waitin' for me if'n I don't say them words?"

"William?" Josiah whispered.

Myra Lynn nodded.

"Listen to me," Josiah said. "The only reason I came after you on the train is because your brother is my friend. One of the few friends I truly have. If you don't tell the judge the truth about what you saw that night, then Scrap will hang, and you'll be all alone after he takes his last breath. There'll be no one left in this world to care enough about you to risk his life saving you from whatever mess you get yourself into next. Do you understand what I'm saying? Caine and William were going to kill you no matter what you said at the trial. My guess is that's why you're on this train. Killing you in Austin would have drawn too much attention to them, would've made everyone question whether Scrap really was the killer, and pointed to one of them, or both, as the real killer. They couldn't risk drawing attention to themselves by killing you right away."

"How do you know what I saw, mister?"

"Scrap told me what happened. That he followed you out of the saloon and saw someone attack and kill Lola. He stopped to help the girl, and you ran off. That's the truth, isn't it? You didn't see Scrap kill Lola, did you?"

Myra Lynn hesitated, and then looked down to the ground, resigned. "No. I didn't see him kill her."

"But you know who did kill her, don't you?"

Myra Lynn nodded her head again. "Yes. I saw who did it."

CHAPTER 38

———◆◆◆◆———

The storm raged on, and the heavy rain offered a much needed rinsing off to Josiah and Myra Lynn. He situated her in front of him on Clipper's saddle, then rode directly over to the remaining Rangers. They were circled around the fallen man.

"Luther Vect is dead, Sergeant Wolfe," the man who was grazed by a bullet earlier said. His sleeve was blood-soaked, and his face was drained of color; sadness hung in his eyes like low-hanging clouds.

"Get him on his horse and take care of him as properly as you can. The rest of you, follow me. We'll return to help Captain McNelly, if we can," Josiah said. He didn't know if Luther Vect hailed from Austin or not; he barely knew the man, but there wasn't time, at the moment, to provide the dead man with the respect he deserved.

"I ain't goin' back to that damn saloon," Myra Lynn said.

"I'll protect you."

"Like I've never heard that before."

Josiah stared at the back of the girl's head, and he

could've sworn he was talking to Scrap Elliot, hardheaded, stubborn, with cotton in his ears. His sister was just like Scrap in a lot of unmistakable—and annoying—ways. No matter how hard it rained, Myra Lynn still stunk. She had a head full of lice, too, all scurrying about, trying to avoid being drowned.

"You've got no worry with me, girl," Josiah said. "I'll look after you." He swung his right hand up and urged Clipper on, heading back toward the Easy Nickel Saloon as fast as he could, unconcerned about the lightning storm that danced over his head. The Rangers fell in behind him, offering their own bit of thunder to all that circled about them.

Captain McNelly had set up a perimeter around the Easy Nickel Saloon, allowing no one in and no one out within a block of the battle. A man on the roof of a three-storey building waved Josiah and his company of Rangers through, offering no challenge. It didn't take long to get to the saloon from there.

The fire had been tamped down by the heavy rain. There were no flames to be seen, just smoke, mixed with sizzling vapors, rising out the roof and through the top-floor windows. Gunfire was silent, and there weren't any ground-shaking explosions to be heard from the Ketchum grenades as Josiah and the Rangers arrived.

"Why are ya bringin' me back here?" Myra Lynn asked, tensing up noticeably. "I hope the whole place burns to the ground."

Josiah ignored Myra Lynn and looked ahead for Captain McNelly.

A group of Rangers stood under the awning of a little shop that sold writing instruments about half a block from the saloon. It looked like they had regrouped and were in the midst of planning their next move. They were doing little to cover themselves from any outlying shooters. Josiah decided that something must have changed. It looked like the battle with Brogdon Caine and his men was over.

Josiah held the reins with one hand, his arms wrapped around Myra Lynn slightly, to keep her from jumping and running, and the other hand holding his Peacemaker, at the ready for any kind of attack or shenanigans that presented itself. "Don't say a word, you understand me?" he said through gritted teeth.

"Why should I listen to you?"

"Because I'll keep my promises to you."

"Oh boy, I have finally been saved by a real man." There was an incredulous tone in Myra Lynn's voice that Josiah had heard before. For a quick second he thought about leaving Scrap and his sister to face their fates alone. But he knew better than to believe he would. He'd risked too much now to turn back.

Josiah brought Clipper to a stop about five feet from the crowd of Rangers. One of them looked up at Josiah, tapped the man he was standing next to, and then as if everyone had communicated silently, the group of men parted, allowing Josiah sight of their concern.

Josiah blinked to make sure he understood what he was seeing.

A man lay on the ground, riddled with bullets. He was no ordinary man, nor was he a Ranger. At least openly. Instead, the man was Mexican. Josiah's mouth went dry and his heart skipped a beat upon recognition of his friend Miguel.

"You stay here," he said to Myra Lynn in a voice that was affected greatly by the sight in front of him. "Don't make me come after you again, okay?"

Myra Lynn was staring at the saloon, unconcerned, it appeared, by the Mexican's state.

"Say you understand," Josiah demanded.

"I ain't goin' anywhere. Like I could anyways."

She was surrounded by at least fifteen men, all with rifles or pistols in their hands.

Satisfied, Josiah slid off Clipper and made his way to Miguel.

Juan Carlos was kneeling alongside Miguel, his leathered face ashen with fear and anxiety. The old Mexican had blood on his shirt, too. But it only took a second to figure out that he wasn't wounded. The blood was probably Miguel's.

Captain McNelly stood at Miguel's head, unmoving, his chest heaving, as he struggled to regain his breath, and his eyes were fixed on Miguel, waiting. There was nothing anyone could do for the man.

The air smelled like it did at the end of a long battle. The clouds' origins were indecipherable, whether from the weather or gunsmoke. Death waited in the shadows, as Miguel coughed, his own chest rattling up through his throat, as he fought to stay alive.

"Ah, Señor Josiah, it is good to see you," Miguel whispered, in between coughs.

Josiah knelt down next to Miguel, opposite Juan Carlos. They exchanged glances, and with a tick of the head, Josiah knew that there was no hope for Miguel.

"Hang on there, friend, help is on the way. We've sent for the doctor."

Miguel forced a smile. "You always were a horrible liar, señor."

Josiah nodded, but didn't agree. "You should be still."

"There's no use, señor. I am a dead man. I dreamed of dying like this, and now it is true. Soon, I will on a new adventure." Miguel moved to genuflect, make a cross over his chest, but his hand fell to the side, too weak to complete the task. "I would've preferred a padre instead of a doctor."

Josiah looked away. His belief in the existence, or nonexistence, of the afterlife was not something he wanted to inflict on Miguel. Religion had always made him uncomfortable, especially after losing Lily.

When Josiah looked back to the man, Miguel arched his back, took a long, grating breath, and then collapsed as the last bit of life escaped from him. His head was turned toward Juan Carlos, who quickly reached over to his neck to feel for a pulse.

"*Él está muerto.* He is dead, señor. He saved my life, stepped in front of the man, there," Juan Carlos said, pointing to a man lying facedown in the street. "If he had not, it would surely be me whose soul now faced judgment, not Miguel's."

Josiah had been so focused on the crowd of Rangers, and Miguel, that he had not seen the dead body. It was William, the barkeep. "I'm sorry," Josiah said. "Miguel was a good man."

"*Sí,* he was, and I will never forget that he paid the ultimate sacrifice so that I should live." Juan Carlos leaned over then and closed Miguel's eyes. "*Que Dios se apiade de su alma.* May God have mercy on your soul."

"This is over, Wolfe. We have Brogdon Caine in custody," McNelly said.

"And I have the witness they were trying to hurry out of town," Josiah answered.

McNelly nodded confidently. "There's only one thing left to do, then."

CHAPTER 39

The rain had eased as the morning moved on, and the sky had grown lighter—but it was still overcast, gray and dismal. There was no doubt that the day to come was going to be gloomy. Any thunder to be heard was distant as it moved east, and the harsh wind of the fiery dawn had pulled back to a steady, southerly breeze.

Josiah was soaked from head to toe. His fingers were shriveled, almost numb, and he was chilled to the bone. *It would be good to be inside*, he thought as he brought Clipper to a hesitant stop in front of the Travis County Courthouse. *But I'm not looking forward to what I have to face.*

The courthouse sat at the corner of Guadalupe and Cedar streets. There were scads of empty buggies, wagons, and carriages parked in front of and around it. Every hitching post within sight was crammed full of horses.

A small brass band had come together under a tall live oak that stood in the middle of the field to the right of the two-storey building. They were playing happy marching music, trying to rouse the crowd that had gathered around the gallows in anticipation of a hanging.

Hucksters tried to spark the crowd, too, doing their best to lift a coin or two from any pocket they could—all to no avail. It was either too early, or the gloom and rain had soaked the crowd to the bone, too. They all stood nearly motionless and silent, waiting patiently, instead of celebrating.

The courthouse lacked the Greek Revival or Victorian style of the buildings on Congress and in and around Old Courthouse Square. It looked nondescript, like it had been built only to serve a purpose and not to make any kind of statement.

Myra Lynn sat securely in the saddle in front of Josiah, and he was followed by Captain McNelly, Juan Carlos, the company of Rangers, and one prisoner who had been taken during the Easy Nickel battle. Brogdon Caine was none too happy to see Myra Lynn, or to be confined, hand and foot, in shackles. He'd been outnumbered by McNelly's company of well-prepared Rangers and surrendered quickly after William, the barkeep, met his death in a blaze of gunfire. From what Josiah had been told, the man's death was not glorious, but resigned; he'd walked out into the street after killing Miguel, firing every bullet he had, taking no cover at all.

Josiah dismounted first, then put out his hands, offering to help Myra Lynn down from Clipper.

"A nickel for a peek," she said, a wry smile crossing her face as she pinched the corners of her skirt, threatening to raise it and show Josiah, and the rest of the men behind him, her private parts.

Josiah didn't flinch, didn't change his expression one bit. "Get down here right now and act like a lady." He wanted to add, *If that's possible*, but restrained himself for fear of leading her into the courtroom even angrier than she already was.

He flexed his fingers impatiently. "Now, Myra Lynn."

The girl frowned, let go of her skirt, then slid down off the saddle, refusing Josiah's show of chivalry. "You probably wouldn't know what to do with it, anyways," Myra Lynn scowled.

Josiah took a long, deep breath as Captain McNelly walked up to his side.

"I think it's best if you let me take the lead on this, Wolfe."

"Yes, sir. I agree. You have far more influence than I could ever hope to have. And this judge might have an axe to grind."

Myra Lynn stood within a foot downwind of Josiah. Her eyes were darting about furiously. Josiah stepped over and took her hand into his, just in case she was calculating an escape attempt.

"Why is that?" McNelly asked as he struggled for a breath.

Myra Lynn shot Josiah a nasty look but remained quiet. To his surprise, she didn't try to pull away.

"From what I understand, the judge is a relation of Pete Feders."

Thunder rumbled in the distance, and the rain continued to fade into drizzle.

"Even more of a reason for you to keep as quiet as possible."

"I agree, sir."

McNelly started to walk forward but hesitated. "You were never in this alone, Wolfe. Elliot is one of my men, and I will go to any length to protect him."

"I know about Milt Fulsum being one of yours, sir."

"I figured you might've stumbled onto that."

"I was never a good spy, but the use of one inside the sheriff's department was not a surprise," Josiah said.

"General Steele was getting a lot of pressure to solve this case, but we hadn't been asked by the sheriff to join in, so my hands were tied—to a degree."

"I understand."

"I never believed Scrap Elliot was guilty of murder for a blue second," McNelly said.

"So you know who the killer is?"

"Yes, I do now, thanks to your work, and Milt Fulsum's."

There was no way to drain all of the humidity and discomfort from the inside of the courtroom. The smell of human perspiration, a mix of fear, boredom, and anticipation, was almost too much to bear. Fans whirled overhead, and all of the women staring down from the mezzanine pushed away the smells as best they could with their own personal fans.

The room was circular, and there was not an empty seat to be seen on either floor. Out of tradition and social expectation, most of the spectators wore black to the trial, funeral clothes, instead of everyday wear, unless they were in the profession of the law.

The judge, Evan Dooley, sat on a slight dais wrapped in an ornately carved walnut rail. Even though Josiah had never seen the man before, the judge looked like he'd expected; tall, full white beard, hard eyes that appeared to be wise and angry at the same time. The only similarity Josiah could see that the man bore to Feders was his birdlike nose. Other than that, he was as unrecognizable as any stranger. He must have been related on Feders's mother's side, considering the difference in his surname.

A big man with skillet-sized hands sat to the right of Judge Dooley. Josiah assumed he was the bailiff. He was the only visibly armed man in sight.

Myra Lynn was securely in the middle of McNelly and Josiah. Two Rangers holding Brogdon Caine upright had followed them inside. The clank of Caine's shackles echoed throughout the courtroom.

The rest of the company of Rangers waited outside, ready at a moment's notice to quell any trouble that might arise.

When Josiah and McNelly had appeared in the doorway,

the courtroom had immediately hushed, and every eye, including the judge's, was on them.

McNelly glanced over to Josiah, gave him a slight nod, and stepped up the aisle that led to the judge. It was then that Josiah got his first good look at Scrap and the rest of the small room. To his surprise, he saw quite a few familiar faces among the crowd who had gathered inside.

Scrap looked withered, like a shadow of his former self. Skinnier, if that was possible, barely clean, even though he was dressed in a fresh white shirt that almost matched the color of his pale skin. His stark black hair was combed but severely in need of being cut. Fear was held tight in the boy's jaw, and he didn't relax one bit when he looked up and saw Captain McNelly enter the room with Josiah and Myra Lynn. Instead his eyes grew more intense and angry as he looked away.

Myra Lynn's hand tensed in Josiah's grip, and her breathing became more rapid.

Woodrell Cranston sat next to Scrap. Oddly, seated together, they looked nearly the same age, and cut from the same impetuous cloth. Cranston's eyes lit up when he saw Josiah, but that was the only hint of recognition. There was no silent message to pass, nothing that Josiah could signal. Cranston was going to have to wait and see what was up, like everyone else.

Another row of lawyers, the prosecutors, sat opposite Scrap and Cranston, their faces dim and less than amused by the disturbance.

Beyond the prosecutors, the gallery was filled with onlookers from the community. Rory Farnsworth, his father Myron, and Paul Hoagland, of course, were in attendance, all in the front row.

A quick glance upward told Josiah that the second-floor mezzanine was full of onlookers, too, as he'd expected. For as uncaring as everyone had made the city out to be about the killing of the whores, there sure seemed to be a lot of people interested in the outcome of Scrap's trial. Maybe they wanted to see justice done. Or they were there for the festivities around the anticipated hanging. This trial lacked the circus environment and fervor that usually surrounded such an event. Maybe it was the weather, but for some reason, Josiah doubted that was it.

Josiah spotted Blanche Dumont, right away, in the mezzanine. Rufous was at her side, his head barely coming to her waist—he had to look through the spindles of the rail to make eye contact with Josiah.

There seemed to be a bubble around Blanche. Apparently none of the other fine women from Austin wanted to stand, or sit, next to her. Her pale white skin was the color of Scrap's shirt, and they could have been related if judged by skin tone alone. Attitude, too, as far as that went. Scrap's condition was temporary—hopefully, if he lived long enough to recover. Blanche's condition was lifelong, and had its fair share of torment that came along with it.

The face Josiah desperately wanted to see, however, but could not find in the crowd was Pearl's.

No matter how he craned his neck, she was nowhere to be seen. The tiff over his visit to Blanche Dumont's house was obviously going to have a long-lasting effect on their relationship. Josiah sighed at the thought, fearing that his disappointment was only going to grow.

He didn't see Milt Fulsum, either, but assumed the man was back at the jail, holding down his position as desk sergeant, maintaining his cover.

A wave of murmurs followed Josiah, McNelly, and Myra Lynn to the gate in the rail that separated them from the judge, lawyers, and Scrap.

McNelly stopped and squared his shoulders. "May I address the court?" he said.

"There had better be a good reason for this interruption, Captain McNelly," Judge Dooley said.

"I object!" one of the prosecuting lawyers screamed out

as he bolted to his feet. He was a middle-aged man, just starting to gray and grow a belly. It poked out of a vest over his tight belt.

"Sit down, Willard, the captain can speak."

"But . . . this is highly unusual," Willard said.

"One more word and I'll hold you in contempt, sir. A day or two in the hole might teach you some respect," the judge snapped. There was little in attitude to compare to Feders, but the sound of the judge's voice was vaguely familiar.

"Thank you, Judge Dooley. May I enter?"

"As you wish, Captain McNelly. Far be it from me to restrain the voice of the Texas Rangers. You are speaking for the organization, I assume?"

"I am, Your Honor. The Rangers and Josiah Wolfe," McNelly said, nodding back to Josiah.

"I am well aware who the man is, Captain McNelly. I will warn you that I am less than partial to anything concerning Ranger Wolfe. But I will respect his right to be in this courtroom and operate as a free man, even though my nephew no longer has that right. Am I understood, Captain?"

"Yes, I understand, Your Honor." McNelly stopped in front of the judge, and the gate that had separated them swung slowly closed, latching with a loud gnash of metal against metal.

Someone coughed. Feet shuffled. The heat was unbearable, and Josiah began to sweat.

"Now, Captain McNelly, what may I presume is the cause for the interruption of this proceeding?"

"I have a witness, You Honor. A witness who saw what happened the night Lola Wellsley was murdered. It is my duty to present her to the court."

"So that an innocent man can be saved." Judge Dooley did not pose it as a question, but glared past McNelly, to Scrap.

"If that is the court's decision, Your Honor. I am in no position to presume innocence."

"Well said, Captain. Who is this witness?"

McNelly turned and motioned for Myra Lynn to come forward. She hesitated at first, tightening her grip in Josiah's hand, but he urged her on. "It's all right, nobody's going to hurt you," he whispered, still holding her hand. "Now, you remember what I told you. Nobody will come for you again if you do the right thing and tell the truth. You understand?" He let go of her hand.

Myra Lynn stared into Josiah's eyes, obviously finding what she needed to understand that he meant what he said, and walked forward then, albeit slowly, to Captain McNelly.

"The witness is Myra Lynn Elliot, Your Honor," McNelly continued. "She is the sister of the defendant, Robert Earl Elliot. He went to the Easy Nickel Saloon to seek her out after not seeing her for several years."

The crowd, including all three of the attorneys for the prosecution, erupted. Judge Dooley began beating his gavel, and the bailiff stood, his hand sliding to his sidearm. It was so loud inside the courtroom that Josiah couldn't hear himself think.

Scrap glared at Myra Lynn, and even though Josiah could only see the back of the girl's head, he was sure she returned the look of distaste.

"Quiet. Quiet. Or I will have you all thrown out!" Judge Dooley screamed. It took several more gavel beats to regain control of the room, but it finally quieted down enough to hear.

"This is highly unusual, Captain McNelly," Judge Dooley said.

"I understand. But Miss Elliot saw who killed Lola Wellsley."

"Is that true, young lady?" Judge Dooley glanced over to the prosecutor who had objected before and warned him of doing so again. "Did you see what happened that night clearly and certainly, without any question at all?"

Myra Lynn nodded yes. "I did."

"Is the man who killed Lola Wellsley in this courtroom, or possibly somewhere else?"

"Yes, sir, I mean Your Honor. That would be him right there," Myra Lynn said as she turned and pointed directly into the crowd behind her.

CHAPTER 40

———◆◆◆◆———

There was less than a second for anyone in the gallery to catch a breath and react to the shock of the what was implied by Myra Lynn's accusation. Once again, the courtroom was enveloped in a deafening roar.

"No!"

"I object! I object!"

"No!"

The judge banged his gavel furiously, and his face turned red immediately with frustration and anger.

Josiah was sure the roof was going to come off of the courthouse, and he wanted to ask Myra Lynn if she was sure of her accusation. But he couldn't bring himself to. Something in the deepest part of his stomach agreed with the girl. It didn't take much thinking to believe that Myron Farnsworth was the killer.

Myra Lynn was pointing without question at the banker.

Abram Randalls had most likely figured out the same thing, which is why he was broken out of the jail and taken to be killed or held captive, for fear he would point his own finger at Farnsworth. There was also the matter of retribution for embezzling, too. Add that in with the time Josiah saw the banker leave the jail, demanding that his son, the sheriff, take care of something, and Blanche Dumont's insinuation that Farnsworth had been a visitor and client of hers—it all just added up and made sense to Josiah. Especially considering the state of Blanche Dumont's business and the coming of the new railroad. Myron Farnsworth had a lot to gain . . . and to lose.

There were still a lot of unanswered questions, but that's what the court was for, to prove the accusation. If it got that far.

Half the crowd was stamping their feet now, and the thunder inside the building matched the storm that had passed by earlier and the report of the grenades that Juan Carlos and Miguel had thrown into the saloon to start the battle in the first place.

Josiah was surprised, and glad, that everything had come to a head in the courtroom instead of out on the street.

The crowd lurched forward, pushing Josiah against the rail that separated the judge, the lawyers, Scrap, Myra Lynn, and Captain McNelly from them.

When Josiah had turned to see who Myra Lynn had pointed to, he'd found himself face-to-face with Brogdon Caine and the two Rangers who were guarding him.

Caine's face held no discernible expression about the accusation, other than that of discomfort. He looked past Josiah and said nothing. Even if he had, there would have been no way any of his words could have been heard. The judge had not yet regained control of the courtroom.

Myra Lynn stood still as a statue, her arm still extended, her index finger unwavering as it continued to point at Myron Farnsworth.

The man's face had drained of color. He sat glaring back at Myra Lynn, his lips moving in a mumble, his hands trembling slightly as he gripped the rail.

Rory Farnsworth's face was flushed red from the surprise of the accusation and from the heat that erupted inside the courtroom. Even though it was spring, most of the men wore proper wool suits, including Rory, who was dressed as fancy as ever, outdone in style and expense only by his father.

The sheriff stood up, shaking his head, joining with the chorus of no's, adding a new chant, "It's a lie!"

Judge Dooley continued to bang his gavel, but the power of it was lost to the roar of the crowd.

"It's a lie! It's a lie! It's a lie!"

As the crowd continued to push forward, Josiah became increasingly concerned about Myra Lynn's welfare, since she was the object of everyone's rage. But he could do nothing, knowing full well that the single show of a gun would send the courtroom into a stampede, instead of a standing-still frenzy. Captain McNelly stood at her side, his eyes darting about, concerned, too, about the girl's safety.

Finally, the bailiff stepped forward and pulled his gun, threatening to shoot into the ceiling, then yelled as loud as he could, "Quiet or you're all goin' to jail!"

The gavel continued to bang as the voices subsided. Josiah felt the pressure of the crowd behind him pull back. He was relieved.

Myra Lynn relaxed her arm, dropping it to her side. She remained standing in her spot, staring angrily at the man she had just accused.

Captain McNelly stood motionless next to Myra Lynn.

Scrap and Woodrell Cranston had remained seated throughout the melee, the looks on their faces matching that of everyone else: shock and disbelief.

Josiah nodded to Scrap, who in return just took a deep breath. The boy still looked shattered, like the solitary time in the hole had changed him forever, like light of any kind was foreign to him, hurtful in some way.

"That will be enough!" Judge Dooley shouted. "Silence in the court!" He banged the gavel again. It echoed throughout the room with absolute finality, and everyone went quiet, waiting with bated breath to see what happened next.

"Do you realize what you are saying, young lady?" the judge asked Myra Lynn.

Before she could answer, the lead prosecutor jumped back to his feet. "I object, Your Honor! This woman is not under oath."

"Sit down, Mr. Smith, or I will hold you in contempt of court. There's a man's life at stake here."

The crowd murmured. Myron Farnsworth had remained seated, and the sheriff was unmoved. He looked like he was about to say something aloud but thought better of it.

The lawyer, Smith, sat back down with a disgruntled thump.

Judge Dooley turned his attention back to Myra Lynn, expecting an answer.

Josiah watched the proceeding curiously, wondering what Myra Lynn was going to do next, thinking back to the last few days, still trying to convince himself of Farnsworth's guilt.

How could a man who could have anything he wanted be a killer? he wondered quietly. His son was the sheriff. He had more money than most men. A place in society. Maybe, Josiah decided, Farnsworth just thought he could get away with anything because of his money and standing in the community. His motive for killing whores remained unknown, at least for now, and his innocence was still a possibility. One thing was for sure, though, Myron Farnsworth was not the typical outlaw.

With a quick thought, Josiah turned to Brogdon Caine and whispered, "If you want to avoid that noose out in the yard, I'd suggest you speak up if you know anything about this. My guess is you answered to Farnsworth. You had a lot to gain if Blanche Dumont was out of the way. If you were an accomplice to the killings in any way, you'll hang, too. I'll see to it."

Caine sneered at Josiah. "You think I'm afraid of dyin'?"

"I don't know what you're afraid of, but Myron Farnsworth has no power over you now. Think about that . . . and what you're risking if you say nothing. Saying something could work in your favor. You're a businessman. I'd consider all of your angles if I were you."

Myra Lynn squared her shoulders, unimpressed with the judge. "I realize what I'm sayin', Judge, I mean Your Honor. That man there killed Lola. He beat her the night before when she wouldn't . . ." She stopped then and looked around her and up to the second floor, making eye contact with Blanche Dumont. "He beat her the night before in places no one could see her bruises unless she was nekkid. He come back the next night to see if she learned her lesson, would do what he wanted her to. That's the way it was with them other girls. He just never knowed when to stop. He's a scary, angry man. I'm just thankful he never took a shine to me, or I'd be dead, too."

"That's a lie!" Rory Farnsworth shouted as he jumped to his feet. "She's just trying to save her brother."

"I don't give a rat's ass about Robert Earl," Myra Lynn shouted back. "Lola was nice to me. She didn't deserve to die like a gutted pig."

Judge Dooley banged his gavel. "That's enough, Sheriff Farnsworth. And Miss Elliot, you need to watch your language. This is a court of law."

"Beggin' your pardon, Your Honor, but I can't see my mouth." Myra Lynn smiled, then curtsied. The crowd laughed, then quieted immediately after the judge swept a wide glare across the courtroom. Even McNelly forced away a smile.

Brogdon Caine pushed up to Josiah so that he was visible to the judge. "Colonel Farnsworth killed them girls, Your Honor. This girl is tellin' the truth." He lowered his head then, avoiding Farnsworth's gaze. "I'll testify to it that that Ranger was just in the wrong place at the wrong time."

The crowd erupted again. It took the judge and the bailiff a good five minutes to get them calmed down.

Colonel. It made sense to Josiah then. The regimental discipline of the jailbreak and the pseudo-uniforms they'd worn all signaled that Farnsworth had been in the war. It also explained the Vigenere cipher. The attempt to kill Josiah at the Tree of Death had failed, and he was surprised that he hadn't considered it before, that the elder Farnsworth might have been an officer in the War Between the States. Josiah was betting that the men in black, and Brogdon Caine, had been in the war, too, and served under Farnsworth in some capacity.

Myron Farnsworth stood up, unable to restrain himself any longer. "You're a dead man, Caine!"

It didn't seem like it was possible for Rory Farnsworth's face to go any paler, but it did. He was as white as snow now, perspiring, his expression confused and certain at the same time. His father had given the first hint that the accusations might just be true.

"I need to see all of the lawyers at the bench now! And one more outburst, and we will empty the court. Do I make myself clear?" Judge Dooley said to no one in particular.

Woodrell Cranston leaned over and whispered something to Scrap, then joined the prosecuting attorneys in front of the judge.

Myron and Rory Farnsworth stood unmoving, shoulder to shoulder. There was no clear escape for the elder Farnsworth, if he was thinking of it. The doors were guarded by the remaining members of McNelly's company of Rangers.

Caine's addition to Myra Lynn's accusation had sent Myron Farnsworth from absolute anger to ashen white. The younger Farnsworth, a shorter version of his father, looked like he just wanted to wither away and disappear.

Josiah felt sorry for the sheriff to a degree. It was only a matter of days ago that Rory had admonished Josiah for his lack of social grace when it came to courting Pearl publicly. Now the social standing tables seemed to have turned. The fall from favor in the circles that the Farnsworths traveled would be quick and painful.

The shadow of his father's deeds would surely dampen, or even destroy, Rory Farnsworth's political and social ambitions. There was no telling how things would play out, but if the accusations were proved true in a court of law, then nothing would ever be the same for either man. Josiah didn't necessarily care for Rory's attitude, but he hated to see a decent man undone by another man's actions—especially if that other man was his father.

The lawyers huddled in front of Judge Dooley for what seemed like an eternity. The crowd behaved, remained quiet. Whispers and objections rose from the bench, but none were clear or decipherable. Still, it didn't take a lawyer to understand what was at stake.

Josiah looked up and made eye contact with Blanche Dumont. She forced a smile, and then a deep nod. He wasn't sure what the nod meant.

Maybe Blanche Dumont was grateful for the apparent outcome, or something else, it was hard to say. But it looked like her business had a chance to survive now. Hopefully, the killings would stop, but her house was still in danger of being taken from her.

After a lot of haggling, all of the lawyers went back to their seats. Cranston was smiling, while the other three men looked like they had just been hit in the small of the back with a two-by-four.

"After much consideration," Judge Dooley said, "all of the charges against Robert Earl Elliot will be dropped. Sheriff, take Myron Farnsworth into custody."

The courtroom erupted in shouts of joy and a mixture of boos. Judge Dooley banged his gavel furiously, shouting, "Order in the court! Order in the court!"

It took a full five minutes for the crowd to obey the judge.

In that time, Myron Farnsworth stood stiffly, glaring at his son. When silence did return, there wasn't so much as a rustle of feet. All eyes and ears, including Josiah's, were on the elder Farnsworth, a man of great stature and wealth, about to be arrested for the murder of a prostitute.

Rory Farnsworth was pale as a ghost. His fingers trembled, but his hands had not moved in any attempt to detain his father.

"I did this for you," Myron Farnsworth said. "I had everything set up perfectly, and you bumbled it, like usual." His disgust was unmistakable.

"Did what?" Rory asked.

"The jailbreak, all of it, so you could apprehend Randalls, put him away, and be assured of the next election. So we would continue to be the law *and* the purse-string holders in this town once the new railroad came through. It was a winning combination, you and me, and now you've ruined it all. Ruined it, I tell you."

"'We'? So 'we' could continue to be the law? I'm the sheriff, Father. And I know nothing of this partnership you're suggesting."

Myron Farnsworth continued to stare at his son, unwavering. Rory, on the other hand, was transitioning from fear to anger. His pale face was turning redder by the second.

"I even had the cipher left behind for you to find. You. Not anyone else. I taught you how to solve them as boy, a gift from my war days. But just like everything else in your pitiful little life, you missed it, allowed someone else to find it, and all of my plans from that moment had to be changed. I am lucky to have had some men who could follow orders, loyal members of the Brigade. But even now, I see I failed to judge their characters as well as I thought I had. This accusation will be reversed, I tell you. It is a great error. That Ranger killed those girls. It will be proven, you'll see."

"*You* killed those girls."

"Don't you understand what is at stake? I did this for you,

for us," the elder Farnsworth repeated, his voice more strained than ever.

"That's a lie," Rory Farnsworth shouted. "All of this is nothing but more of your lies and deceit. Mother was right about you. You're a soulless, calculating man who will stop at nothing to get what he wants, no matter who it destroys. You had Abram Randalls killed to keep his mouth shut about what he knew. This Ranger? He was in the wrong place at the wrong time, unlucky to come out of the saloon just after you had killed that girl, and he was left to answer for your deed. I wanted to hang him. I put him in the hole, and he is an innocent man. A boy. Nothing more than a boy, his life nearly ruined because of your unrelenting greed."

"Again, he is of no consequence. This great city needs me. Needs us. Can't you see that?"

Rory Farnsworth squared his shoulders and reached inside his jacket. "There *are* consequences, Father. You have to answer for what you have done. Give me your hands," he said, as he pulled out a pair of handcuffs from inside his coat.

"I beg your pardon?"

"You're under arrest for the murder of Lola Wellsley." Without any hesitation, Sheriff Rory Farnsworth slapped the handcuffs on his father's wrists. "Bailiff, remove this man from the courtroom, and see him to the hole. I don't want him anywhere near the other prisoners. It's hard telling who is still on his payroll."

Myron Farnsworth started to push by the sheriff but was immediately surrounded by the bailiff and three deputies and put into custody, his hands bound behind him.

The crowd screamed and hollered joyously, as the banker was led out of the courtroom proclaiming his innocence at the top of his lungs.

After his father was out of sight, Rory Farnsworth withered down to his seat and collapsed with his head in his hands. Even above the commotion and noise, there was no mistaking the man's pain, embarrassment, and rising sobs.

CHAPTER 41

—◆◦◆◦◆—

There were still remnants of the morning storm overhead; low-lying clouds that still held drizzle hovered over the courthouse, and thunder echoed in the distance. Any heavy rain was already east, but the day continued to be murky and gray. The band that had assembled was gone, and any anticipation of a hanging had left with it, along with the blood-hungry crowd that had waited outside. Still, there seemed to be hope on a clearing horizon and much relief in the air as Josiah made his way to Clipper.

He stopped suddenly and was nearly pushed aside by the crowd as they rushed to depart, too. A streetcar slugged through the mud, the driver shouting at the mules and snapping the reins as hard as he could to get them to move on.

Two gray geldings stood at the wait, and the horses got Josiah's attention.

Captain McNelly was mounted on one horse, while the other remained tied to the hitching post, its rider nowhere to be seen.

The horses looked like they could have come from the

same sire and mare; they were almost identical. Captain McNelly's horse was almost a hand taller, and maybe in a little better shape from the long rides to and from South Texas, but other than that there were no other distinctions.

"Excuse me, Captain, but do you know whose horse that is?" Josiah asked, pointing to the gelding.

McNelly stiffened and held the reins to his horse tight. He nodded yes. "It is Myron Farnsworth's. I suppose he won't be needing it any longer. Or won't be for a good while."

Josiah sighed. "No, I don't suppose he will."

"I have to apologize, Wolfe," McNelly said, "for General Steele's lack of interest in Ranger Elliot's predicament. Mine, too, as far as that goes. We couldn't risk a public acknowledgment of his innocence, not even to you. As I've shown, we were very well aware that something more diabolical was afoot, we just weren't sure what. The reputation of the Rangers has suffered of late, and we just couldn't risk the appearance of opposing the sheriff, or interfering, which, as it turns out, is exactly what Myron Farnsworth hoped we would do."

"I understand," Josiah said. "If it wasn't for Scrap going into the Easy Nickel to look for Myra Lynn, Farnsworth might have continued on with his scheme. Who knows how many more girls would have been killed?"

"Elliot, and you for that matter, have done a great service to Austin."

"Thank you."

"I will see you tomorrow morning when we muster the company, Wolfe?"

"Yes, sir. Myself and Elliot, if he's up to it."

"Good. You will both be a welcome addition to the company. We must put an end to Cortina and his rustling outfit once and for all. I have no worry that Elliot will be raring to go. He's a free man, after all, and a Ranger to boot."

"Agreed, sir. Agreed."

McNelly loosened his grip, hesitated, then turned his horse out to the muddy street. "Good work, Wolfe," he shouted over his shoulder. "Good work."

"Thank you," Josiah said, though he wasn't sure McNelly heard him. The captain seemed in a hurry to get away from the courthouse. He probably had to report back to General Steele and the governor.

The knowledge that the horse was Farnsworth's satisfied Josiah. It made sense, added to the undeniable conclusion that the man was the killer and the mastermind behind the effort to see Scrap hanged. The only thing that Josiah had come across that hadn't been resolved was the pattern of the three men from Massachusetts. He decided it was only that. A pattern he'd noticed and nothing more. There were obviously more men in Austin from the East than he'd ever realized, Yankees come west to find their fortune and escape the past. That was the thing about patterns. Sometimes they took you down the wrong path and ended nowhere important. It was all part of the process, like considering one letter or another to solve a Vigenere cipher.

When Josiah turned around, he found himself face-to-face with Juan Carlos and Pearl. They had been standing there waiting for him to finish up with McNelly.

A smile wafted across his face as Pearl rushed to him, wrapped her arms around his waist, and buried her face in his chest.

"I'm sorry," she whispered. "I was being ridiculous and immature. I don't want to fight with you ever again."

The world around them vanished, and Josiah was overwhelmed by the sweet spring smell of her toilet water and the feel of her against his body. "There's no need," he whispered. "I should have explained myself better. I have things to tell you, Pearl. Things you may not like to hear, but you have to know."

Pearl angled her face up to him, and Josiah didn't resist, didn't care about the hundreds of prying eyes that might or might not have been following his every move. He kissed her deeply, passionately.

Pearl responded in kind. After a long minute, they pulled apart and started to laugh. Out of the corner of his eye, Josiah saw a wide smile cross Juan Carlos's face.

"I'm leaving in the morning," Josiah said to Pearl.

"I know. But please know this: Our lives start now. Whatever you have done in the past is not my concern. I will never act as I did again, I promise. I know everything I need to know about you, Josiah Wolfe. You're a good, decent man who intends to do good, decent things, like making sure your friend doesn't hang for something he didn't do."

"I don't know about that," Josiah said.

"I do," Juan Carlos said, the smile still on his face.

Josiah nodded a thank-you to his friend, then turned his attention back to Pearl. "I don't know when I'll be back."

"Maybe I can sneak away from Miss Amelia's tonight," Pearl whispered.

Josiah smiled. "I'd like that." He took her hand, then pulled her close and kissed her deeply again, hesitant to let her go. "I'll meet you in the carriage house, just after dark."

Woodrell Cranston and Paul Hoagland escorted Scrap out of the courthouse. The grayness seemed to agree with Scrap, but the light still looked to hurt his eyes. He squinted a bit and came to a stop just short of Josiah, not paying any attention to the small crowd that was waiting to see him.

Scrap stuck his hand out. "Thanks, Wolfe. If it wasn't for you and these fellas, I'd be six feet under by now."

"Just returning the favor," Josiah said. He took Scrap's hand, shook it heartily, then stepped in and wrapped his other arm around him in a slight hug. He let go quickly, but was hardly ashamed of showing the boy some affection. He was glad that Scrap was a free man.

Tears welled up in Scrap's eyes. "I 'spect you're about the best friend me and Myra Lynn could ever hope to have, Wolfe. I'll never forget what you've done."

Josiah shrugged his shoulders and stood back. "These men were determined not to see an innocent man hang. I hope this ends it all. You being free won't bring back Lola Wellsley or the other girls, but hopefully, justice will be served in the end."

Paul Hoagland chewed his stub of a cigar, and slid it to the corner of his mouth. "Hard to say. This could be the trial of the century. Farnsworth isn't going to go to the noose without a fight. He'll bring in the best lawyers in the country."

"Sounds like you're going to be busy for a while," Josiah said.

"It'll be a good story, that's for sure."

"Let's just hope the killings stop," Cranston added. "That the right man is behind bars."

Hoagland laughed. "Spoken like a true lawyer." Both men pushed by them, off to whatever awaited them, leaving Scrap and Josiah standing there together.

"You going to be ready to leave with the company tomorrow?" Josiah asked.

Scrap nodded yes. "I can't wait. How about you?"

"Yes," Josiah said. "I think I'm ready to leave. It'll be good to be back on the trail. Besides, we've got some unfinished business with Cortina to attend to."

"That we do," Scrap said. "That we do."

EPILOGUE

———◆———

Holes had been punched in the roof of Blanche Dumont's house, and the first flame jumped out from one of them, just as Captain McNelly and his company of Rangers passed by.

Josiah and Scrap slowed but didn't come to a stop. The house was completely engulfed in flames, and the heat of it could be felt all at once, like the sun had fallen from the sky and landed a hundred feet to the right of them. The fire had been set on purpose, the battle with the railroad not so much lost as given up. There was no way Blanche was ever going to win, even with Myron Farnsworth behind bars. Still, if there was a deal to be had, Josiah was sure that Blanche had found it when she'd agreed to let her house be destroyed. He had little doubt that when he returned to Austin, she would be in a newer, finer house, open for business.

Blanche Dumont stood in front of the fire, along with Rufous and her collection of girls—including all of Brogdon Caine's girls and Scrap's sister, Myra Lynn, watching her house disintegrate.

"I still ain't happy about her stayin' on here," Scrap said to Josiah.

"You can't live her life for her, Scrap. Besides, Blanche will take care of Myra Lynn the best she can. She'll make sure she gets some education and stays healthy. Maybe she'll come to know something else in life. Maybe not."

"I suppose I have to just live with it."

"Beats lying about it," Josiah said.

"I'm not sayin' another word."

Josiah smiled, and as they passed, Blanche Dumont nodded, and Myra Lynn waved.

All of their good-byes were complete now. Pearl was back at the normal school, her mind on studying rather than on Josiah. Lyle and Ofelia were stocked up and accustomed to their way of life while Josiah was away. Whatever lay behind them all could not be changed, and whatever waited for them down the trail was full of promise, danger, and the hope that somehow they were all making a difference for themselves and the great state of Texas.

Captain McNelly waved his hand forward, ordering the company to pick up its pace. "Let's go," he shouted.

Scrap urged Missy on, his blue roan mare, his eyes full of hope and excitement now that they'd adjusted to daylight.

Josiah held back for a second, looking over his shoulder. He took a deep breath then gently snapped Clipper's reins, moving to a fast trot, leaving Austin, and all he loved about it, behind in a cloud of dust, smoke, and gratitude.

ABOUT THE AUTHOR

Larry D. Sweazy (www.larrydsweazy.com) won the WWA
Spur Award for Best Short Fiction in 2005. He also won the
2011 Will Rogers Medallion Award for Western Fiction and
the 2011 Best Books of Indiana literary competition for his
novel *The Scorpion Trail* (Berkley, 2010). He was nominated
for a Short Mystery Fiction Society Derringer Award in 2007
and was a finalist in the Best Books of Indiana literary competition in 2010. He has published more than fifty nonfiction
articles and short stories, which have appeared in *Ellery
Queen's Mystery Magazine, The Adventure of the Missing
Detective: And 25 of the Year's Finest Crime and Mystery
Stories!, Boys' Life, Hardboiled*, Amazon Shorts, and several
other publications and anthologies. He is member of MWA
(Mystery Writers of America), WWA (Western Writers of
America), and WF (Western Fictioneers). He lives in Indiana
with his wife, Rose, two dogs, Rhodesian ridgebacks, Brodi
and Sunny, and a black cat, Nigel.

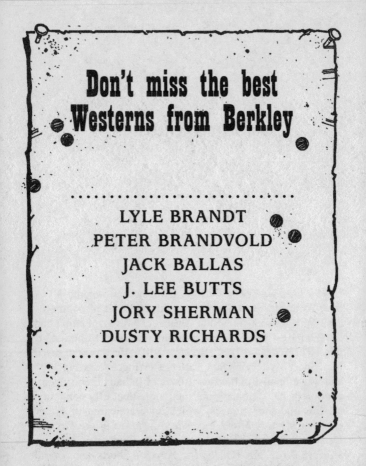

Don't miss the best Westerns from Berkley

LYLE BRANDT

PETER BRANDVOLD

JACK BALLAS

J. LEE BUTTS

JORY SHERMAN

DUSTY RICHARDS

M10G0610